The Men's Club

By

Jeffrey F. Daley

The Men's Club is a work of fiction. Names, characters, businesses, places, events, and incidents are a product of the author's imagination and used in a fictitious manner. Any resemblance to actual persons or locales is entirely coincidental.

Book design by Jordan Daley and Trisha Daley

DEDICATION

For my wife, Trish, and three great kids, Ryan, Jordan, and Matty. With you four, all things are possible. Keep dreaming big until they all come true.

and

For Ken Herrmann, a great friend, who left us too soon. The strongest and most courageous person I have ever known. You are missed.

CHAPTER 1

March 17, 2017

Squirrel's Uber ride got there quicker than he was expecting. The black SUV pulled up and the man lowered the front passenger side window and told Squirrel he was here to pick him up. Once the driver told him he was there to pick up a James Collucci he hopped into the back seat. The man appeared friendly enough but had a much rougher edge than the drivers that usually picked him up. He'd had everyone from college kids to grandmothers and everything in between giving him his Uber rides. This driver was a bit over-dressed in an expensive suit with an overcoat draped over the front seat. He appeared to be in his fifties and looked to be quite physically fit. The driver had one standout feature. He had a long jagged scar starting at his right ear and ending at the edge of his mouth. Squirrel thought it would have been nice to hear the story behind that scar but it would have been rude to ask.

"How are you tonight, Mr. Collucci?" the driver said.

"Doing great. Had a great time. You can call me Jimmy."

"OK, Jimmy it is," he said.

The chit chat stopped and Squirrel found himself in the back seat thinking about the past few hours. The thoughts brought a smile to his face. Things were looking up but that was short-lived. The driver took an unexpected wrong turn.

"Excuse me. You missed the turn."

"I didn't miss the turn. I know where I'm going. It'll get you there quicker," the driver shot back.

"I think I know the best way to get to my house."

Two minutes later the man pulled the car over to the side of the road. This was an old industrial area that hadn't been active for many years. The place was desolate. There were no street lights and the area was pitch black.

"Why are you pulling over?" his voice showing concern.

"I need to get something from the trunk," the driver said as he stepped out of the car. He went to the trunk then opened up Jimmy's door and forcefully shoved a rag over his face. That was the last thing he remembered until he woke up deep in the woods somewhere he didn't recognize. Squirrel was bound and gagged and the driver was holding a flashlight in his face. The man with the scar removed the gag from Squirrel's mouth.

"What the hell are you doing?" he screamed at the man. His head was still groggy from the alcohol and whatever the man had drugged him with.

"My employer is not happy with you. What makes you think you had any chance of getting away with that?" There was a look on the man's face that was all business. Squirrel knew that whatever that man was sent to do would be accomplished. He just wished like hell that he knew what that was.

"What are you talking about? Get away with what? What did I do?" His voice was trembling with every syllable. He had no answers for this man and that was going to be a problem. The man pulled out brass knuckles from his pocket and slowly put them on his right hand.

"I'm going to give you one more chance. If you don't tell me what I need to hear then I will be getting busy with my right fist. Hand over your house and car keys." Squirrel immediately complied with the request but being he had no idea what the man was after he was sure the next few minutes of his life would be quite painful. The first punch came fast and furious and easily broke his jaw.

Squirrel was spitting out teeth and blood and screamed at the man. "I didn't take anything. I don't know your employer. Please stop."

The man continued his interrogation and came to the conclusion that James Collucci was not the guy. He would clean up his mess and arrange for an accident as per his employer's instructions. The man decided a suicide was in order for this one.

The day had started out like many others in the past five years. Squirrel woke up alone in his king-sized bed. He stepped onto his cold hardwood floor and walked to his kitchen and plugged in his

Keurig coffee maker thinking what a great invention this single serving coffee maker was. Always pissed off that he didn't come up with the idea first. He regretted not getting one earlier given all the half pots of fresh brewed coffee that went down the drain. This wasn't an issue five years ago when he would wake up next to his wife every day and they would brew that full pot and consume it in its entirety before getting on with their work days. Of course, his wife didn't call him Squirrel. To her he was just Jim, Jimmy, or Honey depending on her mood. When she needed his attention it was always James Joseph. In grade school he was Jimmy. High school he was Jim. College he was nicknamed Squirrel.

Today was St. Patrick's Day and he had decided he was going to go out and celebrate his heritage. With a last name of Collucci and a dark olive complexion, one might never guess he was almost three quarters Irish. He was the son of Anthony Collucci and Mary Pat O'Brien. His maternal grandparents were both off the boat Irish immigrants and his paternal grandmother was also of Irish descent.

His marriage had run out of gas five years earlier. She lost interest in him and starting taking up with other men. He was married for almost twenty years and they never had any offspring despite significant effort. They could never figure out why they were never blessed like their friends and family. It was probably the biggest reason why she wanted to move on from him. He never saw it coming or never wanted to see it coming. She moved away with whatever she could get out of the marriage and left him behind in their home in Fairfield, New Jersey. She never looked back. Jimmy had been picking up the pieces of his life ever since.

Jimmy had been toiling away in middle management in a telecom office in Morristown, New Jersey. It was a good safe living that provided him moderate financial security. The job was tedious and the days dragged on like Sunday mass for a twelve year old. His circle of friends had dwindled. When he was married he somehow let his wife dictate their social calendar and it rarely if ever involved anyone that wasn't her choice of company. He always took pleasure in his annual three day excursion with the old college buddies. It was always a negotiation with his wife to get her approval for this trip. Despite her controlling ways, he was perfectly happy and always considered himself lucky to have her in his life. For the last six months or so he had been making every effort to move on, something he should have done four and half years ago.

Today some of his co-workers were getting together to throw back some pints of Guinness or Killian's Irish Red with some shots of Jameson's Irish Whisky mixed in. It was a work day but Jimmy decided to take the day off. He had been working hard and thought he could use a three day weekend. His co-workers were a tight group and would often get together on off-work days and after work hours. The work day wound down and Jimmy pulled out his phone and ordered an Uber to pick him up and take him to Flanagan's Pub, which was about fifteen minutes north of him. Jimmy could see from his Uber app that a Kia Sorrento would be picking him up and was two minutes away. Jimmy got to Flanagan's and threw the Uber driver a five spot. He didn't buy into the Uber no-tipping policy.

What he didn't see was the black SUV with the tinted windows driving behind him since he left his home. The SUV then pulled into a parking space in a far corner of Flanagan's parking lot.

Flanagan's was jamming. Juke box Irish music gave way to live bagpipers which was the set up for the always popular Irish step dancers. Applause erupted around for the pipers and dancers. Slowly the juke box Irish music returned in the background. Of course there was no shortage of Danny Boy throughout the day. The waitresses were assisting the bartenders with the three-deep bar crowd. Corned beef sandwiches were flying out of the kitchen. Flanagan's is actually more of a sports bar than an Irish Pub. There are thirty or so TVs on at all times and only one thing gets shown. All sports- all the time. It didn't matter today, with a name like Flanagan's the Irish and Irish wannabees for the day would flock there as if returning to the mothership. The NCAA college basketball tournament was on the TVs without any volume. Despite the blaring Irish music, you knew every time when Seton Hall made a bucket. Every bar stool, table, and high top were taken since 11:00 AM when the doors opened.

For a fifty-four-year-old divorced man, it wasn't really his crowd but he liked spending time with his younger co-workers. Jimmy had a sneaky good sense of humor and the work crew genuinely liked hanging with him. He was always reminded of some story from his college days and he never hesitated telling it. These people had never met any of his college buddies but they all felt they knew most of them intimately from the stories.

Jimmy's goals for the night were simple. He would have some

laughs with his co-workers and eat his once a year meat. Despite all the Irish blood running through his veins, he didn't care for corned beef or any other traditional Irish cuisine for that matter. Tonight he would have his corned beef and be perfectly happy with it. He must have received his taste bud genes from his father. He could eat pizza, pasta, or a good meatball every night of the week if he didn't think it would be odd or unhealthy to do so. His other goals for the evening were to let the Guinness pints and Jameson shots do their thing and to get some one on one time with a certain lady.

One of his co-workers found herself in a similar position. Jessica Adams was recently divorced after she and her husband became empty-nesters. Some thrive on it. Some don't, and the result is usually a quick split. She was fifty-one and her two mid-twenties sons moved out of state after college for careers and left her and her husband staring at each other and the walls. They soon figured out that their children were the glue that had kept their marriage together for so long. Jessica wasn't going quietly to her grave. She was determined to live life on her terms from now on.

Jimmy was a fit fifty-four and despite his post-divorce blues had gotten himself into the best physical shape of his life. It was mostly due to jogging on the treadmill and hiking on the weekends. He was a decent looking man. His forehead was creeping into a five head but other than that he was still hanging on to a thick head of dark black hair with a touch of gray on the sides. Jessica was more of a looker and began dressing younger after her divorce. Until recently Jimmy had thought she was hot stuff but way out of his league. One night they were out with the crew and had a chance to talk about their private lives. Not sure what Jimmy said but she began looking at him differently and acting differently around him. Jimmy felt they somehow may have made a connection on some level.

With all the booze going down and spirits up, it looked like tonight was going to be the night Jimmy and Jessica escalated their relationship. Jimmy had a smile on his face that the work crew hadn't seen in quite a while. Without any notice to anyone, the two of them separated from the table a few minutes apart from each other and went off to a quieter spot on the other side of the restaurant. The younger work crew got a kick out of their lame attempt for a secret rendezvous. They knew exactly what was going on and were happy to see it finally get put into motion.

The conversation between Jessica and Jimmy slowed to a crawl when she moved into his personal space. The talk quickly turned into lips on lips. They both realized that if this was going to happen it wasn't going to be on a night like this when both their heads were swimming in booze. Jessica suggested that Jimmy call her tomorrow so they could talk some more and get together. Jimmy wasn't the one night stand type. This sounded good to him. He had been there about four hours already. If he drank anymore he would wake up and feel like a bus had parked on his head. They both felt they should get back to the table before anyone suspected anything. *Too late for that.*

A few feet away in the crowd the man from the black SUV was sipping his club soda with an eye and an ear toward Jimmy. He was wearing a wide brimmed fedora and had his overcoat on. He didn't exactly fit in but it was St. Patrick's Day and no one seemed to notice or care. He noticed that it looked like Jessica and Jimmy were parting ways for the night. Jimmy pulled out his phone and pulled up his Uber app. He told Jessica that he was getting picked up in five minutes and went back to the table to say good night to the work crew. He didn't realize why they all had smirks on their faces when they said their good-byes. Smiling and hopeful, Jessica stood by the window and watched Jimmy leave.

As Jimmy walked out the door the black SUV pulled up and asked if he was the James that called for an Uber. He said he was and hopped into the back seat. They engaged in some trivial small talk for a minute. The driver didn't seem much for conversation but he liked the roomy accommodations. Jimmy knew the driver already had his destination for where to be dropped off. He didn't know that the driver had no intention of bringing him to that destination. Jimmy was all smiles as he replayed the events of the night in his head. His head was still stuffed with the effects of the beer and whiskey. His thoughts wandered to Jessica and what tomorrow was going to bring. It was probably the happiest he'd felt in five years. He knew he would sleep well tonight. Then the driver missed his turn and all things changed.

CHAPTER 2

I just got off the phone with my human resources department. After thirty years on the job as a police officer and Detective in New Brunswick, New Jersey, I decided to call it a career. I hope I don't live to regret my decision. I love being a cop and never considered retiring until about a month ago.

My wife, Katie, and I went to the Tropicana Hotel and Casino in Atlantic City for our twenty-sixth wedding anniversary on February 19th. We usually take a trip to some resort or casino for a couple of nights. We aren't big gamblers so we never really had any great gambling success stories in the past. That all changed in one spin of a slot machine.

I was playing the three card poker table game and had a few hundred dollars in chips in front of me. Katie was playing her roulette. She could sit there for hours and play the table minimum. If her numbers start hitting then she kicks the bets up a bit. She always places her bets on the family birthday and anniversary numbers. If 1, 15, 18, 19, 21 or 24 come out on the spin then she collects her 35-1 odds bet. I don't even have to watch her to know if she is winning or not. The casinos have the twenty most recent spins posted on an electronic board at every roulette table. I know how she is doing just by looking at the board.

I had bet twenty dollars on my three card hand and twenty dollars on the dealer bonus slot. You get paid for pairs, straights, and flushes. The better the power of your hand, the better the odds you can collect. The dealer bonus is a side bet where you combine your three cards and the dealer's three cards to make your best five card hand. The cards were dealt out and I picked them up only seeing one card. I saw the four of diamonds. Then pinched the cards and squeezed the next card out. Six of diamonds. *Not bad. Straight and flush possibilities.* I squeezed slowly to reveal the third card. I quickly saw it was red card. The view soon confirmed it was a diamond. *Nice. I had my flush.* The final reveal showed it to be a five. My eyes bugged out. I had a straight flush that paid 40-1. I never had a straight flush before but I knew I'd hit big. I didn't know what to do. *Do I call my wife? Text someone? Do I clap? Hug the dealer? Touchdown dance?* Maybe I should just act like most people do when they win and take their chips and move on to the next hand. As I was running these possibilities through my head the dealer flipped over his cards. I thought I was seeing things but it looked like there was a seven and eight of diamonds that got flipped. Now it sunk in. I hit a straight flush on my dealer bonus bet which was another 50 – 1 windfall. *Screw decorum.* It was touchdown dance time.

I have my tough side but also have my fun side. I always liked having a good time and didn't care who knew it. I'm sure Katie had heard some commotion a few minutes ago but she wouldn't have had a view of my table or my embarrassing celebration dance. My dance was a quick spin and some hip gyrations. It couldn't have been pretty to look at. I don't know what twerking is but I just may have added in a twerk or two. My kids would have changed their names and put bags over their heads if they saw their father in action.

I told the dealer to cash me out. I won $1,800 on that hand and combined with my chips before that win, I went to the cashier with $2,250 to cash in. Now it was cocktail time. You don't win $1,800 and not celebrate with a drink or two. I began walking to my wife's roulette table. Maybe it was more like speed walking. I wasn't sure my feet were even hitting the ground. I approached the roulette table and saw the electronic recent spin board. Seeing the last four spins were 18, 15, 24 and 18, I knew she was on a roll herself. I made a quick decision to tell her of our windfall over drinks. I was busting at the seams but somehow managed to keep my win quiet. I was right. Katie was on a roll as she had mounds of single color chips in front of her and a handful of green twenty-five dollar chips. She was so excited that she was up three or four hundred that there was no way I was going to diminish her excitement. I told her the drinks were on her and she was happy to oblige. A quick kiss and we were off to the bar.

On the way to the bar we passed by the high rollers slot machine room, a place we had never even stepped into before. I think I had this idea that each slot machine was occupied by James Bond and a girl on each of his arms. I told Katie that I wanted to check out the high roller slot parlor. She looked at me as if to say, "I only won a few hundred dollars- who do you think we are?" She was feeling good about her recent roll so we went in.

Wow- not what I had imagined. No international spies flanked with gorgeous woman. There was a guy in shorts and a loud Hawaiian shirt who looked bored and was sipping on his coffee. Another old guy with his portable oxygen tank at his side pumping money in like it was on fire. There were a few old ladies with too much lipstick gathering on the cigarette butts dangling from their mouths. These ladies seemed indifferent to the results of their slot spins. They were robotic in how they reached into their purses for another few more hundred dollar bills. Popped them into the machine and three spins later they were reaching for more cash.

I looked and Katie and suggested she give it shot. She thought I was crazy. She didn't yet know I had a wad of hundreds in my pocket. This was clearly not our scene but today and for this moment it was. We saw a progressive $5 Wheel of Fortune machine. That actually meant it was $25 per spin because there was five pay lines. We loved the Wheel of Fortune machines but usually played the twenty-five or fifty cent machines. Sometimes we played the dollar machines if we were feeling lucky. It didn't take much for her to relent. The fun of the Wheel machines was to get a free spin. Whatever dollar amount the wheel lands on is what you win. Katie said "What the hell" and put two crisp Franklins in the machine.

The second spin she got her free spin. She hit the spinner and round and round it went. The payoffs were pretty good on the $5 machine. The wheel was slowing and looked like it was going to land on $150 which was the lowest payout on the wheel. It was better than nothing we thought. The wheel didn't stop on the $150 but went one more space and landed on Jackpot. All of a sudden all sorts of bells were going off and lights flashing over our machine. We knew we did something good but didn't realize how good. She had hit the progressive Jackpot for $1,133,250.25. The attendants ran over and then came a few people in suits. They cordoned off the machine and did their protocol to make sure it was a legitimate hit. Once it was deemed the machine had not been tampered with, we were taken to a back room and given a check. A very large check. Who would have thought? Two touchdown dances in a matter of a half an hour. This time it was a dance for two.

We made a few calls and let our kids know about our good fortune. They knew this was a night to celebrate and were already on their way to meet us. We sat at Tango's bar, which is set just off the casino floor. A Kettle One martini with a stick of olives sat in front of me and an apple martini in front of Katie. We toasted our new found good fortune. We could feel the buzz around us. People whispering "They were the ones" and the like. Word travels fast in a casino when there is a Jackpot hit. I suddenly felt like I should put some of my cash and the check into the safe in our room. Katie thought that was a good idea and had no problem holding down the fort at the bar.

I stepped into the empty elevator to get to the 23rd floor where our room was. A man stepped in behind me. He reeked of alcohol and looked at me awkwardly and said, "Hey". *Quite the conversationalist.* He then moved closer and told me to empty my pockets. The man had a grubby beard and mustache and had me by at least four inches and fifty pounds. I was a hair over six feet tall and a bit above two hundred pounds and could handle myself if needed. He was wearing jeans, a leather vest over a dirty tee shirt, and, of course, his chained wallet. He had a baseball hat pulled down in a lame attempt to hide his identity.

He pulled his knife. It was a nice six inch carbon steel blade Bowie hunting knife. Too bad it won't be doing him any good. I said "You better put that away before you get hurt."

He laughed. "What are you some kind of wise guy? Give it up," he said. He must have seen me at the cashier's window cashing in my chips. The slot machine check would be of no use to him.

"What's your name?" He just stared at me. "I like to address people by name when I talk to them." He just stood there trying to figure me out. I guess he wasn't into friendly conversation. "Okay. You look like a Bob. I'm going to call you Bob."

"Time to shut your fat mouth and give me that wad of hundreds you pocketed." He waved the knife in front of my face.

"Bob, I don't like that option. Do I have any other options?"

"You're a real smartass. I'm going to get that money one way or the other. I'll slice you up if I have to."

"Bob, that's not going to happen. I think you should consider putting that knife away and get yourself off on the next floor." I let him think over my offer then went on.

"Bob, do you like chewing your food?" He wasn't the sharpest tool in the shed and stood trying to figure out where I was going with this. I clarified. "If you want your teeth to chew your food then you better back off now." He laughed again and decided he'd had enough of me. He made his move with a slashing wave toward my right shoulder. I easily swatted it away. Before he knew it, he was on the ground with blood pouring from his face. I dropped him quicker than my junior year college statistics class. My fist went into his solar plexus and drove my knee into his face as he was buckling over. I heard the crack of his nose. His hat flew off his head. *Oh no. He lost his great disguise.* He was face down and I put my knee into his back. I picked up the man's head by the back of his long greasy hair. "Bob, are you gonna be a nice boy for the rest of the day?"

He could only offer "Fuck you" as the blood poured from his face.

"Wrong answer, Bob." I slammed his face into the elevator floor and asked him again. He nodded. "Bob, you be nice today" I said as I left the elevator. I thought I heard him spitting a few teeth out as I was leaving. Not sure what floor he wanted to go to so I hit the buttons for every floor. He wouldn't be getting up for a while. I grabbed his knife and dropped it in the garbage can outside the elevator.

I picked up the courtesy phone in the hallway and called the front desk. "It's a great day at the Tropicana, how may I help you."

I said "Clean up needed in elevator six" and hung up. The front desk clerk was right. It was a great day at the Tropicana.

I rejoined my wife and we continued our celebration. No need to let her know about my little elevator incident. We bought drinks for everyone at the bar. Put five hundred on the bar for the $125.00 bar bill and told Tony the bartender to keep the rest. Tony thanked us profusely as we headed up to our room and waited for our kids to join us.

I smile every time I replay the events of that day in my head. After Uncle Sam got his grubby paws on our money, we cleared a little over $800,000. The casino had used us for promotional purposes by having us pose with the oversized check in our hands. I was on one corner and Katie was on the other. Huge smiles on both of our faces. Our picture and slot win details were pasted all over the casino. We even landed on a billboard for the Tropicana on the Atlantic City Expressway. The check simply said "Pay to the order of John and Katherine MacMasters". John was my birth certificate name only. I was Jack before I was out of diapers.

I had a newspaper delivery route when I was ten years old. I hustled every winter snow storm going door to door to see if anyone would pay me to shovel their driveway or sidewalk, a concept completely lost on my kids and their generation. Once I was able to get my working papers, I began caddying at a local county club. I worked after school in high school and every summer in my high school and college years. After graduating college I immediately took a job bartending while figuring out the rest of my life. I eventually landed a job with the New Brunswick Police Department and spent the last thirty years there. I had enough. Time to live my life. I'm fifty-four years old and have been working for forty-four of those years.

Katie was working as a third grade school teacher in Bridgewater, New Jersey for the past fifteen years. She was a teacher at that school for six years before she took a time out from teaching to raise our three children. She loved her job and her students. Being a teacher, she was given every imaginable holiday off and free summers. Quite a good gig. She also worked part time with an interior designer. That took up quite a bit of time on her weekends and off days. As much as she loved teaching and being with her students, her real passion was taking a room or two or an entire house and putting her design touch on it. The plan for now is for her to teach another year or two and then consider venturing out on her own in the interior decorating world. With me retired and her in a position to make her own hours, it opens up many possibilities for our future.

A few weeks ago we were out for dinner. I said, "I have been giving retirement some serious thought".

She couldn't respond quick enough. "What are you waiting for?"

We'd never really had the conversation but I knew she couldn't wait for the day that I turned in my badge and gun. I had an on the job injury a few years back and she was hoping that would be the end of it. I loved my job and would never let an injury decide my fate. I would only go out on my terms. Our financial situation had obviously improved in the last month. Our financial obligations for our kid's colleges were behind us. Two of my three kids went to college. My oldest son decided he didn't want college and jumped right into the work force. We knew he was a smart kid and would succeed at whatever he decided in life. We had a decent nest egg before the slot machine hit. We agreed that it was time.

After I called my HR department today, I said to Katie, "I just made the call." She jumped into my arms and hugged me almost into unconsciousness. A calmness came over me, something I hadn't felt in many years.

My phone rang and I saw on the caller ID that it was Tim Bollander. He is my lifelong best friend. We went to grade school, high school, and college together. He lives close enough where we still get together regularly. I put it right to speaker. "Yo, Bo, what's up?"

"Hey Mac, did you hear yet?" he said.

"Hear what?" I shot back.

He knew he would be the one to break the news to me. Something I am sure he took no pleasure in. "Squirrel is dead".

CHAPTER 3

"What the hell happened?" I yelled into the phone.

"I don't know. Tommy called me and told me he died," Bo said. His voice was quivering with every word. We'd never had a conversation so serious. I wasn't used to hearing his emotions pouring through the phone. And vice versa. It's not that we weren't capable of it, it's just the way it was.

Katie was in the same room as me and immediately perked up. She knew something had happened. And whatever it was, it wasn't good. I could see her making the "what's up?" hand motions. I put my finger out as if to say "Give me a second so I can find out". I could sense her frustration so I mouthed to her "Jimmy is dead". She had known Jimmy well and also considered him a friend. She hated the name Squirrel and would never call him that. She once asked Jimmy about being called Squirrel. He told her with a smile "I don't mind. It's my name." Katie knew he didn't mind because it tied him back to a time in his life which was among his happiest. She knew it was a nickname from his college days and all the boys still called him that so she tolerated hearing it come out of my mouth. She was tearing up and now pressing for more info. Now my stop sign hand was up. Trying to get her to allow me get some info. She relented for a few seconds.

"Died how?" I pressed.

"Tommy didn't have all the details but said they are saying he killed himself." He said it as if he didn't believe the words that were exiting his mouth. Tommy was Jimmy's younger brother and was also a good friend.

"Bullshit. I can't believe that." That made no sense to me. "I saw him in December before the holidays. We went out for a few drinks. Everything seemed to be going good with him. He told me he was over the bitch and seemed pretty happy."

"Yeah. Well, maybe he wasn't so happy," Bo reasoned.

"I'm not buying it. Who else knows?

"You're my first call" he said.

"All right, we've got to call everyone. I'll take the Jersey boys. You take the rest. Any word on the arrangements?"

"Not yet. We need to find out what the hell happened."

"You're damn right we do. I'll check back with you after I make my calls."

Katie had basically heard the whole conversation. She was in tears and knew I was torn up inside. Squirrel was a close friend and had been for the past thirty-three years. We shared so many laughs and good times that I was dreading facing the fact that his involvement in my life would be reduced to only memories. I told Katie that I would find out more and keep her posted. For now, I had calls to make.

This is the second one of my college friends to die in as many months. In February, Tyler Evigan died in his lake cabin in

Pennsylvania. He would work hard during the week and spend most weekends at the cabin. It never mattered to him what the weather was or what time of the year it was. He was a good friend thirty some years ago but we had lost touch for the most part. He did go to a few of our annual reunions over the past few years. It was always great to re-connect with him. He liked keeping in touch with posts on Facebook. I am not much of a social media person and not on Facebook.

A lot of the boys kept in touch with him. He had a great job in Harrisburg working for the governor. On the night he died, he supposedly fell asleep while smoking and the entire cabin burned down. There was a vodka bottle near his nightstand where his body was found. They concluded he had been drunk and passed out in his bed with a lit cigarette. He always had his demons with booze. I was told that he hadn't had a drink in over two years before he died. I was surprised when I heard alcohol was involved. He must have fallen off the wagon. I wasn't able to go out for any of the services. A few of us chipped in and sent a nice floral arrangement to the funeral home.

I made my calls one by one and broke the news. I didn't get any easier with the repetition of telling it over and over again. There would be a good showing for his wake and funeral. We would make sure of it.

CHAPTER 4

Some of the details of Jimmy's death were coming in. He supposedly jumped to his death from a high peak at one the trails he had been hiking on Friday night and suffered massive internal and external injuries. They found alcohol in his system and apparently concluded that he was depressed and went to a place he was familiar with and ended his life.

I'm sure this was investigated. Four years ago I may have accepted this but not now. He had turned the corner. I was sure of it.

I knew Squirrel's parents well and decided to take a ride to see how they were holding up. They lived only a few miles away two towns over. Katie jumped up and grabbed her coat. I took that to mean she was coming, too. Which was fine with me. My mind was all over the place trying to process everything. I wasn't sure if she was coming to make sure I was okay or to comfort the Colluccis. Knowing Katie, I'm sure it was both.

Katie offered to drive and I took her up on it. I usually do the driving but knew she was the better option for this trip. The ride over was only ten or twelve minutes but it seemed like much longer. The conversation was kept to a minimum. I found myself in the passenger seat with my head turned right and staring out the window.

The world looked like a sad place to me. The scenery was no different today than it was yesterday but it just didn't look the same. I couldn't stop thinking about how Mr. and Mrs. Collucci were trying to deal with this. The thought that the son they raised was so miserable that he had to take his own life would haunt their every thought for the rest of their lives.

The Colluccis lived in a nice upper middle class neighborhood in Bedminster, New Jersey. They had been there for as long as I knew them. We pulled up to their house and didn't see any cars in the driveway. I'm sure their cars were in their two car garage. I wasn't completely surprised they had no company. Jimmy's only sibling was his brother Tommy, who lived out of state. He no doubt was on a plane already or getting on a plane soon. As we pulled up, we saw a tray of food sitting on their front porch in front of the door. It may have been a drop and go. It also could be the Colluccis were not ready for company. Not knowing what to say to people just yet. We would find out soon enough.

Katie parked in their circular driveway about twenty feet from the front door. They must have heard the car pull up. By the time we got out of the car, both of Jimmy's parents were standing at the open front door. I moved quickly to greet them and threw my arms around Mrs. Collucci first then Mr. Collucci, Katie doing the same right behind me.

"Mr. and Mrs. C. I am so sorry," was the first thing out of my mouth.

"Thank you, Jack, and you, too, Katie. So nice of you to stop by.

It means a lot," Mrs. Collucci said. Mr. Collucci nodding his agreement. Then he said "Please, come in."

Katie said, "Thank you" and they walked us to their living room.

"Please sit down. Can I get you something to drink?" Quick declines from both of us. We sat on their leather sofa as Mr. and Mrs. Collucci took the loveseat. They were holding hands. We did the same.

"We are devastated," she started.

"I don't even know what I can say to you right now." Not sure what to say or how to say it.

"I know, Jack. We don't know what to say either. Tommy is on his way. He is taking this hard. They were close as you know," she said.

Katie jumped in. "We know they were. Jimmy talked about Tommy all the time. Jimmy was obviously proud of him." Tommy had found success on Wall Street and moved out west. He now did some consulting work. Jimmy never found the success Tommy did but there was never even a hint of jealousy. He always felt Tommy was a hard worker and had earned every nickel he ever made. Tommy was never the smartest guy in his class but he put in maximum effort and got the grades. That effort led him to earning his MBA and Certified Financial Planner designation. I had known Tommy for almost as long as I had known Jimmy. He would come to visit Jimmy a couple times a semester when we were in college. He must have had some wild times because he kept coming back. Tommy was a ball buster just like the rest of us. He fit right in. Katie had known Tommy and Jimmy for as long as she has been with me. They both came to our wedding. Tommy brought his girlfriend at the time, which is now his lovely wife. And Jimmy brought the bitch.

"How are you guys holding up?" I switched gears. I immediately hoped this came across the way I intended. On the surface, it was a stupid question. *Of course they are not holding up well. Their son just died.*

"We're hanging on by a thread," Mr. Collucci offered. "The next few days are going to be rough."

"Have the arrangements been made yet?" I asked.

"We just got back from Simmons Funeral Home. Wednesday wake and Thursday funeral at Immaculate Heart of Mary in town here," she said, fighting back the tears. I could see Mr. Collucci squeeze her hand hoping it offered her some comfort.

"Is there anything we can do?" Katie jumped back in.

"I wish there was," they both seemed to say softly at the same time.

The conversation quickly turned to an awkward silence, all of us dwelling on the same sad reality in our own way. After a minute or so I broke the silence. "Does anyone know what happened yet?"

Mrs. Collucci was shaking her head and shrugging her shoulders as Mr. Collucci said, "We don't know much. Some detective stopped by and asked us a few questions. He didn't come out and say but gave us the impression he thought Jimmy took his own life. The guy was a bit abrupt and wouldn't give us any more information when we asked."

"Who was the detective?" I asked.

Mrs. C got up and walked toward her dining room table. "Rizzolo or something like that. I have his card here." She grabbed the card and said "Rizzo, Detective Robert Rizzo."

"What did he ask you?" I asked.

"Not much. Was Jimmy depressed? Did he have a girlfriend? Any traumatic events in his life recently? Who were his friends? He didn't ask much more than that," Mrs. Collucci responded.

"What did you tell him?"

Mr. C took over. "We told him about his divorce five years ago. We don't know of any girlfriends. We told him he moved on from his ex-wife. That's about it."

"Anything else?" Mrs. C was now openly crying. I didn't want to press any further.

Fighting through the tears she had anger in her voice. "My boy didn't take his own life. That I'm sure of."

"I know he didn't. He would never do that. I will go see this Detective Rizzo and see what he knows." I didn't know what I would find out. I would need a lot more convincing before I accepted this as a suicide. It just didn't add up.

Mrs. C moved in quickly for a quick hug. "Would you do that for us? Tell us he's wrong." I only hoped that was the news I could bring them.

We were getting ready to say our goodbyes when the front door opened. In walked Jimmy's brother Tommy. He was carrying just a small canvas bag for quick travel. He saw me first as I was walking toward him. "Tommy, great to see you."

"Great to see you, too, Mac." He looked past me and saw Katie. He reached around for a hug. "Nice to see you Katie," he mouthed without much volume, "How are they doing?"

Quietly, Katie nodded and said, "I'd say pretty good. Considering."

Tommy moved into the dining room and embraced both his parents. One arm around each. They held the hug.

When they broke from the hug, we went over and I said "We'll head out so you can catch up."

Katie added, "Let us know if there is anything we can do. Anything at all."

They thanked us for stopping by. We could tell it meant a lot to them. Tommy said, "I'll walk you out."

When we got outside Tommy asked if I thought it could be true. "I'm having a hard time believing it. I just can't wrap my head around it. It makes no sense."

Tommy shot back, "Trust your gut. I don't care what this asshole detective says. He didn't kill himself. I talked to him last week and everything was going great for him. He was telling me that he finally got tickets to go The Masters next month." Going to see the best golfers in the world compete for golf's top prize was a bucket list item for Jimmy. He enjoyed playing the sport and watching it on TV. Seeing the final round of The Masters is something he always dreamed of doing. "He also told me he was thinking about getting back into the dating world. Said he had his eye on some lady in his office." He let it sink in and continued ,"Why? Why now? Things were definitely on the upswing for him."

I couldn't argue with that. "Tommy, I told your parents that I was going to talk to the detective and see what I can find out."

"Great, Mac. We really appreciate that. Will see you on Wednesday. Who's coming from the crew?"

"Pretty much everyone. We'll be there in full force," I said as we headed for our car. I turned back to Tommy and said, "I'm thinking we should be canceling the reunion this year."

"Don't even think about it. That was the highlight of Jimmy's year every year. You can't cancel it, Mac." He paused for a few seconds as I was digesting his thoughts. He then continued, "We'll hoist a glass in Jimmy's memory. Jimmy will find a way to be there. He'll be watching from above. He'll find a way to send us a sign."

"You're right, Tommy," I said. Jimmy never missed one of our annual reunions. He would never want to be the reason for the trip to be canceled. The more I thought about it, the more I was convinced this was the right thing to do. For now, this was one small way we could honor Jimmy's memory.

"Great. Then it's all set. The reunion goes on as planned. Plus, I was giving some thought to this whole situation and I want to make an announcement to the boys at our reunion dinner."

"Anything you want to share now?" I asked.

"No. Not yet. I still need to work out all the details in my head."

"Okay. Sounds good. We'll see you tomorrow."

Every year since we graduated from college, we'd have had an annual three day reunion filled with drinking, golf, drinking, eating, drinking, gambling, and some more drinking. We always kicked off the reunion with a nice dinner at a steakhouse. We started out with great turnouts for the first five or so years. Then the marriages and kids began to enter the picture. This cut the numbers down quite a bit. On our good years we would have a dozen or more make the trip. During the lean years we were lucky to get six of us to show up. The numbers have been back to where they should be for the past fifteen years. We all needed this trip every year. It was a great way to get away from the real world and blow off some steam for a few days. The ball busting and laughs were plentiful. It didn't matter that we rehashed the same stories every year. We laughed just as hard as if we were hearing it for the first time. Tommy didn't go to school with us but he was a regular attendee. I'm glad to hear he is coming this year.

Going to see Mr. and Mrs. Collucci and Tommy was a good call. We found out some info that we didn't know before. As we headed out I couldn't help think that I went there looking for some answers but left with only more questions.

CHAPTER 5

The man with the scar on his jawline was sitting in his black SUV. His assignment was not over and he was staying in New Jersey awaiting further instructions. He had killed two people already and was thinking more bodies would fall if he didn't get what he was sent for. The man simply viewed himself as an independent contractor. Failure was not an option for him. He was given an assignment where his unique skill set was needed and he completed the assignment. It was no more complicated than that to him. He was always paid handsomely, half up front and the balance upon completion. He had yet to fail to collect the balance. The phone rang. The man picked it up and heard his current employer's voice. "Status?" was the only word uttered.

"It wasn't Collucci."

"I'm running out of patience. I thought this would have been taken care of already," the employer said.

"After I finished up with Evigan and confirmed he wasn't the one, I started the backround on Collucci and paid him a visit," the scar man said.

"What happened in New Jersey?" the boss man asked.

"I interrogated him. He knew nothing. He doesn't have anything either. He turned out to be a loose end so I arranged for his suicide.

He doesn't know who it is. With the pain he endured, nobody is that loyal."

"Damn it. I want this done. Get it done. What the hell am I paying you for?" the employer yelled into the phone.

"Listen here," he shot back. "I will get this done. I don't care if I have to kill every damn one of them." He paused. "None of this will ever get tied to you. Like I told you before, anyone I have to get rid of will be made to look like an accident."

"Good. I don't want anyone investigating any homicides. I don't want some detective poking around and asking questions or stumbling into my past."

The employer hung up. The man with the scar on his jaw sat in his SUV trying to figure out who the hell he would target next. He was working off a list of names. He didn't tell his employer but he had a good idea who he would visit next.

CHAPTER 6

Katie and I drove to the funeral home together with Bo and his wife, Faith. The parking lot was full and the surrounding on-street parking was full as well. We would have to park two blocks away but that was all right with us. It meant there was a good turnout for Jimmy's wake. We approached the door and there was a funeral home employee in a black suit holding the door open for us. He was nodding "Good evening" in his solemn voice to all that passed him. The line formed immediately as we entered. It looked like it would be at least a half hour before we would make it to the casket.

As we were waiting, I saw Charlie Logan and the Delpino brothers in line. They were ahead of us by at least fifteen minutes so they weren't going to get out of line to come join us. They tried to wave us up to join them. Not a good idea. Cutting in line at a wake was worse than trying to cut in line for Star Wars movie tickets on opening night. Wakes reeked of death and despair. People wanted to get in and out as quick as possible. There would be hell to pay if we cut the line. I didn't feel like seeing some of Mr. and Mrs. Collucci's friends whip out their light sabers. We stayed and the line moved quicker than I thought.

We got to the casket and saw Mr. and Mrs. C and Tommy

greeting the mourners. It was all very robotic. All of the people say basically the same thing while giving their hugs. We paid our respects to Jimmy and walked over to Tommy and his parents.

A few rows back sat the bitch, Patty. She was sitting with some guy. Of course he looked like an asshole. Whether he was or wasn't didn't matter to me. If he was with her, he was an asshole. I could hardly look at her. She was responsible for so much of the pain in Jimmy's life over the past five years. Jimmy had finally closed the book on her and then this happened. Some things in life are just not fair. We expressed our condolences again and they were as well received as could be expected. The Colluccis were holding up well.

We made our way to the back of the viewing room. Charlie Logan and the Delpino brothers were already there. Bro hugs around.

Tommy Delpino knew I had been over to see Tommy and Mr. and Mrs. C and said, "How are they doing?"

"As good as could be expected," I said. "They're tough. Tommy being back is huge."

We were catching up when we saw a few more of the boys in line. Eddie Vincent and Anthony Puglisi were together as well as Marty Davidson and Brian Kavanaugh. They made their way through the line and then joined us. More bro hugs around.

Brian Kavanaugh came from Maryland. The Delpino's came from Connecticut and Anthony Puglisi from Ohio. Eddie drove in from Pennsylvania. The rest of us were local in New Jersey. It was nice to see the boys making the effort to be here for Jimmy.

We decided to go to Dorsey's Pub for a bite to eat and a few beers. Katie and Faith decided to pass on the invite and headed home. I think they knew they would be welcome but felt it best if it was just the boys heading over. Brian hadn't made reservations at any hotel yet. I suggested he crash at my house. This way he didn't have to shell out for a hotel room and we now had a ride home. Sounded like a win-win to everyone.

I kissed Katie goodbye and told her we shouldn't be too late. I told her that Brian was going to stay over. She appreciated the heads up. She said she would put fresh sheets on the bed in the guest bedroom. Bo said his goodbyes to Faith and off they went.

I told the guys that Dorsey's was only a mile from where we were and gave them quick directions. Bo and I started to leave with Brian when I got a quick tap on the shoulder. I turned around and there stood Patty. At that point, Katie came back in. I forgot to give her the car keys. I handed her the keys and she decided to stay and see what Patty could possibly have to say to me.

"Hey, Jack. Do you have a second?" she said

"Why are you even here?" I said to her. "I see you brought a date to a wake. Real class move."

"This isn't easy on me, you know. I needed someone to be with me. I couldn't do this alone. He's not *my date*." There were a few seconds of silence and then she continued. "I heard Jimmy killed himself and I feel responsible."

"Responsible? How so?" Kate now joining in.

"He must have been depressed because of me."

Katie seemed to have had enough. "You don't know anything.

You've hardly spoken to him in five years. You have an awfully high opinion of yourself. First of all, we don't even know for sure if Jimmy took his own life. And secondly, you sure as hell would have had nothing to do with it. He was long over you." She took a breath. *You go girl.* "You expect us to feel sorry for you. You're not the victim here. Are you here for some type of absolution?" Katie spoke her peace and I could tell she felt better for it.

Patty didn't know what to say at this point. She realized Katie was right. Patty shouldn't be coming to Jimmy's wake and playing the role of victim.

I took over. "Listen, Patty, we appreciate that you came and paid your respects to Jimmy. You owed him that. But staying around is only making people uncomfortable."

She grabbed her wake-date and took off.

.

CHAPTER 7

The three of us drove over to Dorsey's. The rest of the guys were there ahead of us and were seated at a table in the bar room. They had already ordered a few pitchers of beer. The waitress brought us over some cold beer glasses when she saw us join the table. I thanked her for the extra effort. She could have left glasses on the table when she delivered the pitchers. They would have been warm by the time we got there. I, for one, like a cold beer in a cold glass, so I would remember this at tip time.

We were lucky that they had a table to fit all of us. There were nine of us at a table that usually seats eight. It was the biggest they had in the bar area. I sat on one of the ends. Looking down the table there was Bo, Brian, Marty, Anthony, Chuckie, Eddie, and the DelPino brothers.

Bo raised his glass and started. "Men, Squirrel was a great friend to all of us. We had so many good times." We all had our glasses raised. "Tomorrow is going to be a tough day. It's great to see everyone. It sucks that it has to be under these circumstances." Bo paused but obviously not done. "Men. To Squirrel. Gone but never to be forgotten." Glasses were clinking as we all added our "Hear, Hear".

Chuckie stepped up. "Guys, let's not forget Ev." Glasses up again. "Here's to Ev. He may not have seen many of us a lot in the past thirty years but he is still one of us. To Ev." More clinking glasses.

The mood would quickly change as we started re-hashing some old stories involving Squirrel and Ev. The somber mood from the toasts was gone and the laughter began with the stories.

Brian said, "Hey, Mac. I heard Squirrel and Bo got you good." He was right. They did get me good. Now I am going to have to relive it again while getting laughed at the entire time. Last October, I received a letter in the mail from The New Brunswick Police Department. It said that due to my age, I needed to report to Dr. Pranav Singh for a colonoscopy or end up being placed in a higher risk tier for my insurance rates. This would mean more money out of pocket for me. The letter went on that this was a requirement from Aetna as part of their preventive medicine program. Aetna is the health provider for my medical insurance through the department. It had the official department letterhead and signed by the human resources manager. It looked pretty damn official to me. According to the letter, I was to schedule my colonoscopy before November 1, 2016. There was also a pre-test instruction sheet attached. The pre-test instruction sheet told me exactly what I needed to do before the test.

I scheduled the test for 9:00 am on a Friday in late October. According to the pre-test instructions, I had to fast for sixteen hours. No liquid or solids for sixteen hours. So I didn't eat or drink a thing after 5:00 pm on Thursday. It seemed excessive but I didn't give it much thought. The instructions also told me that I needed to remove any excess hair in my "rectal area". I should have known there that something was up but I marched on. I got out my razor and shaved my own ass. The worst part of the instructions was the super laxative that I had to buy and take at 5:00 am so I would completely flush out my system. I did as instructed and sat from 6:00 am to 7:30 on the toilet. Needless to say, the laxative did its job.

I arrived for the appointment and went through with the procedure. As I was leaving I asked the nurse at the desk if she was going to send the report to my human resources department. The letter I received gave explicit instructions to send the report to the human resources manager. She looked at me puzzled. She said she couldn't do that under any circumstances due to the HIPAA regulations that protect people's privacy. I showed her the letter from my employer. She read it and said, "This is not right. We can't send them any medical report nor can they compel you to have an intrusive medical procedure."

I knew that instruction sheet looked hokey. I grabbed the letter back from her and shot out of there. When I got to my car, I saw Bo and Squirrel standing next to their car hysterically laughing. "You sons of bitches," is all I could come up with. The good news was the test results were all good.

I got done finishing the story and said, "I have to give those pricks credit, they made me fund my own prank, give myself a laxative and somehow got me to shave my own ass." I found out later that they went onto the department website and downloaded a form with the department letterhead on it and transposed it to their own hand crafted letter.

Bo was practically choking on his laughter. He said "Shaving your ass was Squirrel's idea. He never forgot you shaving his eyebrow in college. Payback may not be immediate but is still a bitch." The boys got a great laugh. It was true. I did shave Squirrel's one eyebrow one night in college after he had a hard night of drinking. I thought it was much crueler to shave just one eyebrow. This way he would have to decide the fate of the other one. He chose to keep the remaining eyebrow and color in one with an eyebrow pencil. He looked ridiculous for a good month or so. I guess that was a good one because he seemed to never forget it.

We were having some much needed laughs. A few tables away I couldn't help but see two guys sitting at a high top bar table pestering the nice waitress every time she was near them. They looked like two blowhard ex-jocks. The bigger guy was wearing a New York Rangers hockey jersey and the other had a New York Knicks hat on. Mr. Ranger was obviously the alpha male out of the two. He was the loud one and the one doing the most bothering of the waitress. I heard Mr. Ranger snap his fingers at the waitress and say "Two more beers, Honey."

You never snap your fingers at a waitress or bartender. They are not dogs. I could see her reaction. She seemed to cringe every time she heard their voices or got near their table. Unfortunately, the waitress did as told. She brought the beers to their table. As she was walking away, Mr. Ranger gave her a pat on the rear end and said,

"How about a couple more cold glasses, sweetheart?"

She looked back at the man and said "I'm not your sweetheart and don't ever touch me."

He started laughing at her and said, "Take it easy Honey, we're just having some fun here."

She said "I'm not your Honey, either," and walked away while Mr. Knick and Mr. Ranger sat there laughing.

Bo was watching me watch those two idiots and knew I wouldn't let it go. Bo has known me forever and sometimes he knew what I was thinking before I did. This was one of those times and he was right. I could also tell that Bo was thinking of taking care of this. Bo could handle himself. He was always big, athletic, handsome, and strong as an ox. He is still all of those things with good husband, good father, and good provider added in.

Bo began to rise. I put my hand on his shoulder and quietly said, "Thanks, but this one is mine."

He dropped back down in his seat and was waiting for the show. I think he was the only one at the table that knew what was going on. Everyone else was still engaged in storytelling, ball busting, and laughter.

I walked to the table and apparently Mr. Ranger sensed what was about to come and didn't like me intruding on his good time. "What the hell do you want?" he barked. These guys looked to be in their mid-thirties and fairly well built.

"Do you know that you just assaulted that waitress? If you put your hand on someone that doesn't want to be touched it's an assault," I said.

"What are you some kind of cop or something?" the Ranger fan said.

"Not tonight."

"What are you gonna do? Arrest me?" as he laughed. "I didn't assault anyone."

"I have no plans to arrest you."

"What are going to do? Get your crew over there to take us outside?" his laugh was now down to a snicker.

I told him "Those guys won't be going outside. It will be just the three of us."

"No, thanks," Mr. Ranger said. "I ain't hitting no cop."

"I'm going to put my badge and gun away. Then it's just us three old boys. We can either dance outside or you two can pay your bill and get the hell out of here"

Mr. Knick finally piped in. "Look, we're not looking for any trouble."

"You may not be looking for trouble but you found it," I said.

Back to Mr. Ranger. "Keep quiet. We're not going anywhere. Get the hell away from our table." Mr. Knick correctly sensed that they were in a bad spot. The big dumb Ranger fan not quite getting it yet.

"I'll give you the choice, I can take you apart one at a time or both at once. I think you will find it far more embarrassing when you are re-telling the story of how I took you both out at the same time. Like I said, your choice." Now it was put up or shut up time. Fight or flight. *Choose carefully.*

Mr. Ranger finally saw the end game. "We were heading out after these beers anyway." Mr. Knick breathed out an obvious sigh of relief. Maybe he would think twice about choosing a loud mouth obnoxious jackass for a friend.

"You don't get it. You're leaving now. How much is your tab?" I said

Mr. Ranger said, "Okay, pal. We're outta here."

"How much is your tab?" I repeated.

"What do you care?" Mr. Ranger said.

"How much?" in a voice that he knew demanded a response.

"About fifty bucks," said Mr. Knick as he was reaching for his wallet.

"Put your wallet away," I said to Mr. Knick and turned back to Mr. Ranger. "Get out your wallet."

He hesitated as if to try to figure if he had any out. He didn't and pulled out his wallet. I grabbed the wallet from his hand and opened it up as Mr. Ranger sat there looking stupid and defeated. I took out everything he had which was about a hundred and twenty bucks and put it on the table. I tossed his wallet back at him, hitting him in the chest before it fell to the floor. He bent over and picked it up and then looked at me. He looked like he wanted to say something but thought better of it. The two of them put their heads down and quietly headed for the door. They went out of their way to avoid walking past our table. As they were about at the door I couldn't help taking one more shot.

I yelled out to them, "Leaving early tonight guys? You take care now."

Mr. Ranger and Mr. Knick didn't even break stride but were obviously seething, heads still down as they opened the door and left the restaurant. They would have to find another place to drink and be obnoxious being I was quite sure that they wouldn't be visiting this place again anytime soon.

I walked back to our table and Bo had a big grin on his face. "Nice job, Mac. You must be getting soft in your old age. You let'em live." Bo was quite sure both men would be tending to their wounds by now. Bo was one of the few people that knew what I was capable of. It was something that only a few people knew about.

I had my own smile. "Who me? Mr. Nice Guy?"

The waitress came back to our table with two fresh pitchers of beer. Chuckie said, "I don't think we ordered those."

She said, "These are on the house, boys." She walked away giving me a wink and a smile.

We had been there for about three hours and had a big day tomorrow. Eddie grabbed the bill and paid the entire tab before anyone else had a chance to. I easily could have taken care of it given my recent good fortune but he seemed quite happy with his nice gesture. We all thanked Eddie for a night out on him. We broke up our little party and went our own ways. Brian, Bo, and I were walking toward the door when a woman came up to us.

"Are you Jack MacMasters?" she said.

I nodded.

"Can I talk to you for a minute? My name is Jessica Adams."

CHAPTER 8

"Hi, Jessica. You can call me Mac. This is Tim Bollander and Brian Kavanaugh." They exchanged hellos.

Bo said, "You can call me Bo."

"Okay. Will do, Bo."

Brian just stood there trying to figure out what this gorgeous woman wanted with me. Brian had been divorced for about ten years. Ever since his divorce, he had dated occasionally but nothing ever became serious. I could tell Brian liked what he was looking at. Brian, who never was at a loss for words, seemed to be having some sort of brain lock. He would snap out of it soon but I would enjoy it while it lasted.

"How can I help you, Jessica?" I asked.

"I saw you at the funeral home and I kind of followed you here. I'm not a stalker but I overheard that you are a cop and I wanted to talk to you about Jimmy," she said.

"Sure. Are you a friend of Squ...I mean Jimmy. What's on your mind?" I asked.

"There is no way Jimmy killed himself," she said as if to leave no room for debate.

"Wow. You get right to the point. What makes you say that, Jessica?" Bo now taking over. "Do you know something we don't?"

"I worked with Jimmy for the past few years. He had no reason to kill himself. He wasn't depressed at all. I was probably the last person he knew to see him alive. I was with him at Flanagan's on the night he died."

I quickly said "you were at Flanagan's that night?" We had known that he was out that night at a bar. Having alcohol in his system was likely one of the reasons the handling detective concluded it was a suicide. Depressed people often turn to the bottle and sometimes make irrational decisions while under the influence. "If you don't mind, I would like you to tell me everything you know about that night."

"Jimmy talked about you guys all the time. He would tell stories from back in the day that would crack us up at work." She now looked at me. "He told me you were a police detective."

"I am or was. I'm about to be an ex detective. I just put in for my retirement."

"Congratulations. You must be so excited."

"We are. Thank you." The "we" was an obvious quick reference to my wife Katie. "You were saying that you were with Jimmy that night."

"Oh, yeah. I'm sorry." She went on to tell us how close knit a work crew they had with she and Jimmy being the elder statesman and stateswoman. She told how the work gang loved having Jimmy around. They thought he was fun and funny. She then got to the meatier part of the evening. "Jimmy and I left the table and found a quiet area in the bar where we could talk a bit." Bo and I listened intently. Brian still catatonic. "We had been semi-flirting for a little while in the office over the past month. We both found ourselves in similar situations and it looked like things were about to go to the next level with us."

Brian's eyes and mouth were now wide open. It looked like he was snapping out of it. I knew exactly what was going through Brian's head. *Jimmy was a decent looking guy but they weren't even from the same planet.*

Brian finally found his voice. "You… You… You and Jimmy?" I never knew Brian to have a stuttering problem.

Jessica now felt she had to defend Jimmy. "What's wrong with that? Jimmy is…was a great guy." She was getting glassy eyed and began welling up with tears. Obviously realizing that she had to use the word "was" instead of "is". Her genuine care for Jimmy was coming through loud and clear.

Brian backed off immediately. "I'm sorry, Jessica. We're all hurting here."

I decided to get this back on track and looked at Jessica. "What did you mean by the next level, if I may pry? Did something happen that night?"

"I thought for sure something was going to happen that night

47

between us. We started kissing a bit at the bar." *Brian back into his catatonic state.* "I was kind of expecting that maybe we would spend the night together." *Brian close to needing CPR.* "Jimmy didn't want it to happen that way. He didn't want us doing anything that one or both of us would regret because there was alcohol involved. I think that in his mind, if we were to get together, that it would be done when we both had clear minds. I think he is sweet and somewhat old fashioned. I don't think sex with me after a night of drinking is what he had in mind. When it happened, it would have to be real for him." *Earth to Brian. Earth to Brian. Come in Brian. Too late. That last one did him in. Time to bring Brian back with the living.*

I said to Jessica, "How did you leave it with him that night?

"He asked me if I wanted to get together with him the next day. I told him that I sure would and he was going to call me and set something up. I really felt good about it, too."

"Did you leave first or did Jimmy? I asked.

"Jimmy did. Why?"

"Did you see him leave?" Bo asked.

"Yes. He called for his Uber ride and then went back to the table and said his goodbyes and paid his bill. A few minutes later, he was getting into his ride. That was the last I saw him. I can tell you one thing. He left that bar that night and there is no way he left to go kill himself."

"Did you tell any of this to the police?" I asked.

"Some detective came by the office and asked a few questions to a few people and then he left. He never even spoke with me."

Jessica now got to the heart of the matter and looked at me. "Can you look into this? I don't know what happened to Jimmy but it's not what they're saying."

This just sealed the deal for my initial gut reaction. I never thought Jimmy killed himself and now I was sure of it. "I most definitely will be looking into this. And I am going to start with that Detective Rizzo."

Jessica asked if she could join me when I spoke with him. Tomorrow was Jimmy's funeral and we would all be attending. The following morning I had to go to my department to take care of some retirement issues. I told Jessica that I would be available that afternoon after I was done with my work business. We exchanged phone numbers and Jessica left.

Brian could now speak again. "I'm gonna tell you guys something. There is no way Squirrel committed suicide when his alternative was a date with that piece of ass. Is it just me or is she smoking hot?"

Bo jumped in. "Shut up, you idiot." He may have been talking like an idiot but he was absolutely right. There was no doubt that Jimmy had a lot to look forward to.

Bo told me he would be joining me and Jessica when we met with Rizzo and left no room for rebuttal. Brian said, "I'm coming, too." I can't be sure if Brian was coming for Squirrel or Jessica. I assume a little of both. Either way it was fine by me.

We headed home to get some sleep. Tomorrow we had to bury our friend.

CHAPTER 9

September, 1983

"Here comes White Thunder," Bo said as we sat on my front porch in Somerville, New Jersey. I don't know if he saw the car coming or heard this bucket of bolts lumbering down the road. We had finished three years of college and just spent the summer with our parents. We both had summer jobs and earned a few bucks heading into our senior year. We sat on my porch waiting for Eddie Vincent to pick us up. Bo's parents had dropped him off at my house about an hour ago and we were waiting for Eddie to come get us. He lived in Connecticut and this was kind of on the way to Wilkes-Barre, Pennsylvania. It didn't matter, he was happy to come get us. Eddie was a year behind us but we had become good friends last year. He was also one of my few friends that actually kept a car at school. Our parents had driven us up to start each school year until now. I have to think both sets of parents were thrilled when we told them we had a ride this year.

I sometimes think that Bo and I are one person in two bodies. Without any prior discussion on what we were bringing to school, an hour ago Bo had walked up my driveway with a suitcase, two hockey sticks, and his golf clubs. I watched him walk up as I looked to my right and saw my suitcase, two hockey sticks, and golf clubs.

My parents have known Bo since we were in first grade together and loved him as if he was one of their own. Bo was always welcomed with open arms in my house. My parents even told him where the spare house key was kept. I can't think of any more welcoming gesture than that. In return, Bo loved my parents and always offered to help them out any way he could. He was always handy with tools and helped build my father a shed in the back yard after his one car garage got maxed out of storage space. Bo actually did ninety percent of the design and construction but my father got ninety percent of the credit. Bo never minded. He was happy that my father was happy. I was the opposite. I had no carpentry skills. My father once volunteered me for a community project where the townspeople were building a barn for a needy family. Bo and I joined the volunteer crew. Bo did his normal quality work. My lack of skills may have been quite apparent. When we were leaving the job site, the coordinator asked Bo if he was coming back tomorrow. Bo said he would be glad to give him another day. I was waiting for the same invite but it wasn't coming. I asked the coordinator if I should come back, too. He quickly told me he had enough help. I told him I was available and willing to come back. He pulled me aside and said "Jack, I appreciate you helping out today."

"Thank you," I said as I absorbed his appreciation for my help today.

"But" he let hang in the air. *But what?* "You kind of slowed us down a bit today. It's nothing personal but I don't think carpentry is your thing." I was stunned. I thought I killed it out there today.

I tried to defend myself and my skills. I think I had a much higher opinion of my skills than the reality of it. He finally said, "Jack, you're a great kid. But when it comes to you and carpentry and hammering- I would rather be the nail." *Point taken.*

Eddie pulled into my driveway in his 1971 white Chevy Chevelle. He loved this car and felt the need to name it. That would be fine if the pet name was just between him and the Chevelle. That wasn't the case. Every time we would go somewhere he would have to insert the car's pet name in the conversation. We indulged this mainly because he was the only one of the boys that had a car at school and we liked getting our rides in it. He walked up the driveway and said, "Come on boys. White Thunder is ready to roll." *Ugh.*

The truth of the matter is White Thunder is a piece of shit. It is a rust bucket with a barely functioning engine and a disgusting interior. None of that mattered when you are twenty years old and in need of a ride. We threw our suitcases, hockey sticks, and golf clubs in the trunk and off to senior year of college we went.

Before we left Wilkes-Barre at the end of our junior year, we arranged for our off-campus apartment. Our group arranged to rent three adjoining row-houses on Jackson Street. The landlord owned quite a few properties off campus and easily could be labeled a slumlord. We didn't care. We were familiar with the housing being we knew the guys that lived there before us. They were graduating and we were looking for housing. Ten of us ended up renting three of the townhouses. In 19 Jackson Street were Brian, Bo, and myself. 21 Jackson was leased by Squirrel, Tyler Evigan, and Eddie Vincent. 17 Jackson had Charlie "Chuckie" Logan , Anthony Puglisi, and the Delpino brothers. Tommy "TD" Delpino became friends with us early on in freshman year. Eddie and Timmy "Junior D" Delpino were a year behind us and were dorm roommates when they were freshman.

Our landlord had a reputation for wanting to rent to the college kids but was also known for disappearing if any work needed to be done to the place. The townhouses were dumps but the rent was cheap. Bucky G was our landlord and was also a local businessman. He owned a paint store in town and seemed to operate all of his business interests out of that store. His store had this oversized spilling paint can sitting on the roof with Bucky G's written in different bold colors. The prop paint can seemed to be twice the height of the building and looked ridiculous sitting on his roof. I will give him some credit. You couldn't miss it.

Bucky offered us a one year lease for three hundred a month. This place was a dump so it was not three hundred a person. My share was a hundred bucks a month. We agreed to sign the lease despite having to endure Bucky as our landlord. Our landlord for the next year was officially Bucky G Properties LLC. We later found out he offered us a cheap one year lease being there were talks to sell off all his townhouses to the college so they could demo them and put up their own housing or a parking area. It was a bit of a shady move but it didn't matter, for three hundred bucks a month we couldn't get hurt too bad.

When White Thunder pulled into Jackson Street, most of the guys were already there. There was a keg of beer on tap in the back. We kicked off senior year in style.

Except for Eddie and Junior D, the other eight of us became friends when we connected as freshman. We were all on the same floor of the dorm. Bo and I were huge hockey fans in high school and brought that with us to school. On day one, we broke out our hockey sticks in the hall and were passing a street hockey ball back and forth. Soon after we started, Brian Kavanaugh and Tommy Delpino came out and joined us. It didn't take long for us to find a court on campus where we could play our street hockey. We were only a few days into our freshman year when we were playing on the fenced in macadam outdoor basketball court when some guys came up and told us to beat it. These guys brought their equipment and had two goals to set up. There was about twelve of them and they didn't seem to have any interest in us joining them. They told us that they had the court every day at 2:00 o'clock. We watched them for a few minutes and could see they were a talented group and had a very organized game. They had a goal for each end of the court and their goalies were fully equipped with masks, leg pads, waffle boards, and gloves. We ended up leaving as directed.

We got back to the dorm and were feeling shitty for getting pushed off that court. Bo was strong and athletic and not accustomed to being pushed around by anyone. We went back the next day at 1:30 and sure enough the street hockey players were back at 2:00. We were six strong this time. They were about ten or twelve deep. We weren't getting pushed off today. The guy who dismissed us yesterday was walking over to handle us again. His name was Larry Woods aka Woody. He was a big guy with red hair and a full red beard and mustache. We gathered in the middle of the court as Woody made his way over. I think he was expecting us to just leave but we stood there waiting for him. "All right, guys, time to go. We have the court now."

Bo stepped right in front of him. "Says who?"

Woody wasn't expecting the blowback. "We have this court every day at two."

"Not today you don't. We're not done yet." Bo now threw down the gauntlet. It was Woody's move.

"We get a serious game here every day. Can you guys play?" Woody said. By this time most of Woody's upperclassmen crew were coming out to the middle of the court to join him.

My turn to join the conversation. "We can play. We saw you play yesterday. We're every bit as good as you."

One of Woody's cronies piped in. "You're a cocky fuck."

55

"Call me what you want. We'll play you for the court," I snapped back

Woody didn't seem threatened by any means but I could tell he was actually taking a liking to us. They were serious players. We looked to be serious players. I think he respected our defense of our court time.

Woody said, "We're a bit short today anyway. You guys want in?"

We looked at each other and Bo said, "Hell yeah". We did some introductions and they chose up teams. Bo was the first one chosen from our crew and for good reason.

The game was rough and competitive. We all held our own with these upperclassmen. I scored one goal and Bo had three. They could tell we were as serious as they were when it came to street hockey. The game broke up for the day and Bo looked at Woody. "Same time tomorrow?"

Woody smiled. "Two o'clock. Don't be late."

Chapter 10

2017

Yesterday was tough. Tommy did Squirrel's eulogy and did a beautiful job. I don't think there was a dry eye in the house. Mr. and Mrs. Collucci were very happy with the turnout as it showed how loved their son was. It clearly meant a lot to them. Katie and I went to the repast lunch after the funeral mass and burial. All of our crew attended. We pushed two tables together in a corner near the bar and all sat together. While it was nice to gather with the boys, we all knew why we were there. Bo stood up and had his drink in his hand.

"Men", a pause, "and Ladies" as he looked at Katie and Faith, "we lost our good friend this week. We all have great stories and memories of Squirrel. And we are all blessed for that. I can't think of anyone who ever had a cross word to say about him. You either loved him or you hadn't met him. He would give you the shirt off his back and not think twice about it. All I know is that when we talk about him, and we will, it will bring a smile to our faces. I know we all feel the same way. We just have to march on. One thing is for sure, he will be missed and never forgotten."

Bo started drinking his beer and we all followed suit. Nothing more needed to be added. The repast lunch went well and we then went our own ways for the day.

Today I had an appointment with my human resources department to go over some of the details of my upcoming retirement. I had my meeting at 9:00 am with Judy Feingold, the HR Manager. She was a pleasant enough lady and was a long time employee with the department. She was in HR when I was hired and would ultimately outlast me. She said I needed a firm date that would serve as my last day. I told her I want to retire immediately. She said, "We typically require thirty days notice when an employee retires in good standing. They would prefer that your cases were cleaned up to avoid starting some of them back from square one."

"I don't have any critical active cases that can't be reassigned. I really think this may be a good time for me to stop working," I said.

"Is your Captain in agreement that your caseload could be easily distributed without any transition issues?"

"I just talked to him and told him what I was thinking. He told me to not think twice about it. The case transition would not be a problem. He just wanted me to make sure the case file notes were up date and I assured him they already were."

"We still need a final date. Why don't we make it May 5th? You can use your unused vacation bank. I don't think you will miss them. You have over a hundred of them accumulated."

I told her, "Sounds like a plan."

We had some things to go over regarding continuing health benefits and my 401K and pension distribution.

When we wrapped all of that up she said, "Well, Mac, this just may be your last official duty as a New Brunswick Police Detective. Good luck with everything."

"Thanks, Judy. I hope you're not too far behind me."

I left her office and walked back to my desk. I quickly ran into my partner, Kevin Sullivan. There was no way I was leaving the office that day without talking to him. We had been paired together for almost ten years and not a day went by when I wasn't appreciative of that fact. We had an excellent case clearance record as a team, something we were both proud of. He knew why I was there today and he genuinely couldn't be happier for me. He was a few years younger than me and he had no thoughts of retirement. I walked up and saw Kevin. "I'm done, Sully. My last official day is May 5th but I am using my vacation bank from now til then. Can you believe it?"

"Why not, Mac? You earned it. You put in your thirty and now have the means to do it. I'd be pissed if you didn't hang it up," he said.

"Thanks, Sully. Katie really wanted this, too, as you know."

"I do know. She will get off your back now about it," he said but didn't mean anything by it. He knew what she was put through five years ago.

Five years ago Sully and I were investigating a smash and grab robbery case of a gas station. The people broke the window of the station's mini-mart and stole all of the cigarettes, lottery tickets, and whatever cash they could find. We caught the case. This wasn't our typical assignment but due to a manpower shortage because of vacations and the fact the serious crimes were light, they threw this dog in our laps. We viewed the surveillance video and had a good shot of the two perps. We had still photos made and were going to show them around.

Sully and I were doing a routine canvass for witnesses in the neighborhood. We were hoping someone could give us info on the theft itself or provide a name to go with our photos. I took one side of the street and Sully took the other. This neighborhood was quite urban but by no means was it the seediest part of city. There were certainly areas of the city where we always had to be on full alert and with back up. This wasn't that type of neighborhood. Shortly into the canvass, I knocked on a door which was on the first floor of a four story apartment building. I had my badge out and photo in hand. As

I knocked, the door pushed in and it opened about halfway. Before I knew it, I was bull rushed by a muscular guy in shorts and a tank top. I had stumbled into a large gun and drug deal. There were two other guys that followed and were all over me before I could pull my gun. I tried to yell to Sully. One of the guys grabbed my gun and they were kicking and punching at me as I was in the hallway on my back. I heard one of the guys yelling "Shoot em. Shoot em."

I think he was having trouble getting clear shot because the guys were so actively beating on me. The gun went off and then another shot was heard. I felt the impact of the bullet in my shoulder and blood was freely flowing out. I didn't feel a second bullet. The second shot took out the shooter. Sully had heard me call out and rushed over. He put a bullet into the chest of the shooter as the other two tried to hightail it out of there. Sully clipped another one as he was running. They were both caught soon after and bought themselves a thirty year trip to Rahway State Prison.

Sully received well deserved praise and an accommodation for valor in the line of duty from the department. He also got some local press for his heroics. Sully never felt worthy of the accolades as he felt guilty for not getting there sooner. I will always owe him for this. This was also a life altering incident for me. I felt I let myself down, my department down, and my partner down. No cop worth a damn loses his gun to some punk. I did and I would have to carry that around with me for the rest of my career.

I'm quite sure some of the guys in the department felt far less of me after that incident. *How could he give up his gun?* Sully always defended me and I knew he always did and always will have my back. On some level, I could deal with the haters but having Sully's support meant everything to me. In reality, most of the guys supported me and wished me a speedy recovery but there were a few guys that never looked at me the same again. These guys rely on their partners to make sure they went home healthy every night to their families after their shift. It's not that they didn't want me to recover from my injuries, it's that they would never welcome me if I was assigned as their partner. Most of the guys were younger and likely felt I was on the downside of my career and had lost my edge. If your partner couldn't protect you then what good were you? The problem was that they were right. I could deal with the physical injuries but nobody was more pissed off at me about this incident than me.

After that incident I was in the hospital for ten days. I sustained a gunshot wound to the shoulder, six broken ribs, a collapsed lung, and multiple contusions and abrasions. I was on disability for almost three months after the attack. I think people were wondering if I would lose my nerve and my ability to perform my job duties after this. I had to see the department shrink before I would get cleared to return. I hadn't lost my nerve. I didn't lose my ability to perform my job duties. I came back more determined than ever. I would never ever let anyone get the jump on me again. I was willing to do whatever I had to do to make sure of it.

I said my good-byes and walked out the door. I was now off to pick up Bo, Brian, and Jessica to go see Detective Rizzo to see what we could find out. Not exactly what I had in mind to begin my retirement but it had to be done. I certainly didn't expect my first post-retirement visit to be to another police station.

Chapter 11

A few months after I returned from disability I attended a mandatory self- defense training seminar in the department's conference room. About every two or three years the department brass brought in a self-defense expert to sharpen our skills. This was a very basic course and only took two hours. If I didn't know better, I would have thought this was direct knee jerk reaction to my screw up in the field earlier in the year. My captain assured me that it is just coincidental timing and had nothing to do with it. I accepted his explanation but wasn't so sure he was being straight with me.

I sat with Sully as the training seminar got underway. The instructor introduced himself and gave the basic run down of the agenda and said he would open it up for Q and A at the end. The instructor was not quite what I would have expected for a self-defense expert. He appeared to be in his late sixties or early seventies and had a slender build on his six foot frame. He had a full head of white hair and close-cropped white beard and mustache. Except for the faded tattoos on his arms, he looked like everybody's grandfather.

He said his name was Jamison Trotter and told everyone to just call him Trotter. He gave us a thumbnail sketch of his backround. He said he was a marine with two tours in Vietnam and did contract work in Iraq during Operation Desert Storm. He retired from the military and had been a self-defense trainer for the past fifteen years. I'm sure that being a military lifer was the reason he was only known by his last name. I had a feeling there was much more to his resume than he was telling us.

We have had different instructors over the years for this training session. Trotter was by far the oldest. Most of the guys ran dojos somewhere and were martial arts instructors by trade. All of their sessions were pretty much the same. They would show us how to block a punch or kick and how to do some generic arm bends and shoulder flips. I was hoping Trotter's course had more to offer than what we had become accustomed to.

It became immediately apparent that Trotter's session would be different. He was more focused on using aggression to defend yourself rather than the passive punch and kick blocks. He had the blue mats set up in the front of the conference room so he could demonstrate some of his techniques. There were about twenty of us attending this training. He asked for volunteers and I raised my hand right away.

Trotter was showing the class some of the pressure points on the body that can be used to your advantage when in a confrontation. Every one of Trotter's predecessors had preached a passive approach to a peaceful resolution but taught their self-defense programs only as a last resort. Trotter gave no such drivel about passive approaches or peaceful resolutions. I liked that. He was all about there being a winner and a loser and he wanted to make sure we were the winner.

I joined Trotter on the mat. He saw I was getting up in age and asked if I was up for mixing it up a bit. He wasn't being cocky. He just wanted me to know in advance there would be physical contact. He was probably twenty years older than me and twenty pounds less. *I think I can mix it up with you.* Trotter was telling the class about points of weakness on the opponent. He clawed his fingers into my eyes, chops to the throat, jabs to the solar plexus, wrists bends, and foot kicks to the knees. None of this was done at full speed or I would have felt it quite a bit more than I did. He used me to show some other techniques to the class. He did show some punch and kick blocks but also added a quick aggressive response to all of the blocking techniques which would render the opponent useless. When he was handling me I could feel a strength on him that belied his physical appearance. *Just like they say- never judge a book by its cover.*

I knew there was much more to Trotter than he let on. After the class broke up I followed Trotter out to the parking lot. I formally introduced myself. "Trotter, you got a second?"

"Sure. What's on your mind?"

"I'm Jack MacMasters. I would like to hire you."

We moved our conversation to a Starbucks across the street. I'm not much of a coffee drinker but assumed Trotter was. I hopped in line to get us both some coffee. I sometimes wonder if I live in the same world as everyone else. The lady in front of me ordered a venti half caf latte macchiato with skim milk two sugars and a drizzle of caramel on top. *I didn't understand one word she said.* She then whipped out her phone and pointed it at the barista. *What the heck is a barista?* The barista scanned her phone and off she went waiting to hear her name called. I stepped up and ordered two large back coffees and handed her cash. *Her big smile was gone. I felt like apologizing for ordering something with less than eighteen words.* I thought she was going to call a manager over to explain to her what a cash transaction was. She figured it out. "May I have your names, please?"

"My name?" I was puzzled.

She was all smiles again and said, "We write it on your cup, Sir."

"I'm Flintstone and he's Rubble." I could have gone with Starsky and Hutch or even Cagney and Lacy but they were the first two names that came to mind. It wouldn't have mattered. She wouldn't have heard of any of them.

"Thank you and have a great day, Mr. Flintstone. We will call you when your order is ready." *Ugh.* I left her a few dollar tip and we went to the waiting pit.

By this time he knew to call me Mac. "So Mac, what is it you think I can do for you?"

We grabbed a table and opened up our coffee lids to cool them down a bit. I figured a little small talk might be the way to go before getting right into it. I saw a tattoo on his right forearm. It was a tattoo of the scales of justice with the words *Lex Talionis* over the two scale plates. "That's a nice tattoo. What does it mean?"

"I'm sure you heard of it but maybe not in the Latin form. Lex Talionis is the Law of Talion." I was still a bit puzzled and he picked up on it. "The eye for an eye principal." That I heard of.

"I see. Makes sense," was all I could come up with. I'm sure Trotter lived by that code and then some. In his case if someone poked out Trotter's eye then he would poke out their eye, cut off their ear, and then kick their dog. Trotter seemed to be a man of few words so I decided that was enough of the small talk. Time to get down to business.

"I want it all. I want to learn it all. I'm not looking for some basic self-defense techniques." I went on to tell him about my work incident and how I needed to make sure it never happened to me again.

He said, "What makes you think I am the one to help you?"

"You are. I know you are. I can feel it. I'm assuming you were Special Forces and were quite accomplished at it." He nodded. "I also assume you have a lot of experience with combat and death." He nodded again. "I want to know what you know."

"Mac, sorry to hear about your injuries and your situation with your department. I get why you are here and I respect that." I wasn't sure where he was going with this.

"Will you help me or not?" I said with a touch of frustration.

"I would love to."

Chapter 12

I was on my way to Trotter's house and found myself on a dirt road somewhere over the New Jersey border in Bucks County, Pennsylvania. It quickly turned into a remote area. I hadn't seen any pavement for at least three miles. My GPS didn't recognize where I was. I was just following the directions that Trotter gave me. I felt I was getting close as I saw a ten foot high metal fence with barbed wire straddling the top. I followed the dirt road another mile or so right to the end where a heavy duty metal sliding gate was staring back at me. I pulled up to the intercom box and hit the button.

"Mac, right on time. Come on in," Trotter's voiced boomed through the intercom. The gate opened and in I went.

It had been two weeks since I met Trotter. He told me that he had an intensive combat training program that he instructed on occasion. He said he had two brothers coming for this session and invited me to join them. I talked it over with Katie and she was a little skeptical at first. She was concerned I was getting in over my head and possibly doing this for all the wrong reasons. I explained to her that my only reason was to be prepared if I ever had to protect myself at work or my family out of work. She ultimately was satisfied with that explanation but on some level I think she was more for it than she let me see. I know she never again wanted to sit by my bedside in a hospital for days on end watching me recover from injuries. She knew I would be gone for a week but she would manage without me.

Trotter invited me to his house for this training but when I pulled up his half mile dirt driveway I saw it was more of a compound than a house. I parked next to his old beat up pick-up truck. There was a small cottage which I assumed was where he and his wife lived. There was also a large barn and a structure that looked like an army barracks. I later found out it actually was the barracks for his soldiers in training. I got out of the car and was greeted by Trotter and his wife.

"Mac, meet my best friend and soulmate, Annie." He turned to Annie. "Annie, meet Mac." We exchanged hellos. It was a curious introduction. I later found out that they were in fact husband and wife. Trotter never used the term wife or spouse when introducing Annie. He felt those terms were for churches, governments, and lawyers. He felt those terms didn't speak to the depth of the union. Any two people can be married and called husband and wife. Not all wives are the husband's best friends or soulmates. Trotter wanted to reinforce that to Annie every time he had the chance.

They invited me in. It was not what I was expecting for a small cottage in the middle of a combat training compound. The inside was immaculately clean and tastefully decorated with impressive looking antique furniture and a quaint southern charm. Annie had long graying hair that she kept in a ponytail that went most of the way down her back. She appeared a little younger than Trotter but not by much. The graying hair was the only giveaway to her age as her skin and energy were more suited for a woman twenty years her junior. She was a pleasant woman and I enjoyed being in her company.

"Hey, Trotter. Can you grab the tray of drinks?" Annie asked.

It cracked me up that she called him Trotter too. I guess Trotter was right when he told our class at the department that everyone calls him Trotter. He obeyed his lovely wife and he emerged from the kitchen with a tray holding a pitcher of lemonade and three glasses. *Gotta love that southern charm.* I noticed that there was no TV and had to ask. I have seven TVs in my house and figured every home in America has at least one. He said they love TV but don't own one. He told me the television industry peaked in the 1950s and 1960s. He opened up a wood hutch and showed me his DVD collection. I was impressed. I was looking at full sets of The Honeymooners, I Love Lucy, Hogan's Heroes, Get Smart and The Dean Martin Celebrity Roasts among others. He also had a boat load of movies. Of course The Dirty Dozen and The Great Escape were front and center. He said they pop a DVD into their computer when they want to watch some TV. With all the crap on TV these days, I couldn't argue. I could just picture Trotter teaching his maiming skills by day and kicking back with Annie at night and watching Ralph Kramden and Ed Norton getting into some mess. You never really do know what goes on behind someone else's closed doors.

We chatted for a few minutes while sipping on our lemonades when a car pulled up with the radio blaring. Trotter explained that it was his other two guests. They were two brothers that had plans to enlist in the Navy with an eye on becoming Seals. They knew they would need an edge being they would be up against some pretty strong competition. Many attempt to become a Seal but very few succeed.

Trotter wasn't driven by money and didn't charge much for his services. Mostly because the people that come to him are young and haven't yet enjoyed financial success in life. Trotter's payment was watching these young men turn into fire-pissing soldiers. He never took credit for any of their successes but felt satisfaction knowing they were off to a good start. I wasn't the typical trainee for him. In fact, I was by far the oldest one that ever attempted his week long program.

We went outside and Trotter greeted the Nichols brothers. Eric was twenty-four and Stevie was twenty-three. They were in excellent physical condition and both had a cockiness about them. These guys didn't know Trotter. Their uncle was also a military lifer and knew Trotter from way back. He told his nephews that if they wanted to learn how to kick ass then they should spend some time with Trotter.

Their uncle arranged things with Trotter and now here they were.

Eric looked at me and said, "Are you Mr. Trotter?"

"No," I said. I could see him look at Trotter in disbelief. I'm sure he was wondering what this old guy could possibly teach him.

Trotter already knew everything about the Nichols brothers. He did that with all his guests. He knew these guys were from Long Island and had no criminal record. He also knew they were highly intelligent and would be highly motivated to learn. These guys may have been cocky but they were here to better themselves and to learn whatever Trotter had to offer.

Trotter spoke up. "I'm Trotter. Not sir. Not Mr. Trotter. Just Trotter." I wonder if that is what he told Annie when they first met. She's probably afraid to call him anything but Trotter. "This is Mac. He is joining us this week and will be staying in the barracks with you two. You can leave your bags in your car. Everything you need for this week is at your bunk."

Annie walked out of the house with a small rattan basket and placed it in front of the two men. Trotter continued, "Wallets, keys, and cell phones," and pointed to the basket. They gave a slight hesitation but complied. Mac did the same. I had known in advance that Katie wouldn't be able to reach me on my cell for the week that I was away. I gave her Trotter's phone number in case of emergency.

"There is only one rule here. If I say it, you do it. If you don't like what I am telling you to do, you do it anyway. You never question my decisions. If you have a problem with this arrangement, then turn around, start your car and get the hell outta here." We all nodded our acknowledgment. If it wasn't already clear, it was clear now who was in charge. "You guys head to the barracks and get changed and meet back here in a half hour."

The barracks were as dull on the inside as it looked on the outside. There were twelve beds, twelve foot lockers, twelve small windows and army green paint on the walls and slab floor. The bathroom had three shower stalls, three toilets, three urinals, three sinks, and three mirrors. I took one look at his accommodations for the next week and was wondering if I would come to regret this. The foot lockers contained their clothes for the week as well as their toiletries. We got changed and reported for duty.

Trotter brought us to the barn. A bit oversized but on the outside it was just like any other ordinary barn. He gave us the tour inside which included an open area where he had blue mats in place for the physical training. There was a locked room where a retinal scan was required from Trotter to enter. In there was a room full of computers and technology well beyond my comprehension. There were security monitors covering every inch of his property. Within the tech room was a stairway that led to an underground firing range. He opened another door with his retinal scan that housed all of his weaponry. Trotter was ready for Armageddon. The room was loaded with a cache of weapons that included explosives, hand guns, automatic rifles, knives, swords, martial arts accessories, and enough ammunition to last several lifetimes. All of it was arranged with a purpose and was well cared for.

We soon learned that Trotter was a master of Krav Maga. He gave us the history of this discipline. He told us that it is a self-defense system that was developed for the Israeli Defense Forces by martial artist Imi Lichtenfeld. The discipline is known for its focus on real-world situations, its extreme efficiency, and brutal counter-attacks. Krav Maga is derived from the Hebrew words for contact and combat and its philosophy emphasizes aggression and simultaneous defensive and offensive maneuvers. Some of the ideas taught in Krav Maga include developing aggression and continuing to strike an opponent until they are completely incapacitated, attacking preemptively, using any object available to hit your opponent, and targeting the body's most vulnerable points such as: the eyes, neck or throat, face, solar plexus, groin, ribs, knee, foot, fingers and liver. It also teaches to maintain awareness of surroundings while dealing with a threat in order to look for escape routes, other attackers, or to see what objects may be around that can be used to strike the opponent.

Trotter had made it to the level of Master. There are three grades that are divided into Practitioner, Graduate, and Expert. Each of those grades had five levels. Only a small number of people on the planet have ever achieved the Master designation.

The week went by quickly. Most of the work was done on the blue mats where he imparted his wisdom and combat techniques to us. It was a pleasure to watch the Nichols brothers get tossed around like rag dolls by a guy almost three times their age. Trotter did his share of tossing me around as well. He didn't give me any breaks just because I was older. *Hell, I was still almost twenty years younger than him.* He also gave us training on how to be efficient with knives, swords, throwing stars, nun-chucks, among others. We did a little work on the rifle range but not too much. I wasn't there to become a sniper but it was a great benefit to the Nichols boys. The key to becoming an accomplished sniper is all about controlling your breathing. Trotter showed them ways to control their breathing and it paid off immediately. The brothers improved their long range sniper abilities dramatically in the short week they were here.

We parted ways that week and I wished the Nichols boys well. They came here two cocky young men and left two confident young men. Trotter got through to them. People don't respect cockiness. They respect confidence and quiet execution. They thanked Trotter and gave Annie hugs before they took off. They were well on their way to becoming Seals.

You can't learn everything in a week. It was a good start but I wanted more. I went for another week about six months later and have been going for weekend trips to see him about every two months for the past three years. I'm no Master but I wouldn't want to mess with me. As for Trotter, he proved my instincts correct. He feared nothing or no one. He was to be feared. He was every bit as lethal as I thought and more.

I owe Trotter a lot more than the few dollars he wanted for taking me under his wing as his oldest student. He made sure I would never lose my edge again. He knew I would be ready for whatever came my way. After we had our slot machine hit, I sent Trotter a little thank you. I gave him a nice vacation for him and Annie and had a new pick-up truck delivered to his home. While I'm sure he appreciated it, I think he still drives his old beat up pick-up truck. Maybe I should have just got him some Gilligan's Island DVDs.

Chapter 13

1983

King's College is a small Liberal Arts college in Wilkes-Barre, Pennsylvania right off the banks of the Susquehanna River. The town was wiped out eleven years earlier when the banks of the Susquehanna overflowed from the effects of Hurricane Agnes. The city and the college were devastated. The area was mending but still hadn't fully recovered. King's was a Catholic school which for me was just an extension of my previous twelve years of Catholic schooling. Twelve years of Nuns and now four years of Brothers.

I came to college and declared myself a Math major. I quickly found out that Math was not for me. I think I had an inflated sense of my math abilities. When I was in sixth grade, Sister Augustine had her annual math bee. I found myself in the final round standing next to Tommy Willis. He was the class brainiac and later found himself at the top of his class in Harvard Law School. I'm sure he had never lost a bee of any kind in his life. Every dog has his day and that day was mine. He somehow slipped up on a question that I was able to answer. Tommy Willis was eliminated from a brain contest. The class was stunned. Sister Augustine was equally stunned. She begrudgingly declared me the winner and handed me my prize. I proudly accepted that four inch plastic statue of The Mother Mary. Tommy Willis will likely be arguing cases before the Supreme Court someday but he doesn't have that Mary statue sitting on his shelf. And I do.

I switched my major over to Criminal Justice in my sophomore year. I found my passion for law enforcement during my current internship with the Wilkes-Barre Juvenile Detention Center. I was assigned to Mr. Biggs. He had been with the JDC for over twenty-five years. We occasionally had to visit some of his clientele. We went to visit a seventeen-year-old who missed his first probation meeting. He had just been released from the detention center after spending ninety days for an assault on his teacher. We knocked on the door of his home and were let in by his mother. Biggs was not a big guy and used a cane to help him amble around. When the kid saw us, he pushed right through Biggs and ran out the door. Biggs just stood there saying nothing. I didn't know what to do so I took off after him. I chased him down and tackled him a half block away. I had his arms behind his back and my knee in his back. Biggs slowly walked over to me and was laughing. "We don't chase em down. We just call it in and the police will pick him up," he said through his wide smile.

"Why the hell didn't you tell me that?"

"You were gone so quick. I wanted to see what you were going to do," still laughing.

"You're a real winner, Biggs." We were both laughing that this point.

"You're well on your way to getting an A. The guys back at the office are going to love this one," he said.

"You better give me an A, you prick," I shot back. He grabbed the kid and the three of us went back to the detention center. He was laughing the entire way.

I have to admit that I got quite a rush from running that punk down and taking him to the ground. It was that moment that that I knew where my career was headed.

I went back to the house and some of the boys were gathered. They were cooking out in the back and throwing back some beers. They had just got done playing street hockey. I had to miss because of the internship. I hated missing hockey. Some more guys came over and there were about a dozen of us sitting around the back porch area. Chuckie went out for more beer. We were listening to music and drinking our beers when two of our hockey buddies from the dorm came over. Bill Glass aka Willie and Chris Miller walked up. They were a year behind us but we became friends the previous year through street hockey. Willie wasn't the greatest student but was a heck of a hockey player. He liked hanging out at our houses. Willie liked the ladies and for the most part they liked him. He measured the success of his school year by the number of times he got laid and not by GPA.

Willie and Chris walked up and grabbed a beer. "Waz up, boys?" Willie said. "Anyone else coming over?"

Bo was sitting in a lawn chair on the back porch sipping his beer. "No, it's just us" he said.

Willie was looking around and seeing about a dozen or so guys bullshitting and drinking their beers. "Jesus Christ, guys. You ever gonna get some women to hang out over here." We started cracking up. Willie only looks to increase his lady conquests on days that ended in Y.

Willie continued, "What's the deal? Are you guys some kind of mens only club?"

I looked at Bo and Brian.

"I love it. The Men's Club. I like the sound of that."

Chapter 14

2017

We drove to Bo's house and picked him up. We are on our way to see Detective Rizzo of Rockaway police department. He had investigated Squirrel's death and I wanted to know what he developed to support his findings. Squirrel was found at the bottom of a ravine at one of his favorite hiking trails. I had been up there with him a few times but hiking is not really my thing. I know the highest part of the trail has about an eighty to ninety foot drop to the bottom. Any fall from that point would likely be fatal. It would be the equivalent of a fall from a seven story building to a rocky base. *It wouldn't be pretty.* The township put in a low metal wire barrier between the trail and the edge. They also had several warning signs alerting the hikers to the soft edge and to not go beyond the wire barrier. The short wire is only two feet high and can be easily stepped over. Overall it is well marked and safe for hikers.

When I arrived at Bo's house, Brian immediately called the back seat. *Is this like the reverse of calling shotgun?* We knew exactly what he was doing. We were heading to Jessica's house to pick her up and he would like nothing more than to sit next to her for the trip.

Jessica lived in a nice center hall colonial style home with a huge brick paved circular driveway and detached three car garage. It looked like the splitting of the marital assets in her divorce went pretty well for her. *Good for her.* She walked out the front door dressed in jeans, a white tank top with a thin sweater, and her spiked heels. The outfit was fairly basic but enhanced all of her physical gifts. Brian jumped out of the back seat to greet her. *Down boy.* "Hi, Jessica," was all he could muster up.

"Hi Brian." Right back at you, as she hopped into the car with Brian right on her tail.

"Thanks for picking me up, Mac. Hi, Bo" she said and then continued. "So what's the plan?"

"We are going to find how this detective arrived at his conclusions. We'll see what evidence he has and see if he'll show us any of it," I said.

"What if he doesn't want to talk to us or show us anything?" she said.

"I think he will. I think he'll extend me some professional

courtesy. I would do the same for him," I said. "Unless he was a total prick. Then I would give him nothing."

Brian jumped in. "Then please don't be a prick to him until we get what we need,"

"No problem. I got this."

We arrived at the police station and went over to the desk sergeant and asked for Detective Rizzo. I told him I had some info on one of his cases and would like a few minutes. I heard him dial up Rizzo.

"Rizzo, some people here to see you on your Collucci case." He looked back at us and said he would be out in five minutes and for us to take a seat. We sat as directed and waited. Twenty minutes went by and still no Rizzo.

"Hey, Sarge. Is Rizzo gonna see us today?" my impatience getting the best of me. He picked up the phone but I couldn't hear what he was saying. I assumed he let Rizzo know we were getting antsy. Another twenty minutes went by before the door opened. I'm sure that last twenty minutes was Rizzo's way of punishing my bad behavior.

Rizzo barreled through the door. "Who needs to see me?"

I stood up and walked toward him. "I'm Jack MacMasters. I'm on the job. Outta New Brunswick," and extended my hand. He left me hanging for a few seconds but finally shook my hand.

"What's this about, MacMasters?"

"Can we talk about James Collucci? He was a good friend of mine and was hoping you would have a few minutes."

"Not much to talk about. Open and shut. I'll give you two minutes." He escorted us back to his desk. There were a few open chairs but he didn't offer any seats.

Rizzo's desk was devoid of any personal items. No family pictures. No paraphernalia of his of any favorite sports teams. No plants to care for. Nothing to provide any insight on his life outside of work. It wasn't surprising. Rizzo was pushing sixty and the best years of his career were clearly behind him. He was sloppily dressed and was at least sixty pounds overweight. The suit hadn't seen an iron or a dry cleaner in years. His bulging stomach was testing the limits of the shirt buttons. *Someone could lose an eye if one of those lets go.* Everything about him screamed *lazy*. I'm figuring his investigation was also lazy. I dropped one of my business cards on his desk and figured it was time to get down to business.

Rizzo grabbed the file from his desk drawer and opened it up. "Collucci was found dead after he jumped off the peak at Washington Park. Two hikers found him when they moved off the trail to get some pictures. One of the hikers was pretending to jump while the other took his picture. Stupid kids." *Agreed. The stupidity of people never ceases to amaze me.* "They called it in. Collucci had injuries consistent with a fall from that height and with that type of surface for the impact. He drove his car to the park and had alcohol in his system"

"Could he have been pushed?" I asked.

"Wait 'til I'm done, MacMasters. There was no indication he was pushed. I went to Collucci's residence and saw no signs of foul play. And he left a note."

"A note. What note?" I was not expecting to hear that.

"His suicide note. He said he was depressed and wanted to be rid of all his pain. His ex-wife confirmed he was depressed since she left him. Case closed," Rizzo said with a crooked grin. He was obviously proud of how quickly and efficiently he had wrapped up the case.

"Can I see the note?" I asked. The smug look on his face was getting my blood boiling. Bo, Brian, and Jessica were sensing my frustration but kept quiet.

Rizzo paused but decided to let me see it. He pulled out the note which was in a plastic evidence bag. He pulled it out and placed it on the desk. "Look. Don't touch," he said.

I read the note and it was a computer printout. There was nothing in his own writing or anyone's writing for that matter. It wasn't even signed. There were three generic lines about how depressed he was and how he was going to end it all. There was nothing of any personal nature that would be unique to Squirrel.

I looked at Rizzo and said, "This is your suicide note? This could have been prepared by anyone. This doesn't prove anything."

Rizzo defended his investigation. "Who else would have written it? It was on Collucci's computer and printed from Collucci's printer. There was no sign of foul play. He got liquored up and went to a place he is familiar with. He was a hiker and frequented Washington Park. It's not unusual for people to go to places they are familiar with to off themselves. His ex-wife filled in the rest of the blanks."

"His ex-wife is an asshole and doesn't know shit. She has barely seen him in the past five years," Bo getting involved now.

Rizzo was about done with this. "Do you have anything for me or are you people just wasting my time."

"James Collucci was not suicidal in any way. He never was. His wife is so full of herself she would like to believe he was suicidal over her," Bo said.

A computer printout and a delusional ex-wife can be part of his investigation but to serve as the basis for his conclusions was utter incompetence. The last known person to speak to Jimmy was Jessica and Rizzo never even interviewed her.

"This is Jessica Adams. She was the last person that we know that talked to Jimmy. Maybe you want to see what she has to say." My frustration was on full display.

"Listen, MacMasters. Who the hell do you think you are coming in here and stepping all over my investigation?" Rizzo fuming at this point.

Jessica tried to diffuse the tension. "I was with Jimmy earlier on the night that he died. We had a pleasant conversation over some drinks. We talked about starting a relationship. In fact, we were supposed to get together on that Saturday."

"What, for like a date or something?" Rizzo said.

"Of course for a date or something," Jessica shot right back. Rizzo was eyeing Jessica up and down. Even Rizzo would have to know that a date with her would be something to look forward to.

"What are you trying to say? That your friend's fall was an accident? That someone killed him? There's no proof of any of that. How do you explain the note?" Rizzo said.

There was no way to explain the note and call this an accident. That left us with suicide or murder. I knew he didn't kill himself so as far as I was concerned Squirrel was murdered. I didn't know why but I sure as hell would find out.

I was done with Rizzo and his half-assed investigation. "Rizzo, this was no suicide and no accident. You need to re-open your investigation and treat this as a homicide."

"Your friend is either a klutz or he offed himself. This ain't no murder," Rizzo said while cracking a smile. "Now quit wasting my time and beat it. All of you."

"Rizzo, why don't you quit wasting taxpayer's money and hang it up. You're useless as an investigator. I can tell you one thing. When I find out who did this, I'm gonna make you eat that report." *Enough said. Time to go.*

"Fuck you, MacMasters. Now beat it before I throw you out. You don't come into my house and dress me down. Get the hell outta here. Now," he shot back with his beet red face and veins bulging from his neck. *We better get out before those shirt buttons start flying.*

We hurried out of there. We weren't going to get any more from Rizzo. I hoped I gave him enough to think about.

The visit to Rizzo was enlightening. We confirmed Rizzo was a lazy buffoon that had no idea how to conduct a thorough investigation. We knew Squirrel's fall was no accident. He was murdered. We just needed to figure out the "who" and the "why".

On the way out, I asked the desk sergeant if Jimmy's car has been released. He said it was and was at the city impound. He said the closest relative could retrieve it or sign an authorization for a third party to pick it up. I called Mr. and Mrs. C and asked them if they wanted us to pick up the car. I also filled them in on Rizzo's sloppy investigation short of telling them their son was murdered. That was a conversation for another day. They said they would fax over an authorization to the police impound yard.

The four of us were talking as we walked to the car.

"What an asshole that Rizzo is," Jessica said. "Where do we go from here?"

"Let's get Jimmy's car and head over to his place."

Chapter 15

We drove to the police impound yard. There was a small shack inside a gated and chain link, fenced lot. The place was full of all kinds of cars. Everything from old rust buckets to brand new luxury cars occupied almost every inch of the interior. I don't know how the attendant maneuvered any of these cars around. I walked in and asked if they had received the release for the Collucci vehicle. The shack was dirty and smelled of cigarette smoke and dog. I saw a small dog bed and food and water bowls in there but no dog. The clerk immediately put down his crossword puzzle on the counter and jumped up to try to help in any way he could. He was obviously bored and starving for some human interaction.

His crossword puzzle had about eight words filled in, and it looked like only half of them were right. At least two words were misspelled altogether.

"Love my puzzles," he threw out there. I didn't bite. "I was looking for a five letter word for Midwest Hub that starts with O. I wrote in Onion but I'll wait for more letters just to be sure." Not sure what his thought process was to arrive at onion and I wasn't about to ask. "Dem Midwesterners sure love their onions." *And there it is.*

"Sorry, I was never any good at those things." I didn't want to get off track with this guy. "Is the car ready for pick up?"

"What ya say the name was? Carucci? Ya got a lot number?" he asked.

"James Collucci. I don't have a lot number. My name is Jack MacMasters and I am here to get the car. The release was supposed to have been faxed over earlier from the owners."

"That darn fax has been running all day. Lemme take a look." The fax machine was right behind him and had one piece of paper in it. He turned around and acted like he was fumbling with several pieces of paper. "Nice weather we're having today. Aint it?" *Oh no, here comes more small talk.*

"Great weather," was the best I was going to do with the small talk. "Is the release there or not?"

"Oh yeah. I got it. Lemme just look it over and make sure everything is in order."

He was looking it over and taking more time than should be

needed. I was losing patience. "What's your name?"

"Chester Meyers. But my friends call me Chet."

"Listen *Chester*, I'm in a bit of a rush. Any idea how long this will take?"

"No time at all. I just need to confirm you are Mr. MacMasters." I pulled out my license and showed him. He looked at me and then at the picture on my license then at me again and then the picture again. If he looked up at my face again I was going to jump over the counter and stick his head in the fax machine. He gave me a big smile and said, "You sure are Mr. MacMasters and you're all set, Mr. MacMasters." He gave me the keys and told me where in the lot I could pick up Squirrel's Nissan Altima.

"Thanks, Chet."

As I was walking toward the door I stopped and turned to Chet. "Hey, Chet." He popped up and eagerly waited for my question. "Has anyone driven this car since it was impounded?"

"Nope. Not allowed when they got a police hold on em."

"Anyone drive it after the police hold was lifted?"

"Nope. Been in the same spot since the tow driver dropped it there."

"Thanks, Chet." I was about to head out the door but turned back and walked up to the counter and said to Chet, "O'Hare".

"Whadda ya mean, Mr. MacMasters?" obviously confused.

"The Midwest Hub. O'Hare is the airline hub in Chicago" as I pointed to his crossword puzzle lying on the counter.

"Oh, yeah. That's what I thought. Thanks for confirming." He picked up that pencil and put to work what was left of that stubby eraser then proudly wrote in Ohair.

Jessica, Bo, and Brian were waiting for me outside. "What the hell took so long?" Bo asked.

"The clerk was a little chatty. I have the keys and we can take the car outta, here" I said. I looked at Bo and said, "I'll drive Squirrel's car and one of you can take mine."

Brian offered to drive my car. Bo joined me in Squirrel's car and Jessica hopped in with Brian. I'm sure Brian was just fine with the way that worked out. Maybe he could finally have a conversation with her without tripping over his tongue.

I went to the space where the car was stored. I unlocked the door and planted myself in the driver's seat as Bo was getting in the other side. I got in and adjusted the seat forward a few inches. The radio station was tuned to AM 660 WFAN all sports talk radio. No surprise there as Squirrel loved watching, listening, and talking sports. He was a big New York Mets and Jets fan. He liked the New York Islanders in hockey but didn't have much interest in basketball. The drive over was uneventful. Bo and I talked a bit about what we learned from Rizzo.

"Do you think that prick will reopen his investigation?" Bo asked.

"I doubt it. He's too old and too lazy to give a shit. The guy is useless. It's up to us to figure this thing out," I said.

"We will."

"Damn right we will. Now that I am officially retired I have all the time I need to devote to this."

"I'm in for as long as it takes, too. I've got a few jobs going now but nothing that needs me to be on site. I've got good guys running the jobs."

"Sounds good to me, Bo."

We arrived at Squirrel's house not really knowing what to expect. We would look around for anything out of the ordinary. Brian and Jessica were already there and were talking outside my car. We parked behind them in the driveway. Squirrel had a nice bi-level home that looked like it was built in the late 1950s. The place was beautifully landscaped but the lawn looked like it needed to be cut. The key chain that was released to me had only one other key on it and it didn't look like a house key. We started looking around for a hidden key. We checked under the mat, under the flower pots, and in the landscaped area for a rock that didn't quite look like a rock. We found nothing. I checked a few of the ground level windows but all were properly locked.

I went over to the garage door and saw it had an old Stanley keypad. I had a Stanley garage door opener at my house and knew it required a four digit code to access it. I looked at the keypad and saw three of the numbers were worn. The zero was almost completely worn down and the four and one where worn but to a lesser extent. That told me that the code contained two zeros and one four and one one. I tried channeling my sixth grade math skills to figure out how many combinations there were. Quickly figured there are only twelve combinations. I started pecking at the keypad. 1400- no luck. 1040- no luck. 4100- no luck. Then it hit me. I knew the code. I typed in 0041 and the garage door lifted as I expected. I knew that Squirrel was a big New York Met fan and who his favorite all-time player was. In my head I could hear the Mets stadium announcer- *Now pitching for the Mets, #41 Tom Seaver.*

All four of us entered the house. Although I got together with Squirrel fairly regularly, I realized I hadn't been in his house for quite a while.

"Mac, what are we looking for?" Jessica asked.

"Anything out of the ordinary. I would like to check his computer. Look for signs of a struggle. Anything that would show us another person or people were in here on the night he died."

Jessica had grabbed his mail from the mailbox and brought it in and put it on his desk in his family room. I was already heading to the desk to check out the computer.

I sat at the desk and opened his laptop. There was no password required. I first went to his Facebook page. He had a lot of friends, most of whom, I had never heard of. I was scrolling down the posts. It was mostly nonsense from *friends* posting vacation pictures or pictures of their kids at a dance recital or little league game. On and on with tidbits of other people's lives. Facebook wasn't for me. I did not have a personal Facebook account. I had no interest in seeing little Stevie's tee-ball game or little Susie picking up a shell on a beach. It has its place but it's not for me.

I had a Facebook page that was set up for me under an alias for my work. One thing Facebook has taught me is that people will post anything. I had once investigated a burglary where the victim suspected a neighborhood kid who walked by their house every day after school. Someone broke in through the back door and stole a laptop, some jewelry, and an envelope that was sitting on her kitchen counter that contained $500 in cash in $100 bills. She told me that she just went to the bank the previous day and pulled out the $500 to pay her mother's home health aide. We identified the neighborhood kid and used the Facebook account to see if we could check him out. We were able to get *friended* and accessed this kid's Facebook page. It's a good thing that we rely on the stupidity of people to successfully do our jobs. This kid was stupidity personified. Right there on his homepage was a picture of this kid with a big smile holding five fanned out hundred dollar bills. A half hour later he was in handcuffs. A good friend of mine once told me, "Why be stupid unless you can prove it". This kid was an expert at proving it.

I was scrolling down all of the posts from the last few months. Jessica was poking around the kitchen and Brian and Bo were upstairs. One picture caught my eye. It was a picture posted from our friend Tyler Evigan before he died. There was a picture of him and his boss, Andrew Hainesworth, current Governor of Pennsylvania. Tyler was an assistant to the Governors Chief of Staff, Donald Keohane. He had been with both of them for all of his political career. They were attending a bi-partisan photo-op at a new children's hospital that opened in Harrisburg. This was an election year and his opponent was attending as well. The picture posted was of Hainesworth shaking hands with his opponent, political newcomer Michael Guilford, both with big broad smiles and all too long firm handshakes. Tyler and a few of his aides were in the picture with Hainesworth. Guilford was standing with a few of his aides and an elderly couple. There was nothing unusual about the picture. The caption just said "Guess who I ran into?" I looked at the faces but didn't recognize any of the people as someone I would know.

I printed the picture and kept searching the computer. The supposed suicide note was saved as a word document. It was the same as what I saw at the police station. I checked through the emails but didn't find anything unusual. The inbox was mostly filled with junk solicitations but also had some emails from his parents, brother,

Tyler Evigan, Bo, and a few from me.

Brian and Bo came from the upstairs and reported they had found nothing unusual. No furniture appeared to be out of place. No signs of any intrusion.

Jessica reported the same for the kitchen and living room. She was now over at the desk and looking through some of his old mail. Mostly junk mail but there were a few bills. The mail she picked out from the porch looked to be about a week's worth. One envelope was from PNC Bank and looked like a credit card statement. She asked me if we could open it. I said that wouldn't be a problem. Jessica opened the credit card statement. She was reviewing and seeing he didn't use his credit card too often. She saw a few charges from his local ShopRite, his Netflix and EZ Pass monthly charges, a few Uber charges, and a few others.

"Take a look at this, Mac," she said.

"What is it?" I asked.

"The charges for Uber for the night Jimmy died. The last two entries on the list of charges. It doesn't make any sense," as she handed me the bill.

I took the bill and was checking it out as Jessica continued, "The second to last charge shows the Uber cost to get to Flanagan's is $31.00. The last charge for Jimmy leaving Flanagan's is only $5.00. It should be the same as the first trip or close to it."

"Could he have gone to another bar after leaving Flanagan's?" I responded.

"That's a no show fee," Brian joined in. "I had a few of them on my own Uber account. They charge you $5.00 if you order an Uber and don't show up"

"I saw Jimmy get picked up. It was a black SUV. He got in the back seat," Jessica said.

"Whoever picked him up wasn't the SUV he ordered," Brian said. "Then who the hells SUV did he get into?"

"The person that killed him," I said.

It just hit me. I knew something wasn't right when I got into Squirrel's car at the police impound lot. When I got in I adjusted the seat forward.

"Bo, do you remember what I did when I got in Squirrel's car earlier? I adjusted the seat forward a few inches."

"That's right. You did," Bo confirmed.

"Squirrel is at least three inches shorter than me. The guy at the impound said no one had driven the car since it was towed from Washington Park. Whoever drove that car to Washington Park was at least three inches taller than me."

"Holy shit, Mac. I knew it. I just felt it in my bones. No doubt about it. Jimmy was murdered," Jessica added with her eyes welling up as the realization of her friends demise sank in.

I put my hand on her shoulder and said, "You're right. Now we have to find out who was in that black SUV."

Chapter 16

Katie had dinner ready for me when I got home. She was always an excellent cook and an even better baker. It was a good thing that we exercised daily or those meals and desserts could spell trouble. Tonight was pasta and her homemade meatballs with cheesy garlic bread. We split a bottle of red wine to complete the meal. I was enjoying every bite and sip. I filled her in on what we found out. She wasn't surprised being she never for one second believed it was a suicide. I let her know that I was going to see this thing through to the end. She understood and I had her full support.

"So where do you go from here?" she asked.

"I want to talk to the Medical Examiner first then see if we can track down the SUV. I'm hoping Flanagan's or some surrounding business captured the SUV on their surveillance video."

"That would be nice."

"It's not as simple as that. I have a feeling we are dealing with a pro. I'm sure he is being very careful with every move he makes."

"A pro? Why on earth would a professional killer be after Jimmy?" she asked.

"I have no idea. He didn't have any enemies that I know of. He wasn't involved with any sketchy people either. He didn't do drugs and wasn't a gambler. I think I would know if he was leading some type of double life. It just doesn't add up."

We were back at the meatballs and wine while pondering the possibilities. "By the way the food is excellent. The meatballs are fantastic." She gave me a quick thank you and we went back to processing everything we learned.

Katie broke the momentary silence. "It's so strange. Your friend Tyler dies in a fire and a few weeks later this happens to Jimmy. Could there be a connection."

"None that I can think of but I like the way you think. I suppose it's possible. I hadn't heard there was anything suspicious about Tyler's death. Maybe it's worth looking into. Nice job, Hon."

I called Bo and told him that I wanted to speak with the medical examiner and then check out Flanagan's area for surveillance. He said he was on board and I told him I would pick him up at 9:00 AM tomorrow. I filled Brian in. I figured he would want to stay involved as well.

I called Jessica and let her know my intentions. She had already told me she was in for the long haul. I told her I would pick her up after I grabbed Bo.

I went to bed that night and couldn't sleep. I was tossing and turning and my mind was racing. I was trying to put a puzzle together with nothing but round pieces. Nothing fit. Nothing connected. The more I ran everything though my head the less I knew. I needed answers but only had questions. Right then I just needed sleep so I could be ready for whatever tomorrow is going to bring. I started focusing on my fun memories with Squirrel and the many laughs we shared and that seemed to do the trick. I was able to finally drift off to sleep.

I arrived at Bo's house on time. Brian didn't make this trip. He told me that he wanted to stay back as he had a few things he had to take care of with work. He had his computer with him and was able to do whatever was needed without actually having to go back to Maryland. My guess was he was getting ready to take some time off so he could devote his full attention to the matter at hand. The two of us got into my Ford Explorer and we drove to pick up Jessica. A half hour later we arrived at the Morris County Coroner's office. I had made some calls yesterday and found out Squirrel's post mortem was handled by Dr. Alfred Stevens. He is a forensic pathologist and is the lead Medical Examiner for Morris County. I was glad to hear Stevens caught Squirrel's case.

I had met him a few years back when our paths crossed on a

case. We were investigating a missing person's case in New Brunswick. The body was eventually discovered in the trunk of a car in Parsippany which fell in his jurisdiction. His office handled the post mortem on that one. The timing of the death was critical to breaking the perp's alibi. We confirmed the crime occurred in Middlesex County and that is what ended up being the venue for the trial. The handling District Attorney and myself, as the lead investigator, had several meetings with him before the trial. He was the perfect expert witness. His credentials were impeccable and the defense could not impeach one word of his testimony. The jury was out for twenty minutes before they sent back a unanimous conviction.

We arrived at the building and were greeted with a sign pointing us to the basement. For some reason, every morgue I have been to is in the lowest level of the building. The gun metal gray door had a simple sign on it- Morris County Medical Examiner & Coroner. We entered through the door and didn't see anyone at the desk or milling around anywhere. No signs of life. *Pun intended.* A few seconds later the door opened and in walked Dr. Stevens with his Dunkin Donuts coffee in hand and munching on a glazed donut. He looked up and saw the three of us standing near his desk. He then set his eyes my way. "Hey, Mac. Long time no see. Good to see you."

"Good to see you, too, Doc" I did the introductions and continued. We chatted for a bit and I let him know I had in my retirement papers.

"Well, I would say congratulations are in order. Good for you, Mac. Any plans?" he asked.

"Nothing immediate. I really haven't had time to think about it yet."

"I'm sure you'll figure it out in a hurry. So, what brings you here today?"

"Unfortunately I'm not here for business or pleasure." He looked puzzled. "I heard you handled the James Collucci post mortem."

"I did. What's your interest?"

"He was a friend. Rizzo ruled him a suicide. I just want to know what you thought."

He went to the desk drawer and pulled the folder. "I remember this one. Rizzo was pushing me along. The guy has no patience."

"We found out," Jessica said.

"Let me see," as he was thumbing through the report. "Multiple fractures, abrasions, and contusions to the face, torso and extremities. All consistent with blunt force trauma. He was really banged up. Significant facial fractures. He must have landed face first. His face probably hit the hard surface more than once on the way down."

"What about the tox report?" I asked.

"Rizzo didn't order a full tox screen. The ETOH was high but that wasn't unusual. Rizzo told me he was out drinking at a bar that night. Everything else I checked for was within normal limits. I only do a tox work up for what is ordered. I think Rizzo had his mind made up before hearing one word come out of my mouth."

"No surprise there. Rizzo's lazy. I know you just confirm the cause of death and not whether it was suicide or not. What's the official primary cause?" I asked

"Head trauma from blunt force impact."

"Secondary?"

"Chest trauma from blunt force impact. The ribs fractures punctured his lungs."

"Fingernails?" I asked trying to see if there was a struggle of any kind.

"Nothing," he said. "They were clean. No signs of a struggle. No defensive wounds noted. There's no doubt, Mac. The fall killed him."

"Could he have been assaulted before the fall?" I asked.

"He could have but the injuries from the impact from the fall were very significant. It would be impossible to delineate any underlying injuries from an assault to his face from the injuries sustained in this fall."

"Let me ask you this, Doc. If I told you that he was drugged with chloroform, ketamine, rohypnol or some other drug to render him unconscious and said he was assaulted, would you be able to dispute it?" I asked.

"With those injuries and without the full tox screen, I would say it was possible," he conceded. "Those are some big ifs."

"Were there any signs that his hands were bound by any chance?"

"C'mon, Mac. I wouldn't miss something like that."

"I know. I'm sorry. I know I'm grasping at straws." My frustration was on full display.

"He did have on a long sleeve shirt and a coat. So if he was bound over the garments there would be very little chance it would show on the skin," Doc added, trying to give me some hope.

"So, nothing out of the ordinary on this one?" I asked.

"The only thing unusual was Rizzo pestering me to move this along. He told me to make it a priority and then balked when I asked if he wanted a full tox. I know he is typically not too patient so I didn't think much of it. He wanted me to sign off on this before I had the tox screen back. He told me he already knew he was drunk when he jumped and to hurry up with the report. I got the tox results and signed off on it. Sorry, Mac, I wish I could give you better news"

We all thanked him for his time and parted ways. We were going over what we learned while walking out. I told them that I knew Stevens from a prior case and knew he was a quite capable forensic pathologist. They weren't questioning his cause of death findings. The finding of suicide came from Rizzo and no one else. He rushed the post mortem and wrapped up his investigation within three days. *Why the rush, Rizzo?*

We had to put Rizzo aside for now. We had a Black SUV to track down.

Chapter 17

Flanagan's didn't open up for another hour so we went to a local diner for some coffee and a late breakfast. Bo and I ordered a pot of coffee, home fries, and the greatest sandwich on the planet. The pork roll, egg, and cheese on a hard roll was the sandwich that made New Jersey famous. Jessica didn't share our enthusiasm for the greatest sandwich on the planet and she ordered scrambled eggs and wheat toast with orange juice. *Her loss.*

"How can you guys eat that crappy processed meat?" Jessica asked us both.

"Whoa. Crappy processed meat? Don't trash our pork roll. I've ended relationships for much less than that," Bo joked with her as he was turning over the bottle of ketchup and dumping it onto his sandwich.

"Okay Okay. Enjoy your processed meat," she relented. "But

I draw the line at ketchup on eggs. And if you put that Frank's Red Hot on those home fries, I'm switching tables."

We had a good laugh. Jessica had already shown us on several occasions that she was smart and had a great sense of humor. Her great looks were just a bonus. I could see why Squirrel took a liking to her.

"So where is Brian today?" Jessica asked.

"He had some things to take care of at work. I think he is trying to clear some time so he can help us out with this. He was one of Jimmy's good friends and I know he wants to do whatever he can," I said. I thought I saw a hint of a smile on her face.

We finished our breakfast and drove to Flanagan's just as they were opening for business. The three of us went in and were greeted by the hostess. She was grabbing three menus and ready to walk us to a table.

"We're not here to eat," Bo said. Before he could say another word she was directing us to the bar. "We need to talk to the manager."

"Oh. Okay. I'll go get him," she said. I think she was wondering if she was in some kind of trouble. *Was I not polite enough?*

We moved to the bar and sat there waiting for the manager as ESPN blared in the backround on a dozen TVs. It wouldn't be so loud if there was the chatter of customers throughout but we were the only ones in there. After a few minutes of listening to talking heads on ESPN, a man walked up to us and introduced himself as Todd, the manager.

"Hi, Todd. I'm Jack MacMasters and this is Tim Bollander and Jessica Adams" as I extended my hand. He shook my hand and I'm sure he was wondering what I was there to sell him. "We are investigating the death of a friend of ours who died last Friday night. He was here on St Patrick's Day. We think it was the last place he was at before his death"

"A detective came by on Monday and asked a few questions. We didn't know anything," he said.

"We're here to see if you have any video surveillance of the parking lot from that night," I asked.

"We have fourteen cameras covering the inside and the lot. Not all areas of the lot are covered. I burned a copy onto a CD and gave it to the detective. He was a bit abrupt. I was trying to help him and he kept giving me a hard time."

"Can you burn us a copy? We are looking for whatever you have from 7:30 to 10:30."

"I don't know. Why don't you just get this from the detective?"

Bo stepped in. "The detective is an asshole. We talked to him about his investigation and it didn't go too well. He won't be giving us anything anytime soon. He closed his investigation and ruled our friend's death a suicide. We developed information that shows foul play may have been involved. Detective Rizzo didn't want to hear it and said he's not re-opening his investigation. The deceased was a good guy and his family doesn't want the stigma that comes with their son taking his own life."

"Come in the back with me. I'll pull up the video."

We walked back to Todd's office. It was quite organized. The walls were decorated with sports memorabilia from all the local teams. An 11 x 14 picture of his family served as the centerpiece for the front of his desk.

"Nice looking family, Todd" Jessica said. We were getting his cooperation and Jessica wanted to make sure we continued to get it. Todd nodded his thanks and then turned to the surveillance monitor.

"Todd, can you pull up the parking lot at around 10:30?" I asked. He had three different views of the lot. He made some keystrokes and then the three parking lot views were isolated on the screen. He cued it up to 10:20 PM and we sat and watched. The video was being run in real time so it seemed like it was taking forever. 10:30 came and went and still no SUV. We kept watching.

"There it is," Jessica yelled out, and now pointing to the screen. "Right there. That's the car Jimmy got into." We continued to watch and saw Jimmy coming into view. He walked up to the SUV and appeared to stick his head in the front passenger side window. It looked like he was talking to the driver. We had no view of the driver. Jimmy got in the backseat and the SUV took off.

We isolated each of the three cameras on the screen to see if we could get a look at the license plate. Todd cued up the camera that captures most of the front lane of travel. There was no view of the plate or the driver. The SUV came around to the front of the restaurant from the south side parking lot. Todd cued the south side camera and we watched. The SUV first came into view as he pulled from a parking space in the lot. He pulled from the space and made a right turn then he was out of view on that camera. This time the angle of the camera was just right. I couldn't make it out but there was a shot of the license plate.

"Can you enlarge this, Todd?" I asked. He said he could and went to work. There it was in plain sight. Plate # SPJ 47M – registered in Pennsylvania. Todd was already burning the video onto a CD.

"Todd, I hate to be a pain in the ass but I need a huge favor. I'm going to need a separate copy of every angle inside and out covering 7:30 to 10:45. If it wasn't extremely important, I wouldn't waste your time," I asked. I could see Todd was less than thrilled with my request.

He finally responded, "Not a problem. It'll take about twenty minutes."

We waited out in the bar area. The patrons were starting to fill the tables and bar area. ESPN didn't seem so loud now that the place was filling up. Todd came out after about twenty-five minutes with a hand full of discs in paper sleeves.

"Thank you, Todd. This is a huge help," I told him. Jessica and Bo nodded in agreement.

"No problem. I hope you find what you're looking for."

We left Flanagan's and were sitting in my Explorer. We now have a bona fide lead. I called my old partner.

"Sully. It's me. I need you to run a plate."

"Jesus Christ, Mac. You've been gone for five minutes and I'm already running plates for you. Whadda ya need?" I gave him the info and he said he would call me back in a few minutes.

"Mac, we have to really check out those surveillance videos. If this guy was in the lot for a while then maybe he got out of his car. Maybe we can get a look at him," Bo noted.

"It would be nice but I have a feeling this guy is real careful. The SUV is likely a rental and he was probably aware enough of the layout to not get his face caught on camera. Don't worry, Bo, we'll check every second of every one of those CDs." We might be a step closer but we still had a mountain to climb. My phone rang.

"Sully. What do ya got?" He went on to give me the info.

"Thanks, Sully. We'll get together soon."

"Get together? It hasn't even been long enough for me miss you," and he hung up.

I told Bo and Jessica that the SUV was registered to Peterson's Auto Repair and Rental Agency in Palmyra, Pennsylvania just outside of Harrisburg.

Jessica seemed to like the thrill of the hunt and said, "Well, boys, get packed. We're heading to Pennsylvania."

Chapter 18

The man with the scar on his face sat in his black SUV in a parking lot across from Flanagan's. He watched the three people leave the restaurant and get into MacMasters' Ford Explorer. It looked to him like MacMasters was carrying a stack of CDs with him. He could only surmise that he had secured copies of video surveillance for the night of Collucci's death. He had taken it upon himself to keep tabs on MacMasters after he saw him at the funeral home and Dorsey's Pub. His instincts paid off. After seeing him with the Medical Examiner and back at Flanagan's, he knew MacMasters was taking more than a casual interest in his friend's death. He was outright investigating. From the looks of it, he would likely be able to identify the vehicle soon if he hadn't done so already. He was secluded enough where they wouldn't spot his vehicle. He decided to take no chances and pulled out of the lot. He would need to ditch the SUV soon.

The scar-faced man's name was Anatoly Volkov. He had

Russian blood pouring through his veins but had become Americanized over the past thirty-five years. He was known to his business associates in America as Anthony Wolf. His last name was derived from the Russian word Volk and its literal translation was 'the wolf'. He was simply addressed by his employers and associates as Wolf. He liked that just fine. After all they were both skilled predators.

There was barely a hint of his Russian accent left. He had worked hard over the years to shake it. He left behind a miserable and impoverished existence in Russia. Growing up he got into his fair share of fights. Winning most and losing some. Pain never bothered him and still didn't. He killed his first man when he was eighteen. One night he was walking down the street not far from where he lived when he was approached by a man on the street who was wielding a knife and demanding all his money. He had no money to give him. Even if he had anything, he would have never given it up. The crazed man slashed his face from his ear to his mouth. He barely seemed fazed by it. He disarmed the attacker quickly and then used the man's own knife to slit his throat. He calmly wiped off the blood from the knife with his attackers jacket sleeve. He took the knife with him and quietly walked away. He ended up getting the cut on his face stitched up but the quality of work was subpar and he was left with a lengthy scar. That night he learned killing was easy. He would have no problem doing it again.

In America he had made a living out of his passion for killing.

He operated without any conscience or remorse. He was given a job in exchange for money and the objectives of that job would be fulfilled. He had honed his skills over the years. If guns were needed, he had guns and knew how to use them. If it was knives or physical confrontation, he would cut up his victim or pummel him to death if needed. If the job required explosives, he would gather the materials and make his own. If information was needed, he was a skilled interrogator and would go to any extreme to obtain it. He was only hired through referrals and his only clients were the rich and/or powerful. His services didn't come cheap so maximum results were expected on every job.

This job was frustrating him. It was taking way longer than expected. He was given a list of potential blackmailers from his employer. His job was to confirm the identity of the blackmailer and retrieve the item for which he was being blackmailed. It would be merely a bonus if Wolf could also retrieve the money his employer had already paid out. His last instruction was to make sure the blackmailer never blackmails him or anyone else again.

The first two names on the list did not yield the desired results. Both men were properly interrogated per Wolf's standards. If either one was the blackmailer, he would have known. His employer made it perfectly clear that the deaths had to appear to be accidental to avoid any lengthy police investigations. He also didn't want to raise any suspicions in the actual blackmailer, as he needed to find him for his *interrogation* before he realized he was now the one being hunted.

Wolf's phone rang. He was expecting this call.

"Yeah," Wolf answered.

"Status?" Wolf didn't respond immediately. "What have you found out?" his employer asked. He wasn't a patient man and was used to getting results much quicker. He had used Wolf once before and was pleased with his efficiency and results. This would not be a good time to be let down. Wolf received half his pay up front and the other half would come when the job was completed successfully. His employer was a smart man. He figured that would ensure Wolf remained motivated.

"MacMasters, Bollander, Kavanaugh, and a female have been asking questions. They visited the police detective, the medical examiner, and then went back to the bar where I picked up Collucci. As far as I can tell, they didn't get anything from the police or the medical examiner. MacMasters was carrying something when he left Flanagan's. I think it may have been the surveillance video discs."

"What are they gonna find on those discs?" the employer shot back with concern.

"They won't see me. I was careful but they probably will be able to ID the rental. I'm dumping the car. That won't lead anywhere."

"It better not. Listen, Wolf, I'm paying for results. That was sloppy. You better get back to that rental agency and clean up your mess."

"Do you want me to stay with MacMasters and the others?" Wolf asked.

"Leave them for now. I will send two of my guys to keep an eye on them. After you are done with the car rental clerk, I want you moving onto the next name on the list. Same as before, follow him for a bit and learn his schedule and his habits. Find out if he's the guy. You know what to do from there."

Wolf sat in his car mulling his next moves. He knew he had to ditch the rental car and then make sure the rental agent didn't turn into a loose end. Wolf looked at the list. He shouldn't lose too much time dealing with the rental agent. The rental agency and his next target were both in Pennsylvania. It wouldn't be long before he was following Eddie Vincent's every move.

Chapter 19

December 1983

Tensions were running high with our landlord Bucky. All he had done for us, as tenants, was collect our rent. Any repairs we asked from him continually fell on deaf ears. We knew of his intentions to sell off these row houses to the college after this year. We would be his last tenants and he had no intention of keeping us happy. We were onto his game and had every intention of making this last year as tenants as painful for him as he intended to make for us. He had come over to visit twice in the last two weeks. Each visit he was armed with idle threats of eviction.

Last weekend we had a tailgate party in the parking lot behind our houses where about eighty people attended. We had several kegs of beer and were flipping burgers and dogs on the grill. The party was in full gear when Brian decided to have dumpster races. Bucky had two dumpsters in the lot that serviced the entire run of his row houses.

Unfortunately for Bucky, those dumpsters were on wheels.

The race involved a team of three guys pushing the dumpster across the parking lot. First one to the fence at the end wins. As it turned out, a bunch of guys there wanted to make it harder for the combatants and they jumped on top of the closed dumpsters. Each dumpster had four passengers and three pushers. Bo and I were more than happy to sit this one out and watch from the sidelines in our lawn chairs. Before the race started, Tyler said he would take Brian's team and accept any bets. Ten minutes later, all the gambling action was settled and the race began. Eddie was the leader of dumpster number two. Brian and his team and Eddie and his crew approached the starting line. We didn't have a starter's gun, so Willie lit a firecracker. Off they went. Tyler had taken about a hundred bucks in bets and was backing Team Brian. It took them about ten or fifteen yards to get these hunks of metal moving at a good clip. They were neck and neck for most of the race. Somehow Brian's team found some untapped energy and they pulled away easily. The problem was no one thought about how to stop a ton of rolling metal when the race was over. Brian was the big winner. Bucky's chain link fence was the big loser. One guy chickened out and jumped off before impact. The other three were laughing the entire way and went through the fence without incident.

Tyler collected his hundred bucks. Brian's team was celebrating like they won the Super Bowl. We looked over and saw our elderly neighbor looking on. Ruth was about eighty-five years old and had lived in her town house for the past sixty years. She lived in the unit immediately next to our three houses.

The next day we received a visit from Bucky and one of his employees. Bucky was a short barrel chested man in his late forties or early fifties. He was balding and graying in all the wrong places. He was a shrewd businessman and had no problems taking advantage of other people's misfortune to build his own personal wealth. Bucky's paint store was successful enough but his real wealth came from his rental properties. Many Wilkes-Barre residents lost their homes after Hurricane Agnes. The entire area was buried under eight feet of water. Many homeowners did not have flood insurance and the government assistance was minimal. At that time, no one could have conceived the mighty Susquehanna River would overflow its banks. It did on that one fateful day and when people realized they couldn't afford to rebuild their home, they stopped making their mortgage payments. Bank foreclosures ensued. That's where Bucky stepped in. He picked up as many of these foreclosures as he could from the banks for pennies on the dollar. He put in the minimum amount of money and effort to get these places up and running again. I don't know how many properties he actually owns but whatever the number, it made him a very wealthy and powerful man. He had turned being a "slumlord" into an art form.

When Bucky got wind of the fence damage, he was furious. We were sitting on the front porch the morning after the hundred yard dumpster dash when Bucky and company came over to us.

"Good morning, Bucky!" Bo yelled out.

"The hell it is!" Bucky shot back in his raspy voice.

"What's the matter?" Bo knew exactly what was eating at him but wanted to poke at the hornet's nest.

"You guys ain't foolin anyone. I know you guys did it."

"Did what, Bucky?" Bo said with a half grin on his face.

"Listen here, Bollander, you smartass. You're paying for that."

"Pay for what, Bucky?"

"The fence. The god damned fence in the back!" Bucky yelled as the veins in his forehead began to reveal themselves.

"Is something a matter with the fence?" Bo continued to needle him. "I don't know what you're talking about but if there is a problem with the fence, we don't know anything about it. Finals are next week. We were all at the library studying."

"You're not getting away with this. I'll find someone that will tell me the truth. You keep pulling shit like that and you'll all be thrown out. And I mean *thrown* out."

"That sounds like a threat, Bucky. Are you threatening us, Bucky?" Bo kept at him.

"Take it however you want, Bollander."

As Bucky was wrapping up his tirade, Ruth walked out onto her porch. Bucky smiled and turned to Ruth. He knew Ruth was hard of hearing so he amped up the volume. "Hey Ruth. How are you today, honey?" The entire neighborhood was now listening in on the conversation. "I was wondering if you could tell me how my fence got damaged last night?"

"Whaddaya askin me for? I sure as hell don't know." This is not what Bucky was expecting. He knew darn well that Ruth rarely left her house and knew exactly what happened.

"Come on, Ruth. You had to see something," Bucky taking one last shot.

"I ain't seen nothin. I thought you were here to fix my bathroom sink like I been askin ya about." Bucky knew it was time to retreat or he would be getting a pipe wrench out of his truck if he stayed another second.

"Oh,yeah. I'm sending over a plumber. I gotta head out now. My plumber will call you soon, Ruth."

" Ruth knew no plumber would be stopping by anytime soon. That would suit her just fine being her sink was working perfectly. She knew the second she asked him to do anything, he would hightail it out of there. Before Bucky got to his car, he looked back at us and said, "You're not gonna get away with this. Ya hear me?"

"We hear ya, Bucky. I'll tell you what. We'll look into this fence thing and when we find out who did it, you'll be the first to know."

Bo took another poke at him.

"Oh, I know who did it. Someone will rat out you pricks."

"You have a great day, too, Bucky." Bo was determined to get in the last word. With that Bucky and his apparently mute employee got into their truck and sped off. If Bucky was looking in the rearview mirror he would see a porch full of his least favorite tenants getting a huge laugh at his expense.

"Thanks, Ruth." I said.

"Any time, boys. He's been on my shit list for the past twelve years. He's a good for nothing bum." We knew Ruth would never sell us out to Bucky. We got along great with her. She had no problems with our loud parties. This is where her lack of full hearing came in handy. Ruth treated us like the grandsons she never had. We in kind treated her like we would our own grandmother.

Bo was always an early riser. Every day he would go across the street to Charlie's Market and pick up a coffee and a newspaper for her. Bo would leave the coffee and paper on her little table on her front porch. She would always come out around nine o'clock and get her day started compliments of Bo. She didn't have much money and this gesture meant a great deal to her. Every once in a while she would make us a tray of brownies or cookies. She was quite the baker. In Ruth's eyes, we could do no wrong. She also knew that as long as we were neighbors she would be safe. We would make sure of it.

"By the way, you should have asked me if I wanted to bet the race. I would have had a ten spot on Brian," she said with a big laugh. We all joined in on the laughter.

Later that day we were in our house playing darts and having a few beers. Brian, Bo, Ant, Tommy D, Junior D, Squirrel and I were killing a few hours listening to music and having a dart tournament. Somehow we turned the dart tournament into a drinking game. Every point you scored on your opponent cost you a gulp of your beer. As the game was moving along, Willie walked in with some guy I hadn't seen before.

He had a strange smile on his face. "Hey, guys. This is Mickey." We all said our hellos and Willie let Mickey know all of our names.

"We're doing some kind of dart drinking game. You guys want in?" I asked. It didn't take them long to respond in the affirmative. They joined in and cracked open a cold one. We had some small talk with Mickey. We found out he was a sophomore and lived off campus. He and Willie were in the same Theology class. Being a Catholic College, every student is required to take six credits of Theology. They can be taken in any of your four years. It wasn't unusual for freshman to be in the same Theology class as a junior or senior. Mickey was a fairly good looking guy and had a rich-kid vibe about him. He had a bit of a young looking face. He tried growing some facial hair but wasn't quite ready. He did have a great head of hair. There wasn't one hair out of place. I soon found out why. Every time a hair fell out of place, out came his comb and back in place it went. Be that as it may, he was basically a young kid that wanted to hang out and have a few beers with the guys.

I soon figured out why Willie had a strange smile. He was waiting for the right time and finally spoke up. "Guys, promise you won't freak out."

"What the hell are you talking about?" Squirrel piped in.

"Don't freak out." Now everyone was yelling at Willie. "Okay. Okay. Mickey is Bucky's kid."

"Are you friggin' kidding me?" Bo was visibly pissed off. "What makes you think he would be welcome here?"

"Bo, it's cool. Mickey is a cool guy. He knows the problems we have with his father. He's on our side," Willie tried reasoning.

"What do you mean he's on our side?" I asked.

Mickey jumped in, "Look, guys, I'll leave if you want me to. I am not my father. I heard about the dumpster race and was laughing my ass off. If you think I would ever say anything to him about that, you're wrong."

We were digesting what Mickey was saying. It really didn't make any sense that Bucky would use his son as his mole to gather dirt on us. We couldn't be that important to Bucky. I thought Bucky viewed us as nothing more than a mere nuisance in his slumlord empire. After listening to Mickey a little longer, maybe I was underestimating our effect on Bucky.

"My father hates you guys. You should hear him at the paint store. He really hates Bollander." That got a big smile out of Bo. "He said he curses the day he ever let you guys live here." Now we were all smiling. "You guys look like fun to me. I would love to come to your parties. You can trust me. I'm not here for my father."

He seemed to be winning us over but we were still a little bit on the fence about him.

"I don't feel I need to prove anything to you but I can give you some info about what my father is planning."

"Planning? He's actually planning a scheme to get us outta here? You have to be kidding me?" I said.

"No kidding at all. I overheard him at the paint store talking to a couple of the guys that work for him. He wants them to figure a way to get rid of you guys. I'm not sure what he is planning just yet. He was talking about planting drugs or child pornography or something like that. But I don't think that's his plan. He sounded desperate. These guys are in their early twenties and look like they are college age. I think my father wants them to find their way into one of your parties and see what they can find out. Once they find something, they'll somehow use it against you."

"Thanks, Mickey" I said and then looked at the guys. "Maybe we should clean up our act and stop with all the parties," I said with as straight of a face as I could muster up. The guys were looking at me like I had three heads. "We can talk more about it at Friday night's party." *A collective sigh of relief. All is still right in the world.*

Chapter 20

We made sure the word got out for our party. Mickey was going to *accidentally* let it slip to one of his father's young employees that there was a big party at 19 Jackson Street on Friday. That gave us plenty of time to come up with a plan of our own. We had a day and a half to come up with something.

We had just wrapped up the day's street hockey game and were now back at the house. We were throwing around ideas. Some good. Some not so good. Everyone's first instinct was to take Bucky's moles and beat the shit out of them. That was part of the not so good ideas. Bucky would love that. He could care less if his guys got a good beating. It wasn't his face that would be bleeding and swollen. He would no doubt have the police here in a matter of seconds and charges would be filed.

"Enough with the ass kicking ideas. We need to be smart about this," I said.

"Why don't we just not let them in the party?" Tommy D

asked.

"Where's the fun in that? We need to send Bucky a *don't screw with us* message," I responded.

"Mac's right. Bucky needs a message," Bo throwing his support my way. "Think of it like a street hockey game. We know how to play physical when we need to. We also know how to play a finesse game when called for. We need to bring our finesse game to Bucky."

"Wow. Hell of an analogy, Bo. Finesse it is," Tommy D said.

"I think I have an idea," I said. The guys looked my way and listened for the next few minutes. I went through my plan and everyone was on board.

A little while later Brian came back to the house. He stopped by the library after our street hockey game. Most of the guys had left already. Eddie and Willie decided to hang a little longer. It beat hanging in their dorm rooms.

"I think I'm in love," Brian opened with. *Oh no, here we go again.* "I had been staring at this girl in my math class for pretty much most of the semester. I finally got up the nerve to talk to her. Well, maybe it wasn't so much me getting up the nerve. I actually tripped over her backpack in the hall outside of the classroom and she asked me if I was okay."

"You're quite the operator Brian," Bo said through his laughter.

"She said she was sorry. I said thanks."

"Please tell me there's more to it than that?" I said.

"Yeah. I'm getting to it. We got talking and she is awesome. I invited her to tomorrow night's party. She said she would have to sneak out but she would try to make it. She's a commuter who lives locally."

"Did you get her name?" Willie asked.

"Allegra. It's an Italian name. It's such an unusual name I decided to look it up at the library to see what it meant. I thought maybe it would give me something to talk to her about," Brian said and then just stopped the conversation.

After a few seconds Willie said "Well, are you going to tell us or is this some kind of secret?"

"Cheerful, high-spirited, and carefree" Brian said. "It's amazing. Those are the first things you're going to think about when you meet her."

"I guess you're hoping for more of the carefree part," Willie said with his one track mind operating in high gear.

Brian decided to change the subject. "Enough about Allegra for now. Hey, Mac, I think I figured out what to do with my $2,500."

Brian and his brothers had each received a small inheritance from his grandfather. Each grandkid was given $2,500 with the instruction to invest it in a company and let it sit there until they retire. His grandfather was a strong proponent of the stock market but felt too many people panicked and pulled their money too soon.

"What did you decide?" I asked.

"When I was at the library I saw this kid using the library's computer. It had some pretty cool stuff on the screen. He said it was called a Lisa made by a company called Apple. This kid looked like he was pretty into these computers. I don't know shit about them," Brian said.

Willie jumped right in. He always tries to act like he is an authority on every subject. "You don't want to put your money there."

"This kid was telling me they just announced they will be rolling out a new computer in a few months called a Macintosh. It's a computer for your home. They're gonna cost around twenty-five hundred bucks. A home computer might not be a bad idea."

"Why don't you just buy the Macintosh computer with your twenty-five hundred bucks?" Willie said trying to be funny. No one laughed along with him.

"The money was given to me to invest and that's what I'm going to do."

"Nobody is going to buy those things. Who would pay twenty-five hundred bucks for a glorified typewriter? Trust me on this one. I know. My father is a stock broker." Willie was digging in now.

"What the hell do you know, Willie? If he wants to invest in this Apple company, you should mind your own friggin' business!" Eddie shouted out to Willie. They had a love hate relationship. They got along for the most part but they do butt heads quite a bit. Eddie felt Willie was somewhat of a bullshit artist and not one he fully trusted. He had no problem calling him out on his bullshit when he heard it. Eddie wouldn't shed a tear if Willie wasn't part of the crew.

"All right. I'll shut up. If you want to invest in that dog then go right ahead. It's your money." Willie hoped he was making his point.

Eddie wasn't done with Willie. "Hey, Willie. Remind us what kind of car your father drives."

"Don't be an asshole, Eddie." Willie obviously knew where this was going.

"Oh, that's right. He drives a DeLorean. And remind us what company he invested his money in and his client's money in. Oh, that's right. DeLorean Motor Company. And remind us what company went bankrupt last year." Eddie had made his point and then some. Willie wasn't too happy with Eddie at this particular time but he would get over it. He always did.

"I'm outta here. I don't need this shit. I was just trying to help."

"Calm down, Willie," Bo said. "Sit down." Willie really didn't want to leave so he slowly turned around and went back and sat down on the couch right next to Eddie.

"Thanks for the input, Willie. I'll figure this thing out." Brian was trying to diffuse any remaining tension.

We filled Brian in on our ideas to deal with Bucky's moles. He burst out laughing. I think he liked the plan.

Eddie and Willie got up and were headed for the door. I yelled to Eddie, "Hey, Eddie. Make sure White Thunder is gassed up and ready to roll tomorrow night."

"You don't have a thing to worry about. She'll be ready. She always is."

Chapter 21

Classes were over for the day. We had just finished up our street hockey game and now it was back to the house. We had a party to get ready for. When we got back Mickey was already there waiting for us. He was looking like he was ready for a party. He had a nice button down shirt on and as usual not a hair out of place on that head of his. There wasn't too much prep work needed for our parties. Bo made us a bar for our living room. It didn't cost a thing. The head of the theater department was our dorm advisor when we were freshman. We got along great with him and he was more than happy to help us when he could. He built us the goals for our hockey games. He donated all the wood from what he had lying around and Bo did the rest.

The bar was already pretty well stocked with vodka, gin, rum, and whiskey. We added a bottle of Everclear grain alcohol to our stock for tonight. We were expecting a few guests we wanted to drink some of it. Squirrel and Eddie would be taking out White Thunder to pick up the three kegs of Old Milwaukee beer that we ordered. At $22 a keg it was quite the bargain. Our only other expenses were plastic cups, ice, and a few bags of pretzels. When we added it all up, the entire party should only cost about a hundred bucks. A guy we knew from the dorm always volunteered to sit at the front door and collect the $2 entry fee. All he wanted for his services was to not pay the $2 entry and for someone to keep getting his beers. It's certainly a good deal for us. I think he thinks it's good deal for him. We usually get about eighty to a hundred people to show up throughout the night. If we end up making money we put it toward breakfast the next morning for our crew and who ever ends up crashing over our house.

Mickey told us that he made sure his father's employees got wind of the party. He was confident that they would be showing up tonight. He said he would point them out when they got here.

"Wait a second ,Mickey. You can't be here when they show up. If they see you the whole thing could fall apart." I told Mickey.

"What do you have planned?" he asked.

I still wasn't sure if Mickey could be trusted so I wasn't letting him in on anything just yet. "You'll see."

"How can I see if you won't let me be here." He was pleading now.

"Okay, Mickey. You can be at the party but you stay in the back. When these guys come here, you go next door to Evs and don't come back 'til we tell you."

"Great. That'll work," obviously satisfied with the compromise.

"You'll know the guys when they get here. One of them wears a red Mack Truck hat all the time. I'm sure he'll have it on for the party. The other guy is a little shorter and has a bit of a beer gut."

"I'm sure these guys will think they will blend right in but they're going to stick out like a sore thumb," I said. "Thanks, Mickey. Just make sure you don't get seen."

"No problem."

We showered up after the hockey work out and now were ready to set up the party. Brian asked that we keep open the one parking space that we had in front of the house. He wanted that for Allegra. He was pretty confident she would show up. He had walked her to her car yesterday and saw she had a small yellow Volkswagen Beetle. He gave Bo and me a little more info about her after everyone left last night. He said she was flat out hot. Said she had a beautiful dark complexion which obviously came from the Italian in her. She had high cheekbones and long black hair that would go half way down her back if she let it down. She didn't have any make up on and according to Brian she didn't need any. She had natural beauty. She dressed very causally. She wore loose fit pull-over shirts with khakis or jeans and always had sandals on. She had that whole flower child vibe. That vibe turned into a reality when Brian saw her keychain as she was getting into her car. Attached she had a three or four inch in diameter rainbow colored peace sign. It barely fit into her pants pocket. She should carry a purse for it but it didn't look like that was her style. After listening to Brian go on and on about her beauty and personality, I was quite looking forward to meeting her.

The kegs were iced down and the beer was flowing by ten o'clock. The people started rolling in. Our buddy at the door was doing his part. *Two dollars, please. Two dollars, please.* Nobody cared that it was Old Milwaukee. Beer was beer and it was cold. And we were all poor college students. What the heck do you expect for two bucks? Brian was sitting on the front porch waiting for Allegra to show up. Anyone who tried to park in that one open space had to incur Brian's wrath. The space remained open. Eleven o'clock was approaching and still no Allegra. Brian was still holding out hope.

A few minutes after eleven two guys showed up. Our friend at the door knew they would be showing up and were welcome. He wasn't given any more info than that. I was near the front door and saw Mr. Red Hat and Mr. Beer Gut waiting in line to pay. They got to our *bouncer* and we heard "Two bucks, please." The guys dug in and scraped up their two bucks. It's a good thing we didn't charge four bucks. They might not have had enough on them to get in.

The two guys wandered in and were checking out the surroundings. Not much to see at this point. People were standing around drinking beer from red plastic cups and listening to music. The room was busy and the talk was lively. I'm sure they felt like they were blending right in.

Mickey did his part and scooted out the back door when we gave him the word. He was now hanging next door. We had about half the guests in the living room and kitchen on the main floor and the other half hanging in the basement where the kegs were. The two guys walked up to the bar where Bo was standing behind. "What's up, fellas" Bo asked.

"Got any beer back there?" Red Hat asked.

"Beer's in the basement. Cups are down there, too."

Bo pointed toward the basement door. Not even a thank you from them. They just turned and walked toward the door. Bo couldn't help but smile knowing their fate. It couldn't happen to two nicer guys, he thought. There was no rush to put the plan in place. We figured they would be here awhile.

Enough time went by and the two guys were pretty well settled in. They went back to the keg for a re-fill. It was probably their fourth or fifth beer. Two young ladies walked up to them and started getting some conversation going. These ladies/operatives were more than happy to help us out. Their goal was simple. Strike up a conversation, get them to the bar for liquor and get them up to a bedroom.

"Hi, I'm Jenny," the one said to Red Hat. "I'm Ginny," the other said to Beer Gut.

"I'm Daryl and he's Lance. Jenny and Ginny. Are you two like sisters or something?" Red Hat said obviously having left his A game back in his double wide.

"No. Just friends. But we're like sisters. We do everything together. Everything," Jenny said with her full flirt on. Jenny and Ginny were good friends of ours and they were both in the Theater Club. When I asked them if they wanted an acting job, they couldn't say yes quick enough. I was standing near them talking to Squirrel. In actuality, we were listening in on the conversation.

"So Daryl. I haven't seen you around here. Do you go here?" Jenny said.

"Yeah. I go here. I take some night classes. I ain't got time during the day. Gotta work, too," he said.

"Lemme guess," with her hand on his forearm again and smiling through her drunk act, "English major?"

I almost spit my beer out and had a tough time controlling my laughter.

"Naw. I ain't no English major," Red Hat said as if it needed any confirmation.

Before he could say another word, Jenny grabbed his hat and then his hand. "C'mon, I need another shot."

Step one was going well. Of course, we had eyes on these guys the entire time. We saw them poking around our place a bit earlier but it didn't look like they found anything of interest for Bucky. I'm sure they would love an opportunity to get upstairs. The girls were working their magic. The guys didn't have much of a rap. The conversation on the guys end was quite clumsy. Beer Gut even started talking about paint. The girls were hanging on their every word like it was the most interesting thing they heard all day.

Ginny looked at Beer Gut and said, "I want shots, too. Let's go to the bar." Both these guys were fully roped in by now. They were more than happy to get a shot or two. After all, they knew they were getting lucky tonight.

It was a little past midnight and Brian had folded up his tent and headed to the bar. He was commiserating with Bo when he saw the lights of a car pulling into the open parking space. He ran from the bar and out the front door. He was now staring at the yellow Volkswagen Beetle. Allegra got out of the car and gave Brian a big wave and a smile. You could hear her wave as well as she was rattling that big peace sign against her metal keys. Brian ran over to greet her. "Thanks for coming."

"Sorry I'm late. I had trouble getting out" she said.

"Are you thirsty? We have beer and some liquor at the bar," Brian said as he was escorting her inside.

"Some vodka drink sounds good," and off they went to the bar. Bo had a big smile on his face when they walked up. Just seconds ago Brian was in the dumps. Now he was on top of the world.

"Bo. This is Allegra. Can you fix her a vodka drink?"

"Hi, Allegra. Nice to meet you. Cranberry?" he said referring to the vodka mixer.

"That would be great. Thanks, Bo. It's great meeting you, too. I really love this place. You guys must have so much fun here," she said. Bo mixed her drink and handed it to her. He could see exactly why Brian was so excited. She was just as he described. Right down to the cheerful, high-spirited, and carefree as her name suggested. In truth our place was a dump but somehow she saw it differently. She didn't see the dingy walls or frayed carpet. She saw freedom, friendship, and fun. She seemed genuinely happy to be a part of it. Brian and Allegra went over to the couch to chat.

Jenny and Ginny were leading the two guys up the stairs and over to the bar. Mac and Squirrel were not far behind. Jenny had now added a little slur to her words. "Hey, bartender. We need shots. Lossa shots," she said as she grabbed Red Hat's red hat and put it on her head. Bo grabbed four plastic shot glasses. He poured the shots which were strategically placed on the bar. The two guys would not be drinking the same thing as the girls. "Down the hastch," adding a nice slur to her toast. The four drank the shots.

"Four more, Misser Bartender," as she was moving in closer to Red Hat. Ginny doing the same to Beer Gut. The guys were more than happy to do another round. Mac and Bo figured about five of these carefully prepared shots would do the trick.

After the fifth shot, it looked like it was beginning to have its desired effects. It was nice to hear Red Hat look at Bo and said "Hey, Pal. Four more."

"Coming right up," Bo responded. The shots that the two guys were doing included vodka, grain alcohol, and some crushed up sleep aids. Squirrel had a bottle of sleeping pills and knew what they were capable of. Between the multiple beers, vodka, grain alcohol and sleeping pills these guys might sleep until tomorrow night. The girls were getting *drunk* on water.

"Listen, Daryl. I feel pretty good now. You know you're really cute. Let's go upstairs," Jenny told Red Hat. Ginny was doing her thing a few feet away.

"Eggselent idea," Red Hat now doing a little slurring of his own. That was followed by a huge yawn. It was go time.

Jenny and Ginny walked them up to my room. "We all going in the same room?" Red Hat somehow managed to ask her.

"I told you downstairs. We do everything together." She had dropped the slurring act a while back. These guys weren't capable of noticing.

They entered the room and turned the lights down. "You get ready guys. We'll get ready and be back in a second." The guys did as told. A few minutes later the girls went back in and turned the lights on. The two guys were passed out cold lying in the bed next to each other with nothing on but their socks and tighty-whities.

Jenny and Ginny walked out. "They're all yours."

"You guys did great. We owe you one," I told her.

"You owe us more than one. Those guys were Grade A losers. I'm sure you'll figure a way to pay us back," Jenny said and they walked away after a job well done.

"Squirrel, grab the camera and lipstick" I said. He had bought a Polaroid instamatic camera and two packs of film. We went in the room and put the lipstick all over their lips and wherever else it ended up on the face. We propped the two of them up next to each other and put their arms around each other. We snapped the shot and out popped the picture. We set them up for several more poses. The hard one was getting the faces close enough together to make it look like they were kissing. We finished both packs of film and had twenty pictures. We had plans for some of the pictures but we would also keep a few for ourselves.

We got the guys dressed and now we had to do the final step of our plan. I went downstairs and saw the party was winding down. It was a little after 2:30 and there were still about twenty people hanging around.

Eddie yelled across the room "Hey, Mac, you ready for White Thunder?"

"Bring her around back, Eddie," I told him.

We carried Red Hat and Beer Gut to the back porch. We took the keys to Red Hat's pickup truck. Mickey was back in the living room and he showed us where his truck was. We put the two guys in the passenger side of the pickup truck. I got into the driver's seat and told Eddie to follow me.

We drove about four miles to the address we were given. I saw the house and pulled into the driveway. I turned the lights off and drove the pickup onto the front lawn. Eddie, Squirrel, and Bo jumped out of White Thunder and started taping the Polaroids onto the hood of Red Hat's truck. It wasn't too chilly that night but I left the heat on in the truck for the boys. We left them in the front seat of the pick-up truck with their arms around each other and heads on each other's shoulders.

We jumped in White Thunder and went back to the house. We walked back in as conquering heroes. We gave the word that Operation Bucky went off just as we planned it. We thought it was appropriate to have a round of shots. "Bo, do you want to rustle up a round of shots. Hold the grain alcohol and sleep aid," I suggested.

"I threw that shit out. I almost didn't make enough. They drank almost all of it," Bo said as he was pouring the round.

Brian was still talking to Allegra and it looked as if it was going pretty good for him. Brian's not a one night stand type so I knew he didn't have any intentions for romance tonight.

I looked at Mickey and said, "You sure you gave us the right address?”

“I’m sure. After all I do live there,” as we let out a hearty laugh. Mickey was more than happy to join us in the round of shots.

“I wish I could be there to see the look on Bucky’s face when he finds those two idiots on his front lawn this morning.”

Chapter 22

As usual Bo was up early. It didn't matter if he went to bed at 11:00 PM or 4:00 AM, he would be up by 6:30 during the weekdays and by 8:00 on the weekends. That was his idea of sleeping in. My idea of sleeping in was more like noon on many occasions. The party was a success on several levels. Operation Bucky went off without a hitch. Allegra showed up and Brian was on cloud nine. We made about fifty bucks with what our buddy collected for us at the door.

Bo saw there were about ten people that crashed over after the party. Bo took the fifty bucks and went to the Charlie's Market across the street. In addition to the coffees and newspaper, he picked up a few dozen eggs, a few pounds of bacon and sausage, some donuts, rolls, and orange juice. Fifty bucks later he walked out of Charlie's with two bags filled with our breakfast. He didn't forget Ruth. He dropped her coffee on her porch table and the paper would follow when he was done with it.

I got up around 9:30 and walked downstairs to the sound and smell of sizzling bacon. I saw a handful of people. Some were still crashed out and some were beginning to stir. Brian wasn't too far behind me. I went into the kitchen and Bo had most of the feast already prepared. He had cooked all of the bacon and sausage and was now working on the scrambled eggs. He set out paper plates, napkins, and cups at the bar. The rolls, donuts, and orange juice was already out there. He brought out a huge tray of the eggs and meats and set it out with the rest of the food.

"Let's go. Rise and shine." I said to the crashers. "Breakfast is served. Time to eat. Don't insult our chef."

I looked around and saw Allegra was in a chair in the living room. She was just waking up. "Hi, guys." She was way too bubbly for 9:30 in the morning after a late night party. "I had such a great time. You guys are the best. Thanks for letting me crash over here. I didn't want to take any chances and drive home."

Brian walked over to her and told her he was glad she had decided to stay over. Apparently they talked to the wee hours of the morning and all went great. Brian said he finally went up to bed around five.

"Smart move crashing here. No need to ruin a good night by driving. We have breakfast on the bar. Why don't you get some food and juice?" I offered to Allegra.

Brian was sure right about her. She was a looker but she didn't flaunt it. If anything, she played down her beauty. Her personality was infectious. In the limited time I had spent with her, I could see she was genuinely a nice person. It looked like Brian may have hit a homerun with this one.

Allegra was more than happy to eat breakfast with us. She was quite an eater for someone with such a fit and trim physique. "Bo, this is the best breakfast I've had in a long time. You could be a professional chef," she said without a shred of doubt that she meant every word of it. She had a habit of making the person she was talking to feel good about him or herself.

"Thanks, Allegra. I don't think I will be transferring to culinary school any time soon," Bo said.

Allegra went back to the couch and sat down next to Brian. As she was just getting seated the front door opened. In walked Bucky and his mute assistant. "You guys got one hell of a nerve," Bucky started with.

"Hey, Bucky, you can't just walk in here any time you want." Bo got right into it with him.

"Listen Bollander, I own this building and can come in here any time I want. Read your lease," Bucky shot back.

"You mean you own this dump" I said. "What are you doing here, Bucky? We're having breakfast and you're not invited."

"You smart asses think you're so funny. I'll tell you what. I'm gonna make sure you're thrown outta here before the end of the year. I'll see to it," he said thinking this would somehow scare us. It only added fuel to the already burning fire. We knew as well as he did that it's not that easy to evict someone. It takes time and money. He had the money but he didn't have the time and he knew it. He was just trying to make our stay here an unpleasant one. What he didn't know is that we were enjoying our little feud with him. We'd had more laughs at his expense then I could count.

"Is that what you came here for, Bucky? To tell us we're smart asses. We already knew that," Bo said.

"I'm sick and tired of you guys. Especially you, Bollander. I want you outta my house."

"We're not going anywhere. You have no grounds to evict us," Bo kept at him.

"Maybe not now but soon enough you'll screw up and I'll have enough to throw you the hell outta here." His blood was beginning to boil. He composed himself and continued. "You think you can mess with me and my employees?"

"Employees? What employees?" Bo said with a grin.

"You know damn well what I'm talking about. Don't play stupid. You put those guys on my front lawn," Bucky said. Our grins turned to outward laughter. "Yeah, laugh it up now. You'll come to regret it. Believe me."

"Bucky, why would we know anything about your employees?" Bo said.

"Two of my employees went to your party last night and got

stinkin' drunk. They passed out in their truck on my front lawn and you put 'em there."

"Whoa. Slow down Bucky. That's a pretty big accusation. You got anything to back that up?" Bo was on the attack now. "Why would two of your employees come to our party? Did you send them here to spy on us by any chance?" The guys were still snickering and this was clearly pissing Bucky off.

"I didn't send them here. They came on their own." Bucky was trying to defend himself now. Denial and lying was the best option now. The more he thought of it, the more it didn't sound good that he was sending in his people to spy on his tenants. No court would take kindly to that if ever he was able to try to evict us in court. "If I did send anyone here it sure wouldn't be those two guys. They're about as useless as balls on the Pope."

We knew Bucky was lying just as he knew what we did last night. We would have to leave it at that for now.

"Bucky, if your two employees crashed our party, how are we at fault for them getting drunk? They may have started here but could have gone to another party. Don't blame us if they can't hold their booze," I said, deciding to give Bo a break from doing all the heavy lifting with Bucky. "What did they look like?"

"You know exactly what they looked like. One was taller guy with a red hat and the other guy was shorter and stockier," Bucky said.

"Oh, those two guys? Yeah I remember them. Mac, you remember those guys. Don't you?" Bo said and then looked at me.

"Yeah. I remember them. A couple of real assholes. They tried drinking the entire keg by themselves. We had to tell them to leave. I have no idea what happened to them after they left here," I said.

"I'll tell you what, MacMasters and Bollander, if I find out you guys had anything to do with that truck on my lawn, it won't be an eviction you guys will have to worry about," Bucky said. He was seething and obviously didn't care that he had threatened us in front of ten witnesses.

"I'll tell *you* what, Bucky, if you come into my house unannounced again and threaten us, I'll be calling the cops. You understand? Now it's time for you to go. We would like to finish our breakfast and don't care to look at you while we're eating." Bo was an expert at getting in the last word.

Bucky stormed out the front door and left it wide open. He was as mad as we have ever seen him. He knew the laughs he was hearing as he walked out were all at his expense.

"Well, wasn't that nice of Bucky to stop by?" I said with dripping sarcasm. Brian began to explain to Allegra our ongoing feud with Bucky. She seemed to be enjoying the re-cap.

Bucky hadn't been gone five minutes when two other guys walked in the front door. *Doesn't anyone knock anymore?* One guy was wearing a suit with an overcoat and was about sixty years old. The other guy was much younger. He was wearing an athletic warm-up suit with a black tee shirt underneath. He had a heavy gold chain around his all too thick neck. His hair was slicked back and when he spoke it was apparent he was of Italian descent. These two guys were plucked right out of The Godfather. What the heck was going on? Was Bucky sending the mob after us?

We were all taken aback a bit and Bo stepped up knowing it would be wise to tread lightly. "Hi, Guys. Can we do something for you?"

The younger of the two looked directly at Allegra and said, "Get in your car and go home. Now!"

Allegra jumped off the couch and said, "Carmine, what are you doing here?"

"To the car. Now I said" the guy went on. We were a little stunned at this point and didn't quite know what to make of this. Allegra walked out and we heard the Volkswagen start up and take off.

The older man said, "We were sent here by Carmine Selvaggio to make sure his daughter gets home safely. He knew she probably went to some party on campus. We have been driving around and saw her car in front."

We all started to look at each other. We knew exactly who his employer was. You couldn't help but know. He was in the local news everyday recently as he was standing trial for extortion, racketeering, and a host of other crimes. Carmine Selvaggio was the most powerful crime boss on the east coast. And standing in front of us was his trusted associate and someone who I assume was Carmine Selvaggio Jr.

The older man continued, "Mr. Selvaggio thinks the world of his daughter. She tests his nerves with her lifestyle. Mr. Selvaggio wants us to make sure no harm ever comes her way. EVER. Do you understand what I'm saying?"

Brian stood up and said, "I invited her here. I didn't know her last name and we certainly treated her with respect. She didn't want to drive home because it was late and she crashed on the couch."

"My sister likes to have a good time. She isn't always in tune with the wishes of my father. My father doesn't want her going to college parties. You understand. Get it through your heads. She is not to be a guest at any more of your parties," Carmine Jr. added.

"We get it," Brian said.

"You better get it." He snapped and then paused. "My father never wanted her to come to this damn school but my sister has a way of making him say yes to her every request." He looked us over and said "Don't make me come back here again. I won't be so nice next time."

The two men looked around in disgust. They weren't accustomed to dirty walls and carpets and ragged furniture. They left through the door and again it was left open after they passed through. Doesn't anyone know how to close a door? I went over and shut the door. But also to make sure these guys had left. Who the heck was going to walk in next? In a matter of a half hour, we had a visit from our angry slumlord and two henchmen of Carmine Selvaggio.

I looked at Brian. "Did you have any idea?"

"No. None at all. I never heard anyone say her last name. I never asked her. She must have enrolled here under a different last name," Brian said. That made sense. I'm sure her father made that a condition when agreeing to let her enroll here. It didn't matter what state you were from, everyone on campus was familiar with the Selvaggio name.

"What the hell are you going to do now?" I asked.

"What do you mean, what am I going to do? I'm going to say hi to her in class but that's it. I'm not inviting her over here anymore. I'm certainly not going to try to pursue a relationship with her. I don't want some guy coming over here and cutting my balls off and sticking them in my mouth." Brian was clearly disappointed to learn that his pursuit of Allegra was over before it ever got started.

"Sorry, Brian. I know you really liked her. There will be others." I tried to offer him a little comfort.

Brian thought he had met the perfect girl. She may have been as close to perfect as one could hope for. Unfortunately that lone flaw was that she was a Mafia Princess.

Chapter 23

2017

I was in my bedroom packing for my trip to Pennsylvania. Katie didn't quite understand why I was packing to be gone for several days. She thought I would be checking out the rental agency and then head back. Maybe one overnight but several nights was not what she was thinking. Palmyra, Pennsylvania is about three hours from central Jersey.

"How long are you packing for?" she asked.

"I have no idea how long this is going to take. If we find something relevant to Squirrel's death in Pennsylvania then we are going to stay there and pursue it," I reasoned.

"You look like you're packing for a week."

"I'm not packing for a week. Maybe a day or two. Three at the most. You're the one that got me thinking Tyler's death may tie in with Squirrel's. If there is any indication of that, we are going to look into it while we're up there. Tyler didn't live too far from Palmyra and worked in Harrisburg."

Katie knew deep down that we were on the right track and she was thrilled when she heard we had an actual lead. She also knew that Rizzo wasn't going to re-open his investigation. So if Squirrel was to get any justice at all, it would have to start with us.

"You know I always worry about you. I just want you to be safe. I'm glad you're not going alone," she said.

"I'll be careful. You know that." We kissed and I told her I loved her. She returned the "I love you" and I picked up my bag and headed for the door.

"Don't worry, Katie. We'll find this guy and I'll be back before you know it." With that I shut the door and clicked my key chain to unlock the door to my Explorer.

I drove to Bo's house. He was going to ride up with me. Jessica drove her car to meet us there. Brian would drive up with Jessica. Brian had to do a quick shopping for clothes. He only expected to be here for two days. The two days might easily turn into a week. He felt it best to purchase clothes here rather than drive back down to Maryland to pick up his own. He felt we were just starting to get some traction so a seven hour round trip to his house would waste too much valuable time. Besides, he would never pass up an opportunity to spend three hours in a car with Jessica.

We agreed to meet directly at Peterson's Repair and Rental Agency. We would worry about where to stay after checking out Peterson's. We popped the address into the GPS and off we went. Bo and I were going over what we knew already and tried to think of any connection between Squirrel's death and Ev's death. Other than being good friends thirty-three years ago in college, there was nothing apparent to connect their deaths. They seemed to only have limited contact over the past years. Squirrel attended all of our annual reunions and Ev attended a few here and there. There was no crossover with their jobs. They were both on Facebook so they had an idea of what was going on in each other's lives. I printed that picture that Ev posted on Facebook and brought it with me for this trip. I looked at it several times but saw no apparent connection to Squirrel. It was just some politicians and political wannabes standing around at the opening of a hospital. Bo looked at the picture, too and couldn't come up with any connection to Squirrel.,

"Katie planted the seed that maybe we should look into Ev's death. I think she may be right. I don't know why but my gut is telling me they are connected. I was never really a big believer in coincidences," I told Bo.

"But how? Where's the connection?" Bo wondered.

"I don't know. That's what we have to figure out."

"What we do know is Squirrel was murdered. We don't know that about Ev yet, but maybe we should operate on that premise," Bo said.

"Are you sure you run a construction company? You sound like a cop to me." I was impressed with his thought process.

"If Ev was murdered we have to assume it was the same person that killed both of them. We also have to assume he is some type of professional likely hired by someone else." Bo was on a roll and making perfect sense to me. I let him keep going. "He tried to make both deaths seem like accidents or suicides. Why do you think a professional killer would go through all of the trouble to make it look that way? If you're a professional you're not worried about getting caught or tied to the victim in any way. Why the accidental death? Why the suicide?"

Bo was wrapping up. Everything he said was spot on and would require answers if we are to figure this thing out.

"I can only think of one thing. The person who hired him doesn't want any investigation into their deaths. Which tells me he somehow knew both Ev and Squirrel" I told Bo.

The ride got quiet for a while as we pondered the possibilities. Did they have any common enemies? We talked about the possibility of a former friend of ours as a candidate for a common enemy. In our junior year of college, Ev and Squirrel lived off campus with Sal Marchesi. He lived next door to Ev in the dorm when they were freshman. He wasn't a hockey player but they had become friends and decided to room together. Sal was from Long Island, New York and was the son of a well- connected construction company owner. They initially got along fine but that didn't last long. Some people were just not meant to cohabitate with each other. It turned out that Sal was not someone to be trusted. Ev and Squirrel noticed little things were missing. At first it was some small change from their dresser top. Then Ev was missing a text book. He and Sal were in the same class and Ev suspected Sal stole his book. He could never prove it but things went from bad to worse. Ev and Squirrel were fed up and sick and tired of being ripped off. It didn't matter it was only small things. It was the principle of it.

They had no intention of living the second semester with Sal. They decided to take Sal's car and park it about four blocks away. On the last day before leaving for Christmas break, Ev and Squirrel grabbed Sal's car keys and drove the car and parked it. They put the keys back and went back to their homes for break. Sal apparently looked for the car and couldn't find it. He ended up taking a bus back to Long Island. Before he left, he was seen having a fit over having his car being stolen. He told people he knew Ev and Squirrel did this to him. It turned out Sal never returned to school for the second semester of the school year. Word had it that his father was so pissed off about this that he pulled him from school. We never heard from or saw Sal again.

"Is it possible Sal could have anything to do with this?" Bo asked.

"It's hard to imagine that. It's been over thirty years. Why now? Why not when he was pissed off a long time ago?" I responded.

"Maybe he carried it around with him his whole life and the more he thought about it the more he wanted revenge," said Bo.

"I just don't see it. It doesn't make any sense. But then again, nothing about this makes any sense." I had no idea about Sal's whereabouts or how his life turned out after leaving school that year.

"He must have been fuming at Squirrel and Ev if he thought they did it. His entire life path may have changed that day. If it did and he thought they did it, he just may want his pound of flesh before he leaves the earth." Bo was right but it was hard to fathom.

"Have you heard anything about how his life turned out," I asked.

"No. I have no idea. Look Mac, I have no idea if he was involved or not. I'm just spit balling here. Let's see where this rental car lead goes. If it turns up to be a dead end, maybe we give Sal a hard look."

"If I remember right, Sal had a pretty powerful father or at least had pretty powerful friends," I added but didn't really think his father would be bothering with a thirty year old grudge. The guy had to be in his seventies or eighties by now.

"We heard he was definitely pissed off. But would he even know anything about Ev or Squirrel? I'm not sure Sal would have ever mentioned he thought his roommates stole his car. It would probably have been better received if he told his father it was some unknown person," Bo said. He was probably right again. If it were me, I would have gone with the random person story. He wouldn't have wanted to admit his roommates got something over on him.

"You're right, Bo. I'm sure the father would have had nothing to do with it and I kind of doubt Sal did either. The timing is all wrong. Unless we can find some recent contact between Sal and Ev and Squirrel, I think we need to focus elsewhere," I said.

We again found ourselves in silence thinking about the past week's events and today's conversation. We were getting close to Palmyra. Jessica and Brian were following us the entire way. I'm sure she was more comfortable following me rather than trusting her GPS. Every time I saw them in my rear view mirror, they seemed to be chatting away. I'm sure Brian was sad the car trip was coming close to an end. He had definitely taken a liking to Jessica. I don't know if he was wrestling with the dynamic that he might be intruding on his dead friend's girl. There was no precedent for this situation. Brian had not made any untoward remarks or gestures to her. Right now they were just two people with a common goal.

We pulled into Peterson's Repair and Rental Agency. It was open every day except Sunday. We parked and got out of the cars. We all stretched our backs, legs, and arms. That's what you get when four fifty somethings step out of a car after a three hour trip. We would all tolerate the discomfort. We had a mission and a little muscle soreness would not get in the way of that. *Let's do it. Time to find a murderer.*

Chapter 24

Peterson's wasn't a very big place. If fit right in for the
surrounding area. It was located in a mainly residential area
dominated by smallish houses and narrow two lane roads. A one bay
garage and small office served as the centerpiece of this property. To
the right were some older model cars waiting their turn to get
repaired. The left side of the property contained the rental cars. They
actually had a fairly decent amount of cars for such a small location.
They had mostly sedans in stock but had a few SUVs available. I was
eying up the property to see if there were any surveillance cameras
posted. I didn't see any. The garage bay door was open and there was
a man with his head buried under the open hood of some old
clunker.

"Hello!" I yelled out loud enough to get the man's head out from
under the hood. He was clad in his mechanic's garb and had grease
and grime all over his hands, face, and clothes. He walked toward us

wiping his hands with a greasy rag. I wasn't sure if he removing grease from his hands or adding some more.

"Can I help ya with something?" he said.

I introduced us and he said his name was Ralph Peterson. We were not his typical clientele so I don't think he thought we were there to get our cars fixed. We pulled up in two cars so I'm sure he knew we weren't there to rent a car.

"Mr. Peterson, I was wondering if I could ask you about a vehicle you rented to someone. I don't know when it was rented or who rented it." Before I could continue any further he abruptly stopped me.

"What's this all about? What do ya need to know about my cars for?" he said.

"Like I was saying, we would like some info on a SUV you rented. It was a fairly new black SUV. I have the plate number," I responded. He seemed to perk up a bit when I mentioned the black SUV.

"Before I tell you anything, I want to know what this is all about. Follow me," he said. We walked to his office. He went behind the counter and we stayed out in front. The office was far more organized than the garage bay or car lot. He said he would be right back and closed the door behind him. I could hear him talking in a low voice. It seemed as if he was making a phone call. He wasn't gone long. After about a minute, he emerged from the office ready to get down to business.

"You said you had a plate number?" he asked. I gave him the plate number but had a feeling he didn't need it. He knew exactly what vehicle we were inquiring about. He began to fumble around through some papers. He then sat at the desk behind the counter and turned on his computer. He was stalling but I didn't know why. He looked back at me and said, "It'll just be another minute or two."

"Mr. Peterson, I'm a detective in New Jersey and I am looking into a murder. Your car was involved." I didn't feel the need to tell him I was an ex-detective.

"You always go investigating murders as a foursome?" he said. It was a good observation. Detectives didn't travel in packs.

"I'm the only law enforcement person here. The others are friends of the deceased." As I said that the front door opened and in a split second I was not the only law enforcement person in the room. In walked two uniformed police officers. It didn't take long to see who outranked who.

The older of the two looked to be a grizzled veteran of the force. He took off his sun glasses and through his square jaw asked, "Who's asking about the black SUV?"

"I'm Jack MacMasters." I extended my hand. He didn't return the gesture. He wasn't going to play nice until he knew what this was about. "My friends and I came from New Jersey. Our friend was killed. I have a video showing our friend getting picked up by someone driving Mr. Peterson's rental car." The officers just looked at me waiting for me to say more. I would oblige them. "We believe the man that was driving that vehicle is the one who killed our friend. I am a recently retired detective and am trying to get some answers."

"I'm Chief Rodgers and this is Officer Wright. You say you have video of this? Do you have any video of the driver?" he asked. There was more to come but I wasn't quite sure where he was going with this.

"I do and I would be happy to give you a copy of what we have. I think I'm missing something here. What aren't you telling me?" I figured I would try to get something out of him.

"I'm asking the questions here, MacMasters." My attempt to get info from him was a massive fail. "When was this video taken?" I gave him the particulars of the video and then gave him a full run down as to why we were here and what got us to this point. I just kept it to Squirrel's death and left our suspicions of Ev's death out of it. I put it all out there. Now we would wait to see if we were going to get anything in return.

"I'm sorry to hear about your friend," the Chief finally said. "That does explain some things."

"Explain what?" I shot back.

"Earlier today we had a call for a vehicle fire under the Addison

Street Bridge. We checked it out and found it was a black SUV owned by Ralph. He rented it two weeks ago to a man named John Wolf. All his credentials were fabricated. The driver's license was a fake. He paid cash and the credit card he gave was also a fake."

Ralph Peterson jumped in. "My nephew Sammy works for me. He was here the day the black SUV was rented. I was in the garage. Sammy did all the paperwork. He rented the car for two weeks at our weekly rate. He insisted on paying cash. He gave us a credit card but said not to charge anything on it. We took the card being it is our policy. He filled out all the paperwork and paid us the $650.00 in cash for the two week rental. The two weeks was up yesterday and the car wasn't returned. We couldn't reach him by phone so I called Chief Rodgers yesterday."

"This morning the SUV was found burnt to a crisp. Nothing left. If there were any clues in there as to his real identity then they are gone," the Chief said.

"Can we talk to Sammy?" I asked.

"He didn't show up to work today," Ralph jumped in. "I tried calling him but didn't get an answer. He's a drinker and he's done this before. Sometimes he won't show up for two or three days. I really don't need him here every day so I don't mind. He's basically a good kid. Just has himself a little elbow bending problem. He's been pretty good about showing up the last year or so."

I was concerned that he chose this particular day to not show up.

"Can we go see him? I think it's important. I think the guy that rented your SUV was a professional contract killer. Sammy may be in danger if he can identify him."

Chief Rodgers looked at Ralph and said, "You tried calling him? Did you leave him a message?"

"No. I didn't leave a message. I figured he was sleeping one off. Figured he would be in tomorrow. I don't think we have anything to worry about. He's a capable boy. He can handle himself," Ralph said to the Chief.

"Ralph, we're gonna take a spin by his house. Make sure he's okay," the Chief said.

"Can we join you? I have some questions for him. We won't get in your way," I asked.

Chief Rodgers thought about it and told us we could come. We would have to stay out of the way and let him do his thing. He said once he was done with him, we could ask him any questions. I was sure Chief Rodgers was a capable investigator so I doubted we would have too many questions once he was done.

We got into our cars and followed Chief Rodgers and Officer Wright to Sammy's house. The driveway was full so we parked our two cars on the street. I didn't know what kind of car Sammy drove but it appeared he was home. He sounded like a pick-up truck person and there were two of them in the driveway. We met up with

Rodgers and Wright.

"You wait here. I'll see if he's home," the Chief said. This was his show. He made it clear. It was a small driveway and front lawn. We were only about fifteen feet from the front door. We weren't going to miss anything. The Chief knocked on the door and yelled out Sammy's name a few times. Nothing was stirring in the house despite a few lights being on. He tried again and it still did not yield any results. I walked up to the small front porch and cupped my eyes on both sides and pressed them up against the glass for good look at the interior. I didn't see anything out of place. I noticed the lights and some flickering from a room in the back. It could be another light or the television could be on.

The Chief looked at me and said, "I don't think he's home. If he's in there he's probably passed out."

"I got a bad feeling about this, Chief," I tried to reason with him. We needed to get into that house one way or another. I put my hand on the front door handle and saw it was locked. "We should check around back to see if there is a back door open."

Chief Rodgers took a few seconds to think about it. He looked at Officer Wright and told him to call down to McCaffrey's Pub. It was a shot and a beer joint that Sammy was known to frequent. Wright did as he was told and about a half a minute later he told Chief Rodgers that they hadn't seen Sammy in the last few days.

"Okay. We'll check around back," the Chief looked at me and

said. Bo, Brian, and Jessica were out front with Officer Wright. The four of them stayed there.

We went to the back door which led to the kitchen. I again looked into a window and didn't see Sammy. I saw there was a wallet and a cell phone on the kitchen table next to a set of keys. It was starting to look more and more like he was home. Right about now, sleeping off a bender is the best of all of the scenarios. I told Chief Rodgers what I saw. He also figured it was a good bet that Sammy was inside. He tugged on the rear door knob but it was also locked.

"We need to get in there," I said.

"Under the circumstances, I think that's a good idea," the Chief agreed.

He used some force and pushed open the back door. It took some effort but not too much. It wasn't a very secure door. He opened it up and called out to Sammy as we walked in. There was no sign of Sammy in the living room. We walked down a hall where it looked like a few bedrooms were located. We opened the first door. No Sammy. We moved on to the second bedroom door and opened it up. All clear. The last two doors in the hallway were a bathroom and another bedroom. We opened the bedroom door and found Sammy. He was lying in bed with what was left of his head still on his pillow. His hand was draped over the side of the bed with his .38 on the floor below his hand. The wall was a mural of blood and brain splatter. At first look, it could appear to be a suicide but I knew better.

"This is no suicide. He was killed by whoever rented that SUV. He was cleaning up a loose end," I told the Chief. He was still visibly stunned. I don't think they got too many murders in this town.

"MacMasters, we're going to need those videos you have. I'll call it in. You're right. This is no suicide."

Chapter 25

Chief Rodgers asked us to meet him back at his station while they processed the scene. I knew he would be tied up for at least two or three hours. We went out to a local diner to grab a bite to eat and kill some time. We grabbed a booth and started to peruse our menus. We could hear the local rumor mill churning away. *"I heard he shot his ex-wife then killed himself." "I heard his ex-wife shot him." "I heard he stabbed himself to death."* I was pretty sure that if we stayed long enough we would hear someone's theory about him getting abducted by aliens and shot when they returned him to earth.

I filled everyone in on what I saw. They were not allowed in the house once it was deemed a crime scene. I'm not sure they would have wanted to see what I saw anyway. It's the type of image that haunts your dreams. We talked low so we wouldn't add any fuel to the already out of control rumor mill.

"So where does this leave us?" Jessica asked while looking my way.

"I think this confirms we are dealing with a pro. He likely figured out the rental car was compromised and he cleaned up a loose end," I told her.

"How would he know the car was compromised?" Bo asked.

"Not sure. Maybe he didn't know and was just being careful." I paused and then continued. "But that's not likely. He could have ditched the car anywhere. He had to be worried that Sammy could identify him somehow. So I am pretty sure he felt someone would be coming to talk to him."

"We were able to ID the vehicle from Flanagan's surveillance. Is it possible he saw us leaving Flanagan's with the videos?" Jessica asked.

"It may be more than probable. How else would he have known?" I responded.

"We need to be careful," Brian said. "If he saw us leave Flanagan's with those videos then we may be his next target."

"I agree, Brian. If he saw us at Flanagan's, it was probably because he had been following us," Jessica said.

"If this guy is a pro, why not deal with us in New Jersey? Why bring the car back to Pennsylvania and kill the rental agent?" Brian added.

"I can't answer that. But I think you may be right. At this point, we have to assume he knows we are looking into Squirrel's murder."

I tried not to scare anyone but it just might be the reality of the situation.

"What's next?" Jessica asked.

"After we get done with Rodgers, we should grab some hotel rooms. I think we need to go see Ev's wife tomorrow. We need to look into his death. Maybe we can find the link to their deaths." Just as I got the words out, our food arrived at the table. None of us really had much of an appetite. We picked at our food for a while then paid our bill and went to the Palmyra Police Station.

We drove to the station and brought our surveillance videos in with us. Chief Rodgers showed up about twenty minutes later. We joined him in his office. I gave him the videos so they could make their own copies. He knew we were not done with our set. Copies were sufficient for his investigation. I asked him if anything of any interest was found at the scene. He gave me the basic details. One shot to the left temple with Sammy's own Charter Arms .38 Special. There were no signs of a struggle. They found a few unlocked windows but couldn't confirm if there was someone else in there.

"What about the time of death?" I asked.

"The medical examiner places it around mid-morning. Somewhere around ten to ten-thirty" he said.

"Was Sammy right or left handed?"

Statistically almost all self-inflicted wounds are done with the person's dominant hand. Sammy's wound was to his left temple which means it wouldn't be likely that he pulled the trigger unless he was left handed.

"He was right handed. We already confirmed that. It's very unlikely he pulled that trigger." Chief Rodgers was not Rizzo. He knew how to run a thorough investigation.

"What about the GSR?" I asked the Chief but quickly realized Brian, Bo and Jessica might not know what it was. I looked to them. "Gunshot residue."

"We used the carbon-coated adhesive for the test and it was positive for GSR on Sammy's hand," the Chief confirmed. They could have done the test with an alcohol swab but the carbon-coated adhesive typically yields more accurate results. It was good to see they were being thorough. "He may have been drugged before being shot. It would make it easy for the shooter to position the gun in Sammy's hand and assist with the trigger pull. I ordered a full tox screen."

"What about the canvass?" I asked.

"The houses are pretty spread apart. No one saw or heard anything. One person was walking his dog and saw an older model tan pick-up parked near Sammy's house. He didn't think much of it but said he hadn't seen it in the neighborhood before that."

"Did you have any auto thefts reported in your town last night or today?" I asked. If our "pro" dumped the SUV he would have needed another mode of transportation.

"I was thinking the same way as you. I asked the desk sergeant and we had no such reports. I had Officer Wright call the surrounding towns and see if they had any thefts. We checked Gravel Hill, Palmdale, Coffeetown and even Hershey. There was one theft in Palmdale yesterday afternoon but it turned out to be a joy ride for some kids and the car was recovered last night."

I didn't ask about fingerprints. There was no chance our guy could have been that sloppy. I'm sure Chief Rodgers had his forensic team go through Sammy's place with a fine tooth comb.

It didn't seem that Chief Rodgers had much more to offer at this time. The station's computer technician walked in and handed me our surveillance videos. We all gave the Chief our cell phone numbers and he in turn gave us his. I told him where we were staying but likely would be moving on in the morning.

"Thank you for the info. If we come up with anything, we will surely keep you posted," I said as I turned to the Chief and extended my hand once again. This time he reached out and shook my hand back. We walked out the front door and headed to our cars. We were standing outside our cars trying to figure out where we wanted to stay. We decided that maybe it was best to drive to Harrisburg tonight and set up camp there. Our plan was to go to see Ev's wife in the morning and she lived just outside of Harrisburg.

As we were about to leave, Officer Wright came out the front door with some sense of urgency. He was heading over to our cars and was giving the "wait" sign. I got back out of my car to see what this was all about.

He said they just got a call from Gravel Hill Police Department. One of their residents just reported that he discovered his vehicle missing when he got home from work today.

Officer Wright continued, "He said his 2001 tan colored Chevy Pick-Up was stolen. He said there was some shattered glass in the place where the truck was parked."

"How far from Addison Bridge does this guy live?" I asked.

"Gravel Hill is just on the other side of the bridge. He lives three blocks from the bridge. The Chief put out an APB on the truck."

"Much appreciated, Officer Wright. You have a good night now," I said. He responded in kind. He had an air of optimism about him. I didn't share that same optimism. I was quite sure this case would not be wrapped up with Officer Wright pulling over that tan pick-up truck and making an arrest of the driver. Our guy was too smart to keep a stolen vehicle for any amount of time. I wouldn't be surprised if the pick-up was already dumped.

Today had been a trying day. Our best lead had turned into a literal dead end. The body count had increased to three. The lines were getting a little blurred. Were we the hunters or the hunted? I knew one thing was for sure. From here on out, we would be looking over our shoulders every step of the way.

Chapter 26

We found a Hilton Garden hotel in the heart of Harrisburg. It was only about a half hour ride. The day in Palmyra was difficult for all of us. It was a good thing that Brian, Bo, or Jessica didn't see what I saw. I know Bo doesn't spook easily but he was shaken up for a little while after learning of the details of Sammy's death. The reality of the situation was not lost on him. A man was just killed several hours ago by the person we were trying to track down. I had seen my share of violence and death but had never taken another person's life. I know Brian, Bo, and Jessica had certainly never taken a life either. The only person in the equation who had done that was the one we were hoping to track down. We needed to be careful of what we hope for. We just might get it.

We checked into our rooms and decided to meet at a bar across the street to unwind with a few drinks. I called Katie when I got into my room. I gave her the details of what we went through in Palmyra.

I tried to soften it up as much as I could but it's not easy to soften up a gunshot to the head. It didn't work. Her concern for us was coming through loud and clear. I assured her that we were being careful and that we were on the right track. Us being on the right track was what scared her the most. I told her that I loved her and would check in again tomorrow.

We grabbed a table at the bar and ordered a pitcher of beer and three glasses. Jessica ordered a glass of Chablis. We chatted a bit about the day's events. It was also time to see if everyone was still committed to our journey.

"I wouldn't blame any of you of if you wanted to stop tracking this guy and let the authorities handle it," I said.

Jessica was the first to speak. "Mac, I know you're not going to stop and neither am I. We're getting close. You said it before, Mac. He's getting sloppy and starting to make mistakes."

"He may be starting to make some mistakes. But don't forget, he's a stone cold killer. This guy is after something and he doesn't care how he gets it or who he hurts to get it," I responded.

"I'm not going anywhere, Mac. I'm gonna see this thing through," Brian said.

"You know I'm not going back home. I'm pissed. I want to get this prick. He killed two of our friends," Bo added. Bo was never the type to back off from anything or anyone. When Bo is pissed off, I'm glad he is on my side.

"Okay. We press on," I said to all. "We need to have each other's backs and fronts. We don't know if this guy is after us or not. From now on, no one goes anywhere by themselves." Everyone nodded in agreement.

I had brought my gun and Bo brought his as well. Bo's gun was registered and he knew how to use it. He had joined me many times at the shooting range. I'm still a little better shot than he is but he is not too far behind me. Bo's gun was in a case in the back of my Explorer. I told him it might be a good idea to start carrying it on his person. He said he would pick it up when we went back and bring it to the room with him.

"Tell me about Tyler," Jessica said.

"He was a good friend of ours in college just as Jimmy was," Brian said. "He went to law school after King's and became a lawyer in the Wilkes-Barre area. He somehow got connected with Andrew Hainesworth. I think Hainesworth was a district attorney in Pennsylvania and decided to get into politics. Tyler had been part of Hainesworth's team since he was governor. He was the number three guy in the governor's office behind Hainesworth and his Chief of Staff. "

"How does he tie into Jimmy's death?" she asked.

"I wish I knew. That's what we can't figure out," Brian said.

"They're definitely related. We will find this guy and then find out the connection," I jumped in. "Tyler and Squirrel, I mean Jimmy, really didn't see much of each other in the last thirty years but kept in touch. Tyler came to some of annual college reunions but hadn't been to one in a few years. They were both on Facebook but if Jimmy knew of something going on with Tyler, he would have told us."

"I probably kept in touch with Tyler more that most of the guys. I went to his funeral," Brian said. "He never gave me any indication anything was going on. And he never said anything about Squirrel. If the two of them were involved in something, one of them would have said something to one of us."

"What do we hope to accomplish tomorrow?" Jessica asked.

"We will go see Tyler's wife and see what she can tell us. Maybe she knows something. Brian, you take the lead on this one. You know her better than we do."

"Should we be telling her what we know?" Brian asked. "It may not be the best idea to barge in there and start telling her that her husband was murdered."

"We have to tell her something being we are going to be prying into details of his death and his recent actions before it. We can tell her we have suspicions about Squirrel's death and that led us up to this area. We'll tell her we don't know anything about Tyler's death but want to find out more about it to see if there is a connection in any way," I said.

My phone rang and I saw a Pennsylvania number lit up. I answered my phone and heard the voice of Chief Rodgers. "Mac, we just got a call. The tan pickup was recovered."

"Don't keep me in suspense. What did you find?" I said.

"Nothing yet. We're getting it towed in. We'll dust it but I don't expect it will yield any results," he said.

"Where was it found?"

"About twenty miles from here in Steelton. It's about five miles outside of Harrisburg," the Chief said.

"We're in Harrisburg now. Thanks, Chief," I said and then filled my crew in. We finished our drinks and headed back to the hotel. We walked back to the hotel and grabbed Bo's gun from my car while on the way. We all now knew this maniac could be in Harrisburg somewhere. We also knew he could be stalking us as we spoke. What we didn't know was there was someone in a black sedan with tinted windows parked in the hotel lot that was watching our every move.

Chapter 27

None of us slept very well. We had two sets of adjoining rooms that were all in a row. In the morning we had a game plan meeting in my room. Jessica was adjoining my room and entered my room through the interior door. Brian and Bo came together from next door. We decided to take no chances. We would no longer travel in two cars. Jessica agreed to leave her car in the hotel lot and she would pick it up after this was all over. I didn't want any of us exposed by being alone even if it was just for only a few seconds. Brian had called Tyler's wife and asked if we could stop by for a visit. She was glad to hear from him and was more than willing to accommodate us. She said she would expect us around nine o'clock.

Jenny Evigan had been married to Tyler for twenty years. She had been with him for another five years before that. They had a lovely old Victorian home in Camp Hill, which was a smallish suburb about three miles outside of Harrisburg. They lived modestly but comfortably. As we pulled up into the driveway we saw Jenny sitting in a wooden chair on their front porch which ran the length of the front of the home. She walked off the porch to greet us as we poured out of my Explorer. Brian moved ahead and gave Jenny a warm hug.

"Jenny, this is Jessica," Brian said. He knew he didn't need to introduce Bo and me. We may not have seen her since their wedding, but she surely knew who we were. She also knew we were happily married men. I think she was trying to figure out where Jessica fit into this visit. Jenny extended her hand to Jessica and she returned the gesture.

"Nice to meet you, Jessica" Jenny said. She then moved a step towards me. "Great to see you, Mac," she said as she moved in for a hug. Bo got his hug and hello as well. "Come on inside. I just made a pot of coffee." We went into her spacious living room and sat down. Alongside the fresh pot of coffee on the table was a tray of donuts and bagels.

"Jenny, this is so nice of you. I wish you hadn't gone through all that trouble," I said.

"No trouble at all. It's my pleasure. It's so nice to see everyone again," Jenny responded. Her kind welcome to us started to make me feel a little guilty for not attending his funeral. It was three hours away and I hadn't had much contact with Ev in the past twenty years. In hindsight, maybe I should have made the effort. We were close friends at one point in our lives. Maybe I should have gone by the rule that if I was close enough to go to his wedding, I should be close enough to go to his funeral.

"I'm sorry about Tyler's passing. Sorry I didn't make the services," I said to Jenny. I was raised Irish Catholic. My entire upbringing was based on guilt.

"Think nothing of it. The flower arrangement you guys sent was lovely. It was really appreciated." She did a nice job of easing my guilt. "Tyler loved you guys. I know he lost touch with many of you but it never changed the way he felt." *So much for easing my guilt.* I knew she was not trying to make me feel bad. "He really enjoyed your Men's Club reunion as he called it. He worked so hard that he couldn't make too many of them."

"We loved reconnecting with him when he could make it," Brian said.

"His job was so demanding on his time," she said and then paused. "So what brings you up this way?"

Brian decided to get right into it. "I'm sure you heard Jimmy Collucci passed away a few weeks after Tyler. Jimmy's death was ruled a suicide but we have reason to believe Jimmy was murdered."

Jenny was a bit stunned by what she just heard. That's not what she was expecting to hear. "Oh my Lord. What does that have to do with Tyler?" she shot back.

"Maybe nothing," Brian said.

"Maybe?" She wanted to know where this was going. Brian gave her the run down on Jimmy's death and explained that whoever killed him had tried to make it look like an accident. He then explained about the rental car coming from Palmyra. It got us thinking it might be worth looking into to see if there was any connection between the two deaths. "I don't see how there could be a connection. I don't think Tyler and Jimmy talked in several years. At least he never said so to me."

"Do you mind if we ask you a few questions about what Tyler was up to in the weeks before his death?" Brian asked.

"Not at all, Brian, but I don't think I really will be able to help you. He was a good man. He wasn't into anything that could possibly get him killed." She seemed to cringe a little as the word "killed" passed her lips.

She gave us a thumbnail sketch of what he did on a daily basis at the governor's office. He was the right hand man for Governor Hainesworth's Chief of Staff, Donald Keohane. Tyler had been concentrating most of his recent efforts on the election campaign. He had been stumping for Hainesworth at various events.

I took the Facebook picture out of my pocket. "This was on Jimmy's computer. Do you recognize the people in this picture?" She looked at the picture and recognized it instantly.

"I was at that event with Tyler. They were opening a hospital and Andrew wanted to make sure he and his full staff were all visible.

Andrew's opponent was there and he wanted to make sure he had a better showing than Guilford. It's all silly political games."

"Is there anything unusual about that picture?" I asked.

"No. There's Don, Andrew and a few staffers. Guilford is there with his people. I don't know them. I wish I could tell you more but there's nothing unusual about the picture," she said.

"Can you think of anything that happened out of the ordinary leading up to Tyler's death?" I asked.

"Nothing I can think of."

"What about the night of his death. Was it unusual for him to go to the lake cabin by himself?" I was hoping that wasn't going to be received as an insinuation of any extra-marital affair. That was not my intention.

"No. He went there on weekends when he could make it. I went with him many times but he went alone plenty of times. He would go to unwind after a stressful week. I suppose you're going to ask me about his drinking." She offered and we would like to know. "As you may know, Tyler had his demons with alcohol in the past. He had cut down many times and stopped altogether about three years ago. I think he went about two good years without a drop. I began to suspect he was sneaking some drinks from time to time. I didn't see any instance where he was visibly drunk. I can't say I was surprised when they told me he had alcohol in his system. I'm sure you know he was a cigarette smoker. He was a social smoker most of the time we were married but smoked a lot more when he quit drinking and started going to AA meetings."

She was not giving us anything that would lead us to believe his death was anything but accidental. I still was quite sure there was a connection. If I couldn't get anything from Jenny, then we would have to head to the Governor's office to see what we could dig up there.

We made small talk for a little while longer. We talked about Jessica's relationship with Jimmy and why she was driven to seek some justice for him. Jenny liked what she heard from Jessica and I could tell now that she had a healthy respect for her. We were getting ready to say our good-byes when Jenny asked, "How is Eddie's son doing?" Eddie Vincent's son had some significant health problems that required extended hospital stays and various experimental treatments. I felt it was odd that she asked us that question out of the blue like that.

"I don't know much more than anyone else does. I know he has been in an out of hospitals for much of the last few years," I said.

"I heard he was going to undergo another surgery last month and was trying new medications. Eddie had called Tyler in February and gave him an update," she said.

"When did they speak?" Brian asked.

"It was about a week before Tyler passed."

"Did you hear the conversation?" Brian pressed.

"No. I heard them talking but I was in the other room. It sounded like it was a serious conversation. I asked him about it and he kind of dismissed me. He just said they were talking about Eddie's son. I don't think he was telling me everything but I didn't press him. Some of the conversation that I overheard was about something from back in their college days. I had no idea what they were talking about."

I thought it best that we stop in and see Donald Keohane and Governor Hainesworth. We needed to find that connection.

It was now the late morning. Maybe we could catch up with the Governor in his office. I mentioned this to the crew in front of Jenny and she offered to call over there and try to kick a door open for us. She dialed up the Governor's office and was put on hold for a minute. We then heard her thanking whoever she was talking to. She let us know the Governor would be happy to give us a few minutes.

We said our good-byes and went on our way. We weren't sure if anything would come out of this meeting with Governor Hainesworth but it seemed all things were pointing us to Harrisburg. We might as well go right to the top.

After we got in the car, I dialed up Eddie and it went direct to voicemail. "Eddie. This is Mac. Give me a call when you get a chance. Thanks."

Chapter 28

1983

Today was the last day of finals before we all went our separate ways for the Christmas break. Bo and I were done with our finals and were back at the house packing. We had almost four weeks off for break. We were soon to become second semester seniors. We had partied pretty hard for the entire semester. Fortunately, our grades didn't suffer as a result. We made some new friends through our street hockey games and made a few enemies, too, along the way. Eddie was kind enough to offer us a ride back to New Jersey.

We were sitting in the living room waiting for Brian to return from his last final. We needed to get his rent money from him for January. Most people were able to pay Bucky when they returned from break. I don't think Bucky was in any mood to afford us that same courtesy. Bucky always insisted we pay in cash. He knocked twenty-five bucks off the rent for a cash payment. It wasn't a problem for us. As broke college kids, twenty-five bucks could go a long way. I'm sure Bucky had some angle for wanting cash payments.

He probably had some tax scam going. Brian walked in the front door. "Hey guys. I talked to Allegra today."

"What did she say?" I asked.

"She told me she was sorry she didn't tell me who she was. She said she really likes me and wanted to get to know me before I knew who she was. She kind of knows what her father does but I don't think she knows the full picture. It's not like I'm going to tell her that her father is the most powerful man in the state and has probably killed many people or had ordered people to be killed."

"What are you going to do? I know you like her," Bo offered.

"I do like her but I'm not going to do anything. I'd be scared to death to date her," Brian responded.

"It's probably a smart idea to stay away. They are some dangerous people. I personally don't care to cross paths with them again," I said to Brian.

"It's a shame. She is everything I would want in a girl. She's smart, funny, good looking, happy all the time, and has a great outlook on life. I don't think I am in any of her classes next semester so I don't think I will be running into her too often." Brian paused for a few seconds and then continued. "She told me she had a great time at our party. She thought it was so nice of me to save her that parking spot. It was such a little thing but it seemed to mean a lot to her. She told me it made her feel special. It will hurt for a bit but I'll get past it."

"I know you will. If there's anything we can do, just ask," Bo said as he threw his hand up on Brian's shoulder.

"I know. Thanks," he responded. Time to change the subject. "When are you guys heading out?"

"Eddie is picking us up and we are stopping by the paint store to drop off January's rent to Bucky. So we need your share," I said. Nothing like kicking a guy while he is down. The possible love of his life is no more and now time to buck up some money. Brian went upstairs and grabbed his money. In the meantime, White Thunder pulled up and we loaded the car. We said our goodbyes to Brian. We wouldn't see him until we all got back. Of course, I would probably be seeing Bo almost every day during break. He gave us his rent money and off we went to see our favorite person.

Eddie parked in the side parking lot of Bucky's paint store. The three of us went in. Eddie was also paying Bucky for their rent as well. We walked in and saw Bucky behind the counter barking some orders at Daryl and Lance. Daryl was the bigger of the two men. He began to move towards us as we walked through the door and into the store. Bucky extended his hand out across Daryl's chest and said "Stay here."

Bo was never one to miss an opportunity to take a shot at Bucky. "That's a neat trick Bucky. Can you make him roll over, too?"

Daryl wanted to push through Bucky but decided he would let it go for now. He looked over at us and mouthed the words "dead meat". Bucky decided to break up this party and told us to come back in the office with him. The three of us went back in the office to take care of our business. Bucky sat behind his big wooden desk that had stacks of papers covering every inch. It was amazing that this guy was considered a smart businessman after seeing his base of operation. I don't know how he could find anything if called upon to do so. "What do you guys want?" he asked without an ounce of patience in his words.

"We're here to pay our rent for January. We won't be back until mid-January. Wanted to make sure you had your rent on time," I told him.

"I was hoping you punks would try to pay me when you got back. I would love to throw your asses the hell outta there," he said.

"No such luck, Bucky. You're stuck with us," Bo told him. We gave him the rent payment less the twenty-five dollar cash discount.

"OK. You're paid. Now get the hell outta my store."

"Where's our receipts?" Bo asked.

"What's the matter Bollander, don't ya trust me?" Bucky said through a crooked grin.

"Not even for a second. Give us our receipts so we can get out of this dump," Bo shot back. Bucky looked up at him and gave him a few second stare. He obviously couldn't come up with more to say so he put his head down and wrote out the receipts. He handed one to me and one to Eddie. He wouldn't give Bo the satisfaction of taking the receipt from him.

Bucky had one parting shot for us. "Do me a favor. Don't come back early from your break."

"Good one, Bucky. We'll see you in a month," Bo said. Bucky stayed in his office and we closed the door on our way out.

As we were walking out we saw Mickey walking through the front door. He gave a quick head nod but didn't say anything. I don't think he wanted anyone to know he knew us. We gave a little covert nod to him as well.

Daryl and Lance were still behind the counter pretending they were working. No one else was in the store so they had no one to wait on. As we were walking past them Bo looked over and said as he pointed at them "Daryl and Lance? Right?" He knew exactly who they were and what their names were. They looked a little puzzled but nodded their assent. "I thought so. I just didn't recognize you guys without your lipstick on."

Bo started laughing and we walked out the door. We were all laughing and they for sure could hear it. It would only be a matter of seconds before they were right behind us. We could see Daryl's head almost explode after Bo's crack.

We were walking toward White Thunder when the two busted out through the front door and came running at us. We stopped and waited for them. They arrived and were a little out of breath. If they were tired just leaving the store, they wouldn't be lasting too long in a fight. Bo turned and started walking right at them. "You boys need something from me?"

"You mother-fuckers are dead. Nobody embarrasses me like that and gets away with it," Daryl shouted out at Bo. Bo kept walking at them. Eddie and I started to follow. "You must have drugged us or something. I couldn't get out of bed for two days. You think it's funny, taking pictures of us like that. You're gonna pay for that."

"You guys should be apologizing to us. You crashed our party and drank yourselves 'til you puked. Nobody drugged anybody. Anything that happened, you assholes did to yourselves. Now turn around and go back inside where it's safe. If you stay here, you're gonna get hurt," Bo responded.

"You aint hurtin nobody. I'm gonna kick your ass all over this parking lot. Then we're gonna kick their asses." Daryl looked toward Eddie and I and then he looked toward Lance to make sure he still had his support. Lance gave him the nod he was looking for. Daryl moved in toward Bo. I was expecting this to be a two hit fight. Bo knew better than to throw the first punch. As this was starting to go down, we saw some townspeople gathering and looking over at us. They weren't there to break anything up or call the police. They were there for the show.

Bo waited in place for Daryl to make the first move. Daryl was a little taller than Bo and maybe a few pounds heavier. He was definitely a few years older than him. I kept my eye on Lance to make sure he didn't intervene. If he pulled anything, I would be all over him. I'm not sure what was going through Eddie's mind. I didn't know if he had ever been in a fight or not. He could either be scared to death or ready to rumble. We just might find out soon enough.

Daryl took off his hat and work shirt. He stood there in his wife-beater tee shirt revealing his muscular arms and chest. Daryl cocked his fist and threw a wild punch toward Bo's face. Bo easily ducked the punch and threw a vicious right hand punch into Daryl's face. The crack of Daryl's nose was heard throughout the parking lot. Daryl hit the ground and had both hands over his nose trying to stem the tide of the blood. Lance looked over at Daryl then over at Bo. He wanted no part of what Daryl was currently going through. He went over to help Daryl up and get him inside.

I was right. It was a two hit fight. Bo hit Daryl and Daryl hit the ground. Some of the townspeople came over and gave us their names and phone numbers if we needed them as witnesses. They offered to confirm that Daryl was the aggressor and threw the first punch and Bo was merely defending himself. I didn't think Daryl or Lance would be calling the police but it was good to know we had witnesses if it came to it.

"Come on, guys. White Thunder is waiting for us. You know, Bo, I had your back if you needed me. The other guy was all mine," Eddie said. He may have been right but I guess we'll never know for sure. For now I'll give Eddie the benefit of the doubt. I'm sure Bo will sleep better knowing Eddie had his back.

"I don't think they will be bothering us again," Bo said. I wasn't so sure that would be a true statement.

Chapter 29

We returned from our break and now were officially second semester seniors. Nothing ever came of Bo's little altercation with Daryl in Bucky's parking lot. I'll chalk that up to Daryl being embarrassed that a local college kid dropped him with one punch and wouldn't want to be reliving the story on any witness stand. Bo wasn't too worried. He was prepared to defend himself against any charges that may have been brought against him. He had Eddie and I and a few unbiased townspeople to attest that Daryl threw the first punch and Bo was merely defending himself.

We decided to have a party to kick off our return and officially ring in 1984. Even though it was mid-January, it wasn't too late for a New Years Eve party. This had nothing to do with agitating Bucky or poking at the hornet's nest. This is what we did and we weren't changing just because our landlord was fed up with us.

The party was packed with New Year's revelers. We had five kegs of beer and two cases of champagne. We had to upcharge at the door to cover the champagne. We kicked it up to three dollars to get in instead of the standard two bucks. The party was in all three of our houses and went all through the night. There were no visits from Daryl and Lance this time. Mickey was there as expected but I'm sure he wasn't reporting anything back to Bucky.

The party was a success and there were no visits from the police and no after-party morning visit from Bucky. Maybe we finally wore him down. At this point, I'm sure Bucky resigned himself to the fact that we would be there until May and there was nothing he could do about it. No need to get an ulcer over something that you can't control. I think he finally raised the white flag.

We had bigger and better things to worry about than Bucky. We, of course, had to make sure we got all of our credits so when our parents showed up for graduation, we would actually be graduating. Even though we all were somewhat afflicted with *senioritis* we still had to get our grades. The balance was a little tilted toward partying and fun over academics but I was sure we would all find our way to the graduation stage.

The semester was rolling right along. Now it was time to get down to business. There is a longstanding tradition at our college for a year end blowout known as The Enduro. The first Enduro was organized in 1965 and had about one hundred attendees. Last year's Enduro had over seven hundred people attend and even more would be expected this year. The event is always run by three seniors and whatever additional staff that they assemble. Last year's Enduro was run by three of our street hockey buddies. They did a great job coordinating it and it was a complete success. We joined their staff so we got a good look at what was involved in getting an event like this together. There was a lot of planning and effort on their part so seven hundred people could eat, drink, listen to music and have a good time.

One other tradition surrounding the event was the Enduro Bible. It was a book that had captured all of the event data of every previous Enduro. The Bible was a binder and had sections added for each year's event. The data included the names of the event organizers and staff, the budget, the itemized costs, the number of attendees, the drinking contest winners, a picture of the three organizers, a picture of the entire staff, and general event pictures to memorialize the party.

A person gets designated to update the Enduro Bible during the event with the data and pictures. After the party concluded, it was customary to have the ceremonial passing of the Bible to next year's organizers. After Enduro 1983, it was quickly learned that Enduro 1984 would be run by Brian Kavanaugh, Tim Bollander, and Jack MacMasters. I have had possession of the Bible since last May and we have already begun our efforts to keep this long standing non-school sanctioned tradition alive.

Today we were searching for a place to host our Enduro. Eddie was kind enough to lend us White Thunder for the trip. We think we found a location about fifteen minutes away from our campus. Milton's Grove was perfect for us. It was a privately owned farm that had a small lake, one large pavilion, several smaller pavilions, and picnic tables aplenty. There were a few barn type buildings which I assumed were used for storage of farming and grounds upkeep equipment. It was set back about a mile from the main road and had woods on three sides of its spacious grounds. It was ideal for us and was set up to accommodate all of our needs. The small lake was equipped with some small row boats and paddleboats. It was also suitable for swimming if anyone so desired. One of the smaller pavilions could be used to provide cover for the band we hired if we got unlucky and had to deal with rain. The larger pavilion had large barbecue grills on its outskirts. We would use the large pavilion for all of our food and soft drink set up and would be big enough to seat hundreds of people at a time. The place also had plenty of grass acreage for anyone wanting to get a game of football, whiffle ball, or tossing around a Frisbee.

After our brief tour of the grounds, we were sure about this place. We needed to make this happen. We met with the management company that handled the rentals for Milton's Grove and signed a one day lease for the low price of $400.00 for Saturday May 5th.

Today was an unseasonably warm mid-March day. The temperatures got close to seventy degrees. We had known that a bunch of people from campus were heading to the swimming hole at the old and abandoned quarry. This was only about five miles from

Milton's Grove and was on our way home. We had been there many times in the past. We would pack a cooler with some cold beers and hang around on the rocks surrounding the small swimming hole. Being it was such a nice day and we were pretty much passing by it anyway, we decided to kill a few hours over there.

As we drove up the dirt road leading to the quarry, we saw a few other cars parked. One of which was a yellow Volkswagen Beetle. Brian had run into Allegra a few times this semester but none of which were in a social setting such as this.

"There's Allegra's Car," Brian had pointed out but Bo and I had already noticed the car.

"Should we turn around?" I gave Brian an out in case he wasn't up for chatting it up with her. I know he still had strong feelings for her but was resisting all of his urges and keeping his distance. Brian is a level-headed guy. He knows you can't get involved with a girl and not to some degree get involved with her family. Brian wanted every part of her but wanted no part of her family. It was not just because he was afraid they would hurt him if he ever had a misstep in the relationship, he just didn't like them and what they represented. Many people glorify the whole mafia lifestyle and persona. Brian was not one of them. He saw them for exactly what they were and he wanted nothing to do with that.

"No. Not at all. Don't do that," he shot back. "I'm fine. We aren't going to waste this good weather day because I don't want to talk to a girl."

We parked the car and walked the quarter mile or so to the swimming hole. It was jam-packed with people lying out on the rocks, hanging in lawn chairs, and some even in the water. We just knew of it as "the hole". The place was perfect for people to hang out and drink alcohol without any threat of law enforcement crashing the party. The swimming hole was surrounded by woods on pretty much every side. It was a popular spot for kids to hook up and spend some alone time in the woods. Most of the people there were from our school and I either knew most of them or at least recognized most of them. I'm sure most of them were frequent guests at our parties.

Allegra was on the other side of the swimming hole. It wasn't a big area so it wasn't hard to recognize people on the other side. Brian couldn't help himself and was giving frequent glances to the other side. Allegra had on a bright yellow sun dress and threw her hair back in a ponytail. She was talking with some friends and was always animated when chatting it up with people. It was one of the subtle things he really liked about her. She had an infectious smile to go along with all her other qualities. One of Brian's glances was met with one of Allegra's glances. He thought about looking away when their eyes met but decided to hold the eye contact and wave instead. Allegra managed a big smile and gave a return wave. She then gave him the "come on over" wave. Within seconds the three of us were on our way to the other side.

"Hi, guys !" Allegra said through her perfect smile. Her arms shot up in the air and we all got our hugs.

"Hi, Allegra. I haven't seen you in a while. We'll have to get you over for our next party," I said.

"We'll see. My father is trying to keep tight reins on me. It's probably best if I lay low for a while." We could see her disappointment coming through as the words were pouring out. I think she was more concerned about us getting another visit from her brother rather than her incurring the wrath of her father.

Brian decided to get involved but moved the conversation in a different direction. "We were just at Miller's Grove. We signed a one day lease to use their grounds for The Enduro this year."

"I heard about that. You guys are running that this year? I've never been to one but heard it is a blast. My girlfriend went last year. When is it? I don't care when it is, I'm in." She was rambling a mile a minute.

"Awesome. We'll make sure you get a ticket," Brian answered with crooked smile but now wanted to get to the reason we walked over to see her. "Hey, Allegra, can we talk a minute?"

He didn't wait for her answer. He just started walking toward an area near the edge of the woods where no one was hanging around. She followed. As they walked toward the woods to find a nice quiet place to talk, she extended her left hand and grabbed his right hand.

Brian didn't resist. He was happy to be walking hand in hand with Allegra. Something felt very right about it. He also knew it was going to be a short-lived feeling. They both knew that they were going to the woods to talk and nothing more. They found a large boulder and plopped down. They sat side by side but facing each other. Allegra didn't let go of his hand. That was just fine with Brian. Many people escaped to the woods to get busy with each other. They both knew this trip to the woods was not to get busy with each other. The hand holding was just to get though what they both knew was going to be a tough conversation. The both liked each other but that is where it was going to end.

"Brian, I've really missed you."

"I've missed you, too. More than you will ever know."

He paused and tried to collect his thoughts. He hoped the day would come when they got together to talk things out. He had rehearsed what he was going to say but now that he was actually in the conversation, nothing he had rehearsed was at the forefront of his brain. Brian was an old soul and a romantic at heart. Love at first sight was not a concept lost on him. He was just going to wing it.

Allegra started to say something when Brian stopped her. "Allegra, I can't. I just can't."

"Can't what?" she asked but deep down knew exactly what he was saying.

"When I first saw you, I thought I laid eyes on the prettiest girl I had ever seen. When I first spoke to you, I felt like I talked to the most interesting and exciting girl I had ever come in contact with. When you agreed to meet me at our party, I felt like I just hit the jackpot in the lottery. Every second I spent with you accounts for all of the best seconds I spent with anyone in my life." Brian put it all out there. He knew where the conversation was going but felt he needed to let her know how he actually felt and why he couldn't pursue the relationship any further.

"Brian, don't sell yourself short. I felt the same way. I had been working up the nerve to talk to you for weeks. When we finally talked and hit it off, I was thrilled." Allegra was hopeful but already knew there was no future for them as a couple. "Is there any chance we can give it a go?"

Brian paused to digest the moment and squeezed her hand. "I really wish there was. I can't do it."

She removed her hand from his and put both arms around his shoulders and dropped her right cheek onto the top of his chest. She knew why. It didn't need to be said. She knew Brian was a man of integrity and getting into bed with her family was not something he would do on any level.

"I'm so sorry, Brian, but I understand. As they say, you can pick your friends but you can't pick your family. I love my family and I don't make apologies for having them in my life." She broke off the hug and gave him a kiss on the cheek. "Bye, Brian" and she turned and slowly walked out of the woods. Brian sat on the boulder for a few more minutes. He tried to find any justification to change his own mind but he was resolute in his convictions and found no such justification. After all, Allegra's family were people that used others, took advantage of others, and likely hurt or killed others. In short, they were bad people and would continue to be bad people. There was no place for that in Brian's future.

The ride back to our apartment was a quiet one. Brian knew his decision was the right one. The problem was that he didn't know that being right would hurt so much.

Chapter 30

The sun was shining bright. Enduro day had finally arrived. We had been planning this for months. We had over six hundred tickets sold already. We expected to see another hundred or so to walk-ups. Most of the walk-ups would be commuters that we didn't see regularly. This event was well known and commuters and on-campus students flocked in to be a part of it. Brian, Bo, and I drove to Miller's Grove early to set up. We had about twenty staff members to assist us with whatever we asked of them. About half of that group came over with us to get the set-up going. They were a huge help and gave us a lot of their time. All they got out of it was a free entry and a staff T-shirt. Most of them would have done it just for staff T-shirt. The free entry was just a bonus.

In the past few months, we'd had numerous meetings with just the three of us who were running the event and a few other meetings for the entire staff. The food committee was given a budget. They planned and purchased all of the food. I wish I could say we had beef tenderloin and shrimp kebobs but we provided burgers, dogs and chips. The food committee was in charge of everything food. They purchased the food, set up the grills, cooked and cleaned up the food pavilion. Eddie was nice enough to lead the food committee. Eddie was going to be wearing a few hats today. He would also be in charge of taking pictures. We armed him with a polaroid camera and three packs of film. Hopefully there would be a few good ones that would make their way into the Enduro bible.

Brian, Bo, and I scouted the local bars for our entertainment. We found a three piece band at a local hotel bar and signed them right up. They played mostly 60s and 70s rock n roll. They wanted $500 for the day but we bargained them down to $450. Everyone was happy with that. It was a few dollars over our budget but they would each get a buck fifty for the day. They called themselves "We Three Kings". I didn't quite get it being there was nothing religious about them. None of them, much less even one of them, was named King. And they were two guys and a girl. *Maybe they should be Two Kings and a Queen.* We later found out that they started out as a trio of three guys. One dropped out and was replaced by a female. I suppose they were happy with their name and decided to keep rocking on as We Three Kings. We didn't care. They were perfect for us. They would give us four hours of the Beatles, The Stones, The Who, Hendrix, The Doors, and the female lead could belt out Janis Joplin like no other.

Tommy D and Squirrel were in charge of the buses. We arranged to have six buses transport our guests to and from the event. We had them from noon to one o'clock and again from six to eight o'clock. They would continuously go back and forth from the school to the grove for as long as we had them. Being this was not a sanctioned school event, we had to find a place just off campus to do the pick-ups and drop-offs. This was probably the best use of the money we collected. Not only for the safety factor but it is probably the main reason why the school brass turned a blind eye on Enduro day. I think the other reason is half their professors ended up attending the event. A few of them even rode the buses with the students.

We also arranged for all of the beer. Thirty-six kegs in total. Half Miller Lite and half Old Milwaukee. The Old Milwaukee was to keep the price down. It didn't matter, college kids will drink anything. With at least three hundred girls coming, we needed to have a lite beer option. We ended up getting a volume discount and the distributor agreed to provide a refrigerated keg trailer and an employee to change the kegs throughout the day. We were all set.

We had done all of the planning and just had to pray for good weather. We monitored the weather all week and were afraid of a threat of rain as the weekend approached. Fortunately that rain was here and gone by Friday afternoon. We found ourselves with a sunny and eighty degree beautiful day with no threat of rain. The few wisps of clouds in the sky would not prevent the sun from shining on us for the entire day.

We arrived at the grove as scheduled to set up for the day. A few hours later the buses would start spitting out fifty college kids at a time that were raring to go. Brian was manning the parking area and greeting the buses. The staff members provided wrist bands to all of the people from the bus. Brian directed all of the people that drove themselves as to where to park. He also made sure they had tickets. If they didn't, he sold them one and gave them a wrist band.

The first buses started rolling in at noon. Cars were now also starting to mix in. Brian and his parking crew were pretty active for the first hour. Directing and collecting. Collecting and directing. About one o'clock Brian saw the bright yellow Volkswagen Beetle pulling into the parking lot.

Brian had run into Allegra several times since their chat on the boulder. Things were just fine between them. They would talk and they genuinely cared how the other was doing. It was far less uncomfortable than either may have expected. Allegra pulled right up to Brian with the window already rolled down. She was alone.

"Hey, Brian. You guys got lucky. We all got lucky. What a beautiful day."

"You got that right. It's gonna be a blast. You can park right over there."

Brian pointed to a space near the front entrance of the party area that had an orange traffic cone in front it. It was a single secluded spot between some trees and a small equipment shed. Brian still wanted to do whatever little gestures he could for her to make her feel special. Just as she looked over, one of the staff members was removing the cone. Allegra was a rock star. She might as well have rock star parking.

She looked back at Brian and smiled. "Thanks, Brian."

"My pleasure. I'll catch up with you later after I get done with this initial rush of cars and buses."

"Sounds great, Brian. Talk to you in a few." With that she pulled into her primo parking space and went in to the party.

I saw Allegra roll in by herself and went right up to her. "Hey, Allegra. Great to see you here," I said.

"Hey, Mac. What a day. What a turnout." She moved in and gave me a quick hug. "How many people are here? It looks like the entire school is here."

"I think we will be a bit over seven hundred when it is all said and done. Why don't you head on in and grab a bite to eat and get something to drink." The band was just getting started and kicked off with Behind Blue Eyes by The Who. They sounded awesome and worth every penny we paid for them.

"Wow, Mac. That band sounds great." She started walking in and then turned around. "Hey, Mac. Would it be okay if I left my car here overnight? I may not want to drive home."

"No problem Allegra. You can leave it here and pick it up tomorrow. Or we can have someone get it back to campus for you and you can take a bus back. Whatever you want to do is fine with us. Go grab a few beers and have a great time. We will figure out your car later."

"Sounds like a plan. Thanks, Mac." Allegra headed into the party to mix in with the seven hundred or so other partygoers.

Everything was going according to plan or better. People were having a great time. People were in the water. Frisbees were flying. Some of the commuters brought their dog, one of which was an expert at tracking down a long Frisbee toss. That dog was drawing a crowd and heavy applause with every catch. The volleyball pit was full. One handed volleyball. Each volleyballer had to keep their red plastic cup of beer in one hand at all times. Not sure if that was just invented that day or if it was an actual drinking game. I hadn't heard of it before but I liked what I saw. Teams of volleyballers drinking sips of beer with every lost point. If you spilled your beer you had to chug a full one. Some dopes spilling on purpose just so they could show off their chugging prowess. I saw Mickey in the volleyball pit holding on tight to his red plastic cup. Mickey liked his beer but he wasn't a chugger.

I was standing near the beer truck and taking in the sights with Brian and Bo. Brian then said, "Guys, I made an executive decision."

We looked at him and were waiting for him to continue. He

started pointing toward the band and at two guys standing there listening to the music. It was Daryl and Lance.

"What the hell are those two idiots doing here?" I barked at Brian.

"They drove up while I was working the parking lot. They said they wanted to buy tickets so they could listen to the band and have a few beers. They must know the band from town. Eddie was there too. They recognized Eddie from the fight. They said they won't be any trouble."

"Are you serious?" Bo said.

"I told them that I would let 'em in but warned them that if they stepped out of line, they would be run out in a hurry. I took their money and let 'em in. I figured it's the end of the school year. What the hell? Anyway, like I said, I made an executive decision." Brian doesn't believe in grudges. Bo's fight with those two was a thing of the past for him.

There wasn't much I could say. Being Brian felt it was okay to let them in, then that was good enough for me. Bo agreed. Nothing was going to ruin our good time that day.

The main event was less than an hour away. Ever since the initial Enduro, the day was highlighted by a drinking contest. A team of seven guys or ten women would do their best to empty a quarter keg of beer. The teams brought their own kegs with them. The kegs had to have the seal unbroken that was over the tap opening. It was our only way to monitor any potential cheating. We didn't want anyone draining any of the keg before the contest began. There would really be no reason to cheat. There were no prizes for the winning team members. The winners would have to settle for only bragging rights. And of course they would get their names logged into the Enduro bible where they would remain forever.

Today we had ten teams. Eight teams of seven guys and two teams of ten girls. The rules were simple. First team to kick their keg wins. Any participant that vomited was eliminated. We had an area cordoned off near the beer truck. The teams were beginning to assemble their members and move their keg into the drinking pit. Soon the cordoned-off area would be surrounded by people cheering these men and women on. *Chug. Chug. Chug.* I was standing around near the beer truck and was talking to Brian and Bo when Eddie scooted on by with his camera. "Hey, guys. Get together. How about a shot of the three of you? The event runners."

"Sure. You got it," Bo said and then he stood between Brian and me and put his arms around both of us. I put my beer in one hand and my other arm around Bo. Brian did the same from the other side. We all leaned in and had big smiles on our faces. Eddie took his picture and we heard the sizzle of the instamatic camera as it spit out the picture. Eddie grabbed it and started shaking it with his hand while it developed. Not sure why he was shaking it. It doesn't help the picture develop any quicker. After about a minute he said the picture looked good and declared it a keeper. He was now moving into place around the drinking pit to get a good vantage point so he could take a few shots of the contestants.

The teams were all in place and huddling around their kegs. The guys were pushing each other around like football players before the coin toss. The women were far more sedate. They were quietly discussing their strategies to upset the guy teams.

I took center stage in the arena of battle. "Welcome, teams." By now the drinking pit was ten deep with spectators. Most people couldn't hear me but that was fine. As long as the teams could hear, we were okay. "The first team to empty their keg wins. Don't puke. If you do, you're out. You can use cups and pitchers. The keg, cups, and pitchers all have to be empty and all beer swallowed for us to declare a winner. You win nothing for your efforts." That drew a small snickering of laughs from the crowd. "This is the Enduro bible." I raised it in the air for all to see. "This book has the names of every person for every winning team since the Enduro began. If you want to get your name here, you better drink fast."

There was a roar from the contestants as they started high fiving and chest bumping. They obviously wanted their names in print for all future generations to admire.

"Men. Ladies. Tap you kegs. Good luck to all. The contest begins," I gave a few second pause for effect, "Now!"

The crowd gave a loud roar and started cheering on their friends or whoever they were rooting for. The teams were now pouring beer out of their kegs as fast as they could. There were different strategies in place. Some teams got in line and filled their cup and walked to the back of the line. The goal was for their cup to be finished before they got to the tap again. There were a few teams using pitchers to keep the tap open at all times. Then pour from the pitchers to the cups. There was no perfect strategy. The bottom line was you needed people that could handle a lot of beer in a short period of time.

People were dropping like flies. After twenty or so minutes of constant drinking, many of the participants had vomited their way out of the contest. Another ten minutes later, the contest was over. Thirty three minutes and twelve seconds after the start, it was over. One of the guy teams had won. They still had six guys left up to the end. It wasn't a record but it was still an impressive showing. The guys were declared the winners and Eddie went up to them to get their names and take a team picture. Eddie shook his picture into development and liked what he saw. That would be the picture for the bible. On cue, the band played a shortened version of Queen's "We Are The Champions". It was a decent effort but no one can match the pipes of Freddy Mercury.

After the contest, the party began to wind down. Enduro 1984 was a complete success. A good time was had by all. Our clean up staff was doing their thing. The band stopped playing and was breaking down their equipment. The buses were doing their final run. The parking area had some straggler cars still around. The keg trailer was being hooked up to be towed away. We kicked all but one of the kegs. The keg attendant poured us a few pitchers and left them at the picnic table we were sitting at. I was sitting with Brian, Eddie, and Bo. We were soon joined by a few others. We poured off the pitchers into our plastic cups and enjoyed a few cold ones while we unwound from a long day.

I didn't see Allegra's car in her parking space. I thought she was going to leave it overnight. "Hey, Brian, did you see Allegra leave? I thought she was going to leave her car," I said.

"No. I didn't see her leave. I saw her earlier in the day but not much after that. I didn't see her at all after the drinking contest," Brian responded. "She was having a good time. I hope she got a ride. She was definitely drinking a few beers."

"I'm sure she's fine. She doesn't live too far from here," I said and then changed the subject. "Eddie, how did you do with the pictures?"

He threw the stack of polaroids in front of me and said, "Take a look. A lot of good ones. I'll put a few of the good ones in the bible later tonight and I'll give you the rest." I took a quick look and liked what I saw. Eddie did a nice job capturing the highlights of the event.

"Nice job, Eddie. These look great."

The day was giving way to the darkness of night. We wrapped up and headed back to our apartment for the after party. A job well done by all involved.

Chapter 31

We moved the party back to our place. Our plan was to have a late night cookout with the left over burgers and dogs and whatever beer may have been left. No such luck. The Enduro was such a great success that there was nothing left over to bring home. It didn't stop us. We took a few dollars from our profits from the party and grabbed some more beer and a bunch of steaks. Our staff members and a few others joined us to cap off what was a great day and a great event.

We didn't make it a late night as most of us were exhausted from the day and the days of prep before the event. We sat around with our bellies full of New York strip steaks and baked potatoes and sipped on our beers. We went over the events of the day and by all accounts a good time was had by all.

Now came time for the ceremonial passing of the Endure bible to next year's event runners.

"Eddie, hand me the bible," I said. Eddie got up and walked over the bible. He seemed a little sad as I think he was hoping he would be designated to run the event year. His sadness was short lived. I held the bible up and raised it over my head. "Our committee has discussed at great lengths who will receive the honor of keeping the tradition of the Enduro going. We have decided to pass the bible to..." I paused for dramatic effect even though it wasn't necessary. "Drumroll please." More unnecessary pausing. "Tommy D and Eddie Vincent." Eddie jumped up and ran toward me and grabbed the bible. Tommy D was happy but far more restrained. Eddie hoisted the Enduro bible over his head like he had just won the Stanley Cup. I though he was going to give an acceptance speech which was not called for. His speech was one word. "Nice," accompanied by a huge smile.

"Eddie, with the bible comes great responsibility. This tradition must go on and be better than the previous year. You guys will have your work cut out for you," I said.

"We got this, Mac," Eddie quickly and happily shot back. He looked at Tommy D and said, "We should get Willie to join us." Tommy nodded in agreement and now it appeared next year's Enduro event management team was fully in place. Eddie held on to the bible like he was protecting the Ark of the Covenant. "The bible is in good hands," Eddie said. I agreed. There was no better choice than Eddie to take this on.

The party broke up fairly early and everyone got a well-deserved good night's sleep. It was mid-morning and we were all stirring about and getting ready to choke down some greasy eggs and bacon. Bo grabbed some coffee from the market across the street. We were still going over the events of the day before and feeling proud for the success of the event. Everything went so well, we thought we pulled off the perfect event. Those thoughts went quickly out the window.

I was sitting in the living room with Bo when Squirrel slammed the front door open and ran in. He was huffing and puffing. "Did you hear? Did you hear?"

"Hear what?" Bo and I responded. We knew something was wrong. "Spit it out. What the hell is going on?" Bo said.

Squirrel was hesitating as if to find the right words. This was bad. Squirrel had bad news and didn't know how to deliver it. "Squirrel," I shouted. "What is it? What?"

Squirrel just blurted it out. "Allegra is dead". An eerie silence came over the room for a second. Bo and I stared in stunned disbelief. Squirrel went on. "She was found murdered last night at the hole."

"Oh, my God. What happened?" I said.

"I don't know. I went over to the student center this morning to make some copies of notes for my finals and I heard people talking about it. I tried to find out what happened. The only thing I could find out was there were detectives on campus this morning asking all sorts of questions. "Apparently Allegra went to the quarry last night after the Enduro and got killed."

My thoughts quickly shifted to Brian. "Holy shit. We have to tell Brian."

I turned to get up to go upstairs and break the devastating news. When I turned toward the stairs, I saw Brian standing there in shock. He didn't say a word. I knew he had heard everything Squirrel just said. Bo saw the same and got up. The three of us slowly walked over to Brian. Brian walked down the rest of the steps and broke down in tears. We put our arms on him and walked him to the couch. He was inconsolable for the next few minutes. We let him have his cry and get it all out. Brian slowly got up and walked back upstairs. We didn't follow. He wanted to be left alone for a little while to process and collect his thoughts.

"You know, guys, these detectives are probably going to want to talk to us. After all, the Enduro may have been the last place she was seen alive," Squirrel said.

Bo quickly replied, "We have nothing to hide. I'll tell them whatever I know, which isn't much."

"I don't have much to offer. I don't even know when she left," I said. We just started thinking of the events of yesterday and if there was anything that happened that might be relevant to her death.

None of us could come up with one thing. What ever happened to Allegra it had nothing to do with the Enduro.

It didn't take the detectives long to get to our place. We did receive a visit from the investigating detectives later that day. They questioned all of us and we cooperated fully. The problem was we didn't have any information for them that would be of any benefit to their investigation. They gave us their business cards and told us to contact them if we thought of anything.

We didn't learn anything from the detectives. They were tight-lipped as to the content of their investigation. That was to be expected. We only learned that she was found dead in the woods at the quarry and their investigation was being treated as a homicide. The detectives did remind us of who the victim was and who her family was. We already knew who her family was and what they were capable of. Whoever killed Allegra had better hope the police found him or her before the Selvaggios did.

Our last ten or so days of college felt like an eternity. We had our finals and all of our group that were seniors attended the graduation ceremony. Our families were up and it was supposed to be a joyous time. Allegra's death was devastating to all of us. None of us could attend any of the services for Allegra. The family had a private wake and burial. We don't even know where she was interred. If we did, we could have at least gone to her gravesite to say our goodbyes and send prayers her way. Unfortunately, the prayers we sent her way had to be done from a distance. Allegra had such a big heart and pure soul that there was no doubt what direction she was headed for in her afterlife.

Allegra's death would forever be on our minds. All of us wishing there was something that could have been done by any one of us to have prevented this. If we only did this or did that then maybe this wouldn't have happened. We were just beating ourselves up over something we had no control over. We knew there was nothing any of us could have done. We all felt helpless. We did decide that the tradition of the Enduro had to come to an end. There would forever be a black cloud hanging over the Enduro should it continue. The decision to end it was unanimous. Eddie was disappointed but he was fully on board.

Now it was time to go our separate ways and get into the real world. Some of us had jobs waiting for us and some didn't. I didn't have any employment waiting for me. I was going to take the summer off and then try to get hooked up with any police department that would take me. Bo was going to work construction with his father over the summer and then decide what he would do after that. Brian was heading back to Maryland where his family lived. He had no employment waiting for him either. Brian left college with a hole in his heart. Those last ten days of college after Allegra's death were very painful for him. Everywhere he looked, there was a reminder of her. Brian would be fine but it would take him some time. He clearly loved her.

Our college years were behind us and the months had been

passing. Since Allegra was murdered the hours turned into days and the days into weeks and the weeks into months and the months into years. Despite significant effort on this high profile murder case, no suspects were developed and Allegra's murderer was still walking the earth.

Chapter 32

2017

The drive over to the governor's office was a short one. It took us twice as long to find parking then it did to get there. We talked on the ride over as to what we would ask and how we would ask it. I was hoping my backround as a cop would lend some credibility to the situation and the Governor would feel free to talk openly with us. If that didn't work, maybe the Governor would be a sucker for a good-looking lady.

We left our guns locked in my car and entered the Capitol Building. We went through the normal security check points and a few minutes later we made if to Governor Hainesworth's office. We entered the office and immediately saw a pleasant-looking middle-aged woman who I assumed was the Governor's secretary. She looked up as we entered. "You must be the group Jenny called about. Please take a seat. The Governor will be with you in a few minutes."

"Thank you, Ms. Richards," I said as I was looking directly at her nameplate.

"It's Mrs. Richards, but you can call me Elizabeth."

"Elizabeth it is. Thank you for fitting us in on such short notice," I said. "Hopefully we will only take up a few minutes of the Governor's time."

"You actually caught him on a good day. He will be here for at least the next three hours. Then it is off to some campaign commitments," she said. Her demeanor screamed efficiency. Her desk was impeccably organized and she had her computer key board with dual monitors. She was likely a multi-tasking expert. She also appeared to be a long time fixture in that office so I assumed she was well-acquainted with Tyler. After a brief pause, she continued, "Jenny said you are long-time old friends of her and Tyler." She stopped and giggled. We were not sure why. "I mean good friends. I didn't mean to call you old." She laughed again.

"We are his good friends and we are old. So you're not wrong either way," Brian said. "Have you known Tyler long?"

"Oh yes. I have been with Andrew, I should say Governor Hainesworth, for almost forty years. I started with him way back when he was just starting out in the Prosecutor's office. I followed him to the State District Attorney's Office and then stayed with him when he went into politics."

That would make Elizabeth around sixty years old or more. I would have figured she was about my age, but I can buy that she got me by a half a dozen or so years. "Tyler has been with Andrew for many years now. So I have known Tyler for as long as the Governor has. He was such a wonderful man. It is such a shame what happened to him."

"That's nice of you to say," Brian said. As he was saying that, we could hear her phone beep and she picked up.

"You can see the Governor now. It's the second door on the right." She hit a button and a buzzer went off allowing us to access the back offices.

We got to the second door on the right and were about to knock when the door opened up and we were greeted by Governor Hainesworth's extended hand and politician's smile. "Come on in. Come on in. Have a seat wherever you are comfortable." There were four introductions and four handshakes. Each one of us was met with a firm right hand grip followed by his left hand joining the party on the back of our hands. It was a polished handshake that he had done thousands of times. He was a tall man in his mid-sixties with slicked back graying dark hair and wire-rimmed glasses that looked a little small for his face.

His office was large as would be expected. He had an enormous oak desk with an oversized high-back leather chair behind. There were two leather chairs in front of his desk. There was also a sitting area with some couches and a few club chairs. He seemed to be guiding us to the sitting area so that is where we went. The Governor stood in front of one of the club chairs and extended his hand for us to sit anywhere else. We took up three sections of the couch and one of the other club chairs.

The office was tastefully decorated with all of the furnishings for a man in his position of power. There were two curios filled with sports memorabilia and many pictures in frames on his credenza and all over his walls. He obviously liked golf as there were numerous pictures of him in foursomes with the rich and famous standing on the first tees of some exclusive golf clubs.

The Governor was polite and instantly likeable. I can see how easy it must had been for him to get voters to pull the lever with his name next to it. "Can I get anyone anything to drink?" as he motioned to the small bar area in his office. We all politely declined. "So, Elizabeth said you are friends of Tyler. How do you know him?"

I took the lead. "We met in college many moons ago." I didn't feel it was necessary to do a specific response for Jessica. "We lived together at King's College and remained good friends." I felt the need to throw in the Kings name as we could have also been his college friends from law school.

"Ah. The Kings boys. I've heard a few stories," he said as he choked out a big laugh. "The good old days, as Tyler used to say."

"I am sorry for your loss as well as my loss. Tyler was someone I considered a good friend. It was my privilege to work side by side with him for so long. He was an outstanding attorney and an excellent political strategist. I was lucky to have him with me."

"That is nice to hear. I'm sure he was. He was always driven. We all knew he was going to succeed at whatever he did," Bo said.

The Governor looked over to Jessica and asked. "Did you go to Kings also? How did you know Tyler?" Now was time to get down to business. The only way to explain Jessica's presence was to get into the whole reason why we are here.

"I didn't know Tyler. I know these three guys." The Governor seemed puzzled.

"So how is it I can help you today? What brings you to my office?"

I took over and decided to dive right in. "We have reason to believe Tyler's death was not accidental."

"Not accidental? What do you mean not accidental? I personally communicated with the investigating officer and made sure no stone would be unturned. He assured me there was nothing out of the ordinary and his death was officially ruled as accidental." The Governor did not seem to like where this was going. "So, Mr. MacMasters, what makes you make such a statement?"

"I'm sorry I was so abrupt." I went on to tell him about the unusual set of circumstances surrounding Squirrel's death. I went on about what we found at Flanagan's and how that led us to Palmyra. The Governor was not aware of the recent murder in Palmyra. "I have no idea if Tyler's death was accidental or not. I'm not a believer in coincidences so we are looking into the possibility the two deaths are related."

"I wish I could help but I think you're barking up the wrong tree. I trust the investigation into Tyler's death was thorough and the conclusions are accurate. I hope you didn't let Jenny know all of this. I think she has been through enough in the past few months. I'm sure the last thing she wants now is to re-live this horrible tragedy." The Governor had a valid point but we couldn't un-ring that bell.

"I did broach the possibility but I did not provide details to the extent I gave you. I told her we were looking into Jimmy Collucci's death as something didn't seem right with that. I only told her I wanted to be sure there was no connection to Tyler's death," I offered to the Governor. "She was fine with what we said and also said she would want to know if we turn anything up that is relevant to Tyler's death."

"I still don't know how my office is involved or can be of any help."

"I'm not in any way saying *your office* is involved with anything. I just wanted to talk to you to see if Tyler said anything unusual or out of the ordinary in the days or weeks leading up to his death."

"Unusual?" He paused for a few seconds as if he was actually trying to think back to that period of time. "Nothing unusual or out of the ordinary. We had been quite busy around here at that time with the campaign." His effort to recollect and response seemed genuine but he was a master politician.

"Did he mention anything that could be perceived as bothering him?"

"No. Nothing at all. I doubt he would have bothered me with his problems at that time. It's not that I wouldn't have helped him if I could, it's just that he knew how busy we all were. He may have gone to my chief of staff, Don Keohane, if there was something important going on. Don and Tyler were quite close."

Governor Hainesworth got up and went over to his desk and pushed a button on the phone. "Elizabeth, would you be a dear and see if Don is around. Please send him in if he is here. Thank you."

I got up as well and was walking around his office and looking at his memorabilia and pictures. I was hoping to kill a few minutes with small talk while waiting for Mr. Keohane. I was looking at a picture of him and Donovan McNabb, who quarterbacked the Eagles but never won the big one. There was also a picture of him and Mike Tomlin, who coached the Steelers to a Super Bowl victory. He looked much happier standing with Mike Tomlin. The Steelers delivered him multiple championships over the years and the Eagles never delivered him the big one.

I then saw a picture on the wall of a familiar building. One that I hadn't seen since my college internship days. "Governor Hainesworth? Is this you in this picture?" He got up and walked over to me. He knew what picture I was referring to. He took it off the wall and took a good look at it. I didn't interrupt him while he took his brief stroll down memory lane.

"I told you earlier. Please call me Andrew. That sure is me. A few years and a few pounds ago. That's me and Don Keohane. He's aged a bit himself but don't tell him I said that," he said with a little grin. "We go all the way back to when we were young prosecutors in Wilkes-Barre. We cut our teeth together and that picture was taken just after we started there." The two of them were standing on the steps of the Luzerne County Courthouse which was right in the heart of Wilkes-Barre.

There was faint knock on the door and then Don Keohane poked his head in. "You wanted to see me?"

"Come on in Don and take a seat." He was clearly wondering what was going on but just didn't say anything and went and sat down as directed.

The Governor gave a quick overview of what we previously discussed then said. "If there was anything going on with Tyler before his death, it would be okay to relay that to my friends here."

"I can't think of anything. Tyler didn't talk too much about his personal life. We all thought he was doing well staying off the booze. I was a little surprised when I heard he drank a bottle of vodka and passed out. I was surprised but not overly surprised considering his past." Don had the same view on this as we did.

"Did he say anything unusual or out of the ordinary before his death?" I asked just the same way as I asked the Governor.

"I'm sorry. I wish I could help," Don said. "Anything else?" as he looked at the Governor. He saw his friend still holding on to the picture of the two of them standing in front of the Luzerne County Courthouse. Something in that picture must have jogged something in his memory.

"You know, Tyler did ask me a question which I thought was a little out of the blue." He had our full attention and we let him go on. "He asked me about a murder case from thirty some years ago."

"Let me guess. Allegra Selvaggio," I said.

"Yes. How did you know that?" Don asked.

"Tyler knew her back in college. We all did. Why would Tyler ask you about it?"

"Andrew was the prosecutor in charge of that case from our office and I was working for Andrew." Governor Hainesworth seemed a little surprised Don Keohane was bringing this up. It was actually a low point in his young career at the time as no one was ever brought to justice for her murder.

The Governor spoke up. "Don, I wasn't aware of that conversation. When did that occur?"

Don thought for a bit and said, "It was a week or so before he died."

"Why didn't you tell me about it?" the Governor asked.

"I didn't think much of it. I certainly didn't think it was anything I needed to report. It was just a quick question and answer."

"What did he ask?" I asked.

"He just asked if there were any new developments in Allegra's case. He didn't say why he wanted to know. He just asked that if there were any recent developments. I told him I hadn't heard any updates in quite some time. He said he hadn't either. And that was the extent of it." He stopped for a second and went on. "Tyler and I both knew that if we ever heard anything regarding that case, we were to notify Andrew immediately. It is long unsolved but is the highest profile solved or unsolved case in the last fifty years."

Governor Hainesworth seemed a little upset with his Chief of Staff. I can see Don's point. It didn't seem to me that Tyler asked anything unusual considering they all had limited ties to Allegra or her case. I guess the Governor didn't see it that way.

I gave Governor Hainesworth my contact information and he

gave me his private number. He all of a sudden was a bit more interested in what we were doing and wanted to be kept in the loop. I assured him I would do so. We thanked him for his time and left his office.

The question was not why Tyler asked Don Keohane about Allegra's case. It was why he asked him about her death and then was found dead less than a week later.

Time for us to regroup and get a bite to eat. We hopped in the car and pulled out of the capitol building parking garage. What we didn't see was a dark SUV pull out a few cars behind us with our vehicle in its sights.

Chapter 33

We went to a local café a few blocks from Governor Hainesworth's office. It was a quaint place that was filling up fast. We grabbed a table and began to peruse the menus. Our meeting with the Governor and Don Keohane yielded very little other than a long shot lead about a three decades old murder. What bothered me was how uncomfortable Governor Hainesworth became after Don Keohane mentioned Allegra's name. It was likely due to the fact that he had some direct involvement with her case and it was never solved. Perhaps it was nothing more than a black mark on his otherwise stellar tenure with the district attorney's office. We placed our lunch orders with the waitress and started to discuss where we were with our quest.

Jessica felt she was left behind in the conversation. "So, tell me about Allegra. Why would Tyler be asking about her now?"

"She was a friend of ours when we were in college," I responded. "She was found murdered in some woods near our school after she attended a party we threw."

"Wow. Did the police think you guys had anything to do with it" she asked incredulously.

"No. It was not like that. We were questioned by the detectives just as many others were but we didn't know anything. We were questioned but we were never treated like suspects." I paused and then continued. "It was never solved but it wasn't for a lack of trying. This was a high profile case. Allegra's family made sure the detectives gave maximum effort and I'm sure they did their own investigating. Her father was a very powerful man. Her father was Carmine Selvaggio."

I didn't need to elaborate any further. The Selvaggio name was still prominent. Anyone raised on the east coast would know that name and know exactly who they were and what they did for a living. Jessica heard the name while we were in the Governor's office but didn't make the connection.

"My God. What the heck happened?" she questioned.

Brian jumped in. "She was found dead in some woods near this swimming hole that we used to hang out at. Her car was found at the scene. She was found dead by some locals. We don't have any confirmed information but the rumors are that she was either bludgeoned or strangled or both. The last place anyone saw her before her death was at our party. We don't know when she left the party or what she did after she left."

Brian paused to collect himself. To this day, any talk of Allegra brought back an ocean of regret and guilt. Jessica seemed to sense that. "I wish I could have been there for her. None of this would have happened."

Brian had been shouldering this burden since her death. She put her hand on his shoulder to provide a little comfort. We all knew that there was nothing any of us could have done to prevent her murder. We all went through bouts of guilt but worked through it. Brian never seemed to fully get there.

"That's strange, really strange. After all those years, Tyler asks about her and a week later he's dead. It can't be a coincidence," she said as she looked directly at me. "Mac, you said you don't believe in coincidences."

"I don't."

"Could the Selvaggios be involved with Tyler and Jimmy's deaths?" she asked.

"I highly doubt that. That would mean they had something to do with her murder. There is no way they could be tied to her death. I know that for a fact."

I was sure they had no involvement with her murder but I couldn't be as sure about the Selvaggio's having no involvement with

246

Tyler and Squirrel's death. More questions. More coincidences. It just didn't make any sense. The puzzle wasn't coming together.

We all agreed on one thing, it was worth checking out. We had very little else to go on. This lead seemed to be as promising as any other we had. It might not lead to anything but it had to be checked out. We finished our meal in mostly silence as we all continued to try to piece this thing together. We paid our bill and went back to the hotel to pack.

My thoughts still were centered on Governor Hainesworth. He was a man who was used to being in control and not one easily caught by surprise. Why didn't he make mention of Allegra when he found out we were friends with Tyler and went to college with him. He would surely know that if Tyler was friends with Allegra then we must have been as well. I don't think he would have even acknowledged Allegra to us if Don Keohane didn't bring it up in front of everybody. The one thought that came to mind was no one had ever been developed as a prime suspect in the case. All roads of that investigation went right through the district attorney in charge, Andrew Hainesworth.

Next stop – Wilkes-Barre, Pennsylvania – our old college stomping grounds. We needed to do a little poking around and see if we could find out why Tyler was asking about Allegra thirty three years after her murder.

The drive to Wilkes-Barre was uneventful and took about two

hours. We got ourselves set up in a hotel right in the heart of the city. The memories of college began to flood back. We were only about six blocks from our former campus. We drove through it on our way to the hotel. Jackson Street was still there but not in the same shape or form of thirty three years ago. Senunas' Bar and Grill was still there but was now moved across the street where Charlie's Market used to be. Senunas' was a hangout for us in college and was now being managed by an old friend of ours. We would have to stop in before we left town. Our old set of row houses had been long demolished. The college purchased that land shortly after we graduated and demolished all of the old slums in favor of a new multi-level parking deck.

We got ourselves set up in three adjoining rooms. We met in Brian's room in the middle to discuss our game plan. We decided that Bo and I would go to the Wilkes-Barre police station to see if we could meet with the investigating detective. While this was technically considered a cold case, I was sure it still got plenty of attention. While we were there, Brian and Jessica would begin the tedious task of reviewing the video footage we had obtained from Flanagan's.

I was hoping to have heard back from Eddie by now but for whatever reason he hadn't reached back out to me. It was getting late in the day but we decided to visit the Wilkes Barre Police Department to see if the handling cold case detective was available for a chat. We drove out of the hotel parking garage and were making our way through town when I saw a dark SUV a few cars behind us.

It seemed as if we were being followed. I kept an eye on the rear view mirror and side mirrors. I felt quite sure they were following us. They seemed to be doing a pretty amateurish job of it.

We pulled into the police station and the dark SUV drove past the station and kept going. Bo and I got out of the car and went in to see what we could find out about Allegra's case.

The desk sergeant was sitting back and drinking a coffee. He must be just getting on his shift. Second shift was never any fun. I'm sure he wasn't too happy to be there. His name plate said Sgt. James Venters.

"Sgt. Venters, how are you today?" I said with a smile. I waited a brief second but no response was forthcoming. He looked at me with the "state your business" look.

"My name is Jack MacMasters. I was hoping to get a few minutes with the detective handling the old Allegra Selvaggio murder case." This got his attention.

He sat forward and said "What did you say your name was again? MacManus?"

"No. MacMasters, Jack MacMasters." Sgt. Venters wrote it down hurriedly. "Who is handling that case? Is he available?"

"Detective Wheeler and it's not a he. Detective Eileen Wheeler. She's not in today. Is this something that can wait until tomorrow? She gets in a 8:00 AM."

It was already late in the day so we would be able to push this off until tomorrow morning. "We will be here tomorrow at eight o'clock." I handed Sgt. Venters my card and he eyed it up.

"You're on the job?"

"Sort of," I responded. He looked puzzled. "I just put in my papers."

"Well, good for you. I've got four or five more years then I'm done."

"It'll go quick. Don't you worry."

"Thanks, MacMasters. I'll give Wheeler a heads up that you will be coming by tomorrow. If you have anything on the Selvaggio case, she will certainly want to talk to you."

"Have a good shift, Sergeant."

Bo and I headed for the door. Before we opened the glass door I decided to scan the area from behind the glass. "Hold on Bo. Don't go out yet."

"What's up ,Mac?"

"I'm looking for a dark SUV. I think it may have followed us from the hotel."

"Why didn't you say anything before?" Bo shot back at me.

"I wasn't a hundred percent sure. Now I am. There it is. Parked in the strip mall lot across the street." Two guys are occupying the front seats. I thought for a second. "Bo, I need you to be a distraction and get their attention. I'm going to sneak around and pay these two guys a visit."

"What kind of distraction?"

"How should I know? Just do something to get and keep their attention"

Bo went out the front door and I took a side exit. The two would not have a view of the side exit from their vantage point. I walked down a half a block and then headed toward the parking lot from a side angle. I was watching Bo and his brilliant distraction. He was bent over and tying his shoe. *Pretty lame, Bo. You need to do better than that.* He must have read my mind. Bo got in the car and popped open the hood. He went around and was pretending to be dealing with an engine problem. *Much better Bo. Much better.* I was nearing the car and could see they were both focused on Bo and his car problems.

I was able to get behind their car without them noticing me. I swiftly moved to the driver's side window. I took out my gun and rapped it noisily on the window. "Roll down the window now and both of you better keep your hands where I can see them." Both immediately shot their arms half way in the air as if they were being robbed. The driver then slowly put his finger on the power window button and rolled it down.

"Who the hell are you guys? And you better have a damn good

reason for following me." The guys were obviously amateurs and appeared to be new to this kind of surveillance work. They weren't quite sure how to respond now that they were outed. They looked at each other and decided to come clean.

"Relax, please. Put that gun down. It's not what you think," the driver said. How did he know what I thought? I didn't even know what I thought. I had no idea who these guys were and what they were doing tailing us.

"Who sent you? I want answers now. If I don't get them now, this will get ugly real fast. Who the hell sent you?" I yelled toward them.

"Hainesworth. Andrew Hainesworth. We work for his security team," the driver shot back.

"Hainesworth? Why is he sending out his security team to follow us?"

The passenger looked over and said, "Look, pal, we just do what we are told."

"Get your boss on the phone."

The passenger dialed up Governor Hainesworth and said "Governor, this is Sparks. MacMasters made the tail and confronted us. He is here now." After what I suspect was a quick and sharp reprimand, Sparks handed the phone to me.

"Governor, what is this all about? Why did you send these two

Keystone Kops to follow us? "

"Jack. May I call you Jack?" *Always the polite politician.* He didn't wait for my reply and he just went on. "I was a little un-nerved after our conversation about Tyler's death. When the conversation turned to Allegra, I was a little taken aback. I don't see how the two could be related but if they are, I want to know. Tyler was a longtime friend of mine and Allegra's case has haunted me throughout my entire legal career. "

"No disrespect meant but we don't need your babysitters. We don't need you looking after us. Tell these guys to head back to Harrisburg and leave us alone."

"My apologies to you and your friends. It was a knee jerk reaction to our meeting. I will call them back. But Jack, if you need any assistance with your investigation please feel free to call me. I will be sure to take your call. And Jack, please keep me in the loop if there are any developments in Allegra's case or Tyler's death."

"Will do. I'll be in touch if anything develops." We hung up and as I was walking back to Bo and his car problems I saw the dark SUV heading out. I didn't think we would be seeing them again. If Governor Hainesworth wanted us followed he better send his A-Team and not those two clowns.

I filled Bo in on who these guys were and who sent them. Bo was stunned to find out Andrew Hainesworth was behind this. We drove back to the hotel and were trying to figure out if the Governor was being straight with us or if he had other reasons for keeping tabs on us. One thing was for sure, we needed to be careful and alert on every move we made from here on out. We knew we had enemies out there. We just didn't know who they were yet.

Chapter 34

"Status?"

It was almost midnight and that was the all too familiar single word greeting Wolf would get from his employer. Wolf had had enough of this job and this employer. The job had gone on far longer than he expected. Patience on both ends were wearing quite thin. Wolf had a balance due and he wanted to collect it and move on to the next one.

"I feel good about Eddie Vincent. I followed him around today. He spent most of the day at a children's hospital. His son has some serious medical problems and has been in there for a while." He could almost hear his employer processing the information on the other end. No doubt coming to the same conclusion that Wolf had. Eddie Vincent may have had financial problems due to his son's medical issues and might just be desperate enough to resort to blackmail to avail those problems.

"What are you doing about it? Why don't I have my money back yet? Why don't I have that damn picture back yet? "The employer yet again confirming he had completely lost patience for this situation.

"I have it under control," Wolf shot back.

The employer's voice was now in an all-out yell. "I'm sick and tired of hearing you say you have it under control. I want my money and I want that picture. And I want it yesterday. You comprende?"

Wolf sat silent for a second as his employer blew off his steam. Wolf wasn't accustomed to being talked to like that. He would, however, make sure this job was completed. His professional reputation was at stake. Regardless of what he currently thought of his employer, he would make sure he successfully completed the job to the employer's satisfaction just as he had done for every other person that utilized his services.

"I got it. I comprende," Wolf responded. "I expect to have this wrapped up in the morning."

"Why not tonight?"

"I can kill Vincent any time I want. I will go there in the morning in case he doesn't give me the photo or the money. If I have to find it myself, I would rather do it in the daylight. I don't need anyone seeing a flashlight moving around his property. Plus the daylight will give me a better chance of finding it," Wolf reasoned.

"That makes sense. I want this over tomorrow morning." The yelling was replaced by normal conversational tone. "Get this over with. I can't keep having this hanging over my head."

"One more thing," Wolf added. "What do you want me to do about MacMasters, Bollander, Kavanaugh and the girl? They are in Wilkes-Barre now. Not far from me. They paid a visit to the police station today."

"What?" the normal conversational tone was short lived. This was not what he wanted to hear. "What police station?"

"It's under control." Wolf knew right away that was not the right response.

The yelling escalated even further. "Stop telling me it's under control. It's not under control. It's out of control. You hear me? Out Of Control." He paused and then continued but was now slightly calmer. "How do you know this? Did you run into them when you were following Vincent?"

"I put a tracker on his car in Harrisburg before I left to track Vincent."

"That was good thinking by you." This put his mind at ease knowing he was keeping tabs on MacMasters and company. If he felt they were too close, Wolf would be able to dispose of them on short notice.

Wolf had felt that MacMasters and company could be a problem for them down the road. They were getting too close for comfort in Harrisburg. Now it was even worse that they were in Wilkes-Barre asking all the right people all the right questions. Wolf wasn't sure the trail would lead to Wilkes-Barre but here they were. He felt good about his decision to throw that tracker on his car just in case.

"As far as I can tell they don't have any information and are just grasping at straws." Wolf tried to allay his client's concerns but it wasn't working.

"This is not good, Wolf. I need to think about this." A few seconds passed as Wolf remained silent and let his employer process this information. "Maybe he will ask his questions and move on. I don't know what he thinks he is going to find out."

"They are staying in a hotel in downtown Wilkes-Barre in three rooms. I already scoped it out."

"Okay. That is good. We know where they are and where they will be going. I'll figure out what if anything we are going to do with MacMasters and the others. For now I want you to stick to your plan. See Vincent in the morning and make sure he is the one. If he is, get my money back and get that picture. Do whatever you must to get it. Make sure it looks like a clean accident. I don't want this trail of bodies tied together."

"No problem. It will be done in the morning. I'll call you when I'm done."

There were no good-byes or further instruction. The employer clicked off wondering if this thing was finally coming to an end.

Wolf was just staring into space after the phone line disconnected. He was disgusted with his current employer. Thoughts of paying his employer a visit after this job was done were going through his head. Business first. Pleasure second. Wolf was sure the business end of their relationship would be concluded tomorrow.

Chapter 35

I filled in Brian and Jessica on the day's events. They had stayed back at the hotel reviewing the surveillance videos from Flanagan's. There were so many camera angles and hours of video to peruse. They hadn't come up with anything of any use to us as of yet.

"What's up with Hainseworth? That was a bizarre move. He seems to be taking a pretty big interest in what we are doing." Jessica wasn't so sure about Hainesworth when she met him in Harrisburg. Now she was even less sure about this guy and his motives. "Don't you find it strange that all roads ran through him in Allegra's murder investigation and with all the resources available to him, no one was even arrested or not even a prime suspect was ever named?"

"I know exactly what you mean and see how you can feel that way," I responded. "I have my doubts about him, too. The problem with Hainesworth is what possible motive could he have? As far as I know, he never met her or had any connection to her. I'm sure he knew about Allegra's father but that doesn't mean he would have had any dealings with Allegra."

"I can tell you that Allegra never mentioned Hainesworth or the District Attorney's office when I was with her," Brian said. Jessica sensed a hint of pain in Brian's voice when mentioning her name. She put her hand on his shoulder again. She wasn't being forward with him. She just wanted to make whatever small gesture she could to let him know she was there for him. "Did Hainesworth have any involvement with any organized crime task force?"

"I have no idea," I said. The truth was none of us ever heard of Andrew Hainesworth when he was a young district attorney. He may have been an up and coming hot shot attorney but we knew nothing of him. I only heard of him after Tyler connected with him and he began his ascension to the highest elected office in Pennsylvania.

"What is the plan for tomorrow?" Jessica asked.

"Mac and I are going to see the cold case detective tomorrow first thing," Bo responded.

"Should we all go?" Brian said.

"I think just Bo and I should go. You and Jessica need to keep checking out those videos. There has to be something on there. If we can get a good look at the guy, I can send it to some friends back at the department to see if they can run it through a face recognition program."

"Mac, did you hear back from Eddie yet?" Brian asked.

"No. Not yet. He lives close so I think if he doesn't call back, then we can all go to his house tomorrow after we get back from the police station."

They were all in agreement with the game plan moving forward. It was late and it had already been a long day. Time to get some sleep. Tomorrow just might be another long day.

Surprisingly I got a restful night's sleep. I'm a creature of habit. I like sleeping in my own bed with my own pillows and the comfort of Katie at my side. I was exhausted from the day's events and dropped off right after my head hit the pillow. Bo was in the other queen sized bed in the room. He didn't get quite the good night's sleep that I did. He told me my snoring was peeling the paint off the ceiling. He finally got to sleep due to his own exhaustion and my snoring wasn't an issue anymore.

We got up around seven o'clock and got ready for our visit to see Detective Wheeler. We showed up at the police station exactly at 8:00 AM. The desk sergeant told us Wheeler was running late and would get there as soon as she could. We took our seats in the lobby as directed. The desk sergeant picked up the phone and made an internal call as he pushed only one button. He looked up at us as he was talking.

A few minutes had gone by and a man in uniform walked into the lobby. We knew Wheeler was female so it wasn't who we were waiting for. The man came right up to us and stated his business. "Are you the two looking to talk to Detective Wheeler about the Allegra Selvaggio case?"

"We are," I responded. I could now see his name on the little metal plate on his chest. This was Wheeler's boss. "I'm Jack MacMasters and this is Tim Bollander." He extended his hand and we shook.

"I'm Chief Warren Lutes. I was told you two may be coming back this morning. Wheeler should be here any minute. In fact that may be her coming in now."

Wheeler burst through the door and hurried over to us. "Sorry, Chief. My mother again." Apparently she didn't have to say any more as the Chief nodded his acknowledgement as if to say "I understand". Whatever issues Wheeler was dealing with regarding her mother must be pretty serious or at least known to Chief Lutes.

Wheeler looked to be in her mid-thirties and physically fit. She wore her mid-length brunette hair in a ponytail and had an attractive look about her. She was dressed in dark slacks and a white button down shirt with light jacket. She struck me as efficient and competent.

"Wheeler, this is Jack MacMasters and Tim Bollander. I didn't get past the greeting so I don't know what they have to offer. But these are the two who came in yesterday and asked for you," the Chief said.

Wheeler looked at us and told us to follow her.

"Wheeler, find out what they have and report back to me right away."

With that Chief Lutes left the lobby without any further instruction to Wheeler or questions for us. He was the superior but knew to let Wheeler do her job and report her findings up the chain. It was quite clear that the mention of Allegra Selvaggio got a lot of people's attention at this station.

She didn't lead us to her desk. She instead took us to an interrogation room. "We will have more room to talk in here," she reasoned. She pulled out one of the metal chairs and offered me a seat. "Would either of you like some coffee?" Now I was feeling like Bo and I were being treated like suspects. The room was institutional painted block walls with a table and four chairs. There was no two way mirror in this room but there were four surveillance cameras on the ceiling corners.

I routinely used the nice approach when getting some perp in the interrogation room. I would get them comfortable, make sure they were offered a drink, then break them down.

"Detective Wheeler, we came here to discuss some recent events that may or may not be related to Allegra's death. We felt it was worth a discussion with you. We are not here to be treated like suspects," I said.

"You're not suspects. If you were, you wouldn't both be in the same room. We would have split you up. You should know that." She was right. "I also would have read you your rights if there was any thought on our part that you may be suspects." That was also true. "You need to understand that it is much better to speak in here for privacy sake. I don't need anyone out there listening in on anything Allegra Selvaggio related. The Selvaggio's have friends in many places and the mention of her name generally results in a call to her family. This is more or less for your protection." I didn't immediately process the enormous sensitivity this case still had in these parts. "So let's get down to it. What brings you here? What are these recent events?"

I gave Detective Wheeler the run down. I told her about Squirrel's death that was ruled a suicide and Tyler's death that was ruled accidental and not suspicious. So far I didn't capture her attention. I then filled her in on what we discovered at Flanagan's and the death of the rental agency clerk. Still nothing for her to get excited about. I continued with the visit to Tyler's wife and our conversation with Governor Hainesworth and his assistant. She finally became interested when I let her know Tyler was inquiring about Allegra's death and died shortly thereafter. She was also intrigued when I told her we think Eddie Vincent approached Tyler and had asked about Allegra. She was now leaning forward and jotting notes in her pad.

"Could this just be a coincidence?" she asked.

"Could be. You have been doing this for a while Detective. Do you believe in coincidences?" I asked.

"No. Not even a little," she shot back.

"Well, neither do I. So we are just following where this case is taking us and it took us here. I think that Allegra's murder is somehow tied to the deaths of my friends."

She pulled out her case file and put it in front of her. It was about six inches thick. That means there had been a lot of interviews and a detailed investigation.

"Our names are probably in that case file. We were interviewed thirty-three years ago before we left school," I said.

"I know who you two are. You two and Kavanaugh were interviewed shortly after being you ran the event where Allegra was last seen. I know my case. I have to with all the people I have to report to." She paused and went on. "It is also partly why you are not being treated like suspects. You three all had rock solid alibis for the time of her death and were cleared."

"When did you pick up this cold case?" Bo asked.

"Please don't refer to it as a cold case. At least not around here. This case is still the top priority of the department. My Chief would get an earful from the Selvaggios if they ever thought this was being treated like a cold case. I give quarterly reports to the Chief who in turn provides updates to the Selvaggios. It's never fun to give the "no progress" update. I picked up the case two years ago. My predecessor was not making any progress and he was dismissed from the case. The Selvaggios have little patience when it comes to Allegra's case."

"Have you had any solid leads since you took over?" Bo asked.

"Not really, but they are satisfied with my effort. I did a lot of re-interviews and gave the case a lot of attention. I've had the evidence re-examined and I keep re-running the prints that we couldn't match. I just keep hoping that if I keep at it, my break in the case will come." She was right. Hard work and taking different views of the case evidence often lead to new avenues to explore.

She gave us an overview of her case. "Allegra was found about thirty yards inside a wooded area that surrounded the swimming hole at the quarry. She was last seen at the Enduro event. Many people confirmed her presence there but no one could confirm when she left or if she left alone or with someone. Her car was found parked and unlocked at the swimming hole. She was choked and bludgeoned with a large rock by what is believed to be one unknown assailant. The blow to the head was the official cause of death. Given the severity of the blow, death was likely instant. No witnesses were located at the scene. We surmised that most people who normally go to the swimming hole were likely still at the Enduro event. She was found around two o'clock in the morning by two local teenagers that were there to get some alone time. The boy stayed at the scene while the girl left to call the police. They were cleared as suspects. The M.E. said she had been dead for about eight hours which places the time of death at around six o'clock. Forensics bagged and tagged everything. The car was impounded and is still there."

Bo and I sat there absorbing every word. It was a good thing Brian was not here. This would have been far too painful for him to endure.

Detective Wheeler asked if we wanted to view the crime scene photos. We both agreed to see them. She pulled out what appeared to be about fifty or sixty photos. Some were the gory pictures of Allegra lying in her place of death. Blood all over her sun dress and the ground where her head rested. I took a quick glance and moved on. They were hard to look at. I have seen plenty of crime scenes and crime scene photos but this one was particularly rough to see. I wish I didn't see the gory pictures of her lifeless body. Those images will forever be embedded in my brain. Those pictures will certainly keep me motivated. My only thought before moving on to the other photos was about bringing whoever did this to justice. Make sure he gets the death sentence in one form or another. Bo was thinking the exact same thing.

There were many photos of the car. Allegra's purse was hanging partly off the front passenger seat and some of the contents had fallen to the car floor. It was typical items you would see in a purse. We saw her hairbrush, black comb, several different color hair berets, an eye liner pencil, used and unused tissues, a pen, sunglasses, and her wallet. Some loose change was either already on the floor or fell from her purse or wallet. I also saw her car keys hanging in the ignition. I'll never forget that rainbow-colored peace sign attached to her key chain. I found myself smiling at the thought of Allegra and the happier times.

Wheeler was digesting everything she had just heard. "I think I need to pay Eddie Vincent a visit. I would like to know why after thirty-three years he decided to ask an old friend about Allegra. It may not add up to anything but you never know. How can I get in touch with Eddie?"

"I'm going to see him this morning. I left him a few messages but he hasn't got back to me yet," I said.

"Is that unusual?" she asked.

"Not really. Eddie has a child with health issues and his son is back in the hospital. I figure he has been busy with that."

"I think I will pay him a visit today as well. I have to deal with a personal situation this morning." She paused and continued. "My mother is not well. Early stages of Alzheimers. I am interviewing an in-house aide. I will go see him after that." Wheeler didn't have to volunteer that personal information with me. It made me feel good that she felt comfortable enough with us to share that.

I gave Wheeler Eddie's address and phone number. I also gave her the information on the hospital where his son was in case he wasn't home.

Wheeler gave me her card and personal cell number. I gave her my info as well. She said she wanted to be notified of any development no matter how small or insignificant it might seem. She actually looked somewhat relieved. If nothing else, she wouldn't have to give the "no progress" report to all the people scrutinizing her every move.

Bo and I decided to go back to the hotel to pick up Jessica and Brian and then we would be off to see Eddie. If we couldn't track him down at his home then we'd try the hospital. Jessica didn't know Eddie but Brian will want to see him.

We drove back to the hotel and parked in the parking garage. We got out of our car and went to the elevator that led to the hotel. Two men in suits and overcoats approached the elevator waiting area. They were not there to get onto the elevator.

The taller of the two men said, "Mr. MacMasters and Mr. Bollander, my employer wishes to see you." I had a pretty good idea who these two guys worked for. We had left our guns in the car when we visited the police station and didn't take them out after the visit. We were not armed but if they were who we thought they were, then we would not be needing our weapons.

"Who is your employer? Can we make an appointment for later today?" I asked. I knew the answer but wanted to see how they handled even the slightest resistance to their inquiry.

"This will not wait until later. You two are coming with us now. Mr. Selvaggio is not a person who waits for anyone." The man opened his coat to show he was strapped. He didn't have to show me his gun. I knew who they were the second they approached us. I looked forward to meeting his employer. As he was saying that a large black sedan pulled up to the curb at the elevator. The taller man opened the back door and extended his hand toward the back seat. Before we got into the car we were patted down to be sure we were not packing any weapons.

Bo and I got into the backseat followed by the shorter of the two men. The taller man hopped in the front seat. We drove off to see the head of the most powerful crime boss in the state.

Chapter 36

Eddie was an early riser. He had a few things to get done around the house before he went off to see Billy. He was in a bit of a rush this morning as his chores went a little longer than expected. He decided he had done enough and jumped in the shower to get ready for his visit at the hospital. He got himself cleaned up and ready to go. Eddie grabbed his phone from the kitchen table and saw he had a few messages.

Eddie also saw he had a missed call from Mac. Eddie quickly opened his messages and listened to the most recent. The voice was Mac's and he said something about Eddie being in danger. Eddie was intrigued but was in a rush. He decided he would call Mac back on the way to the hospital.

Eddie grabbed his keys and opened the front door. There standing in front of him on the porch was a well-dressed man with a large scar on his face who was pointing a gun right at his head. Eddie stopped in his tracks. Wolf waved his gun in a motion as to tell Eddie to back up and go back inside. Eddie retreated to the inside of his home followed by Wolf. Eddie recounted the recent events in his life and knew this was not a random robbery. This man was there with a purpose. Eddie didn't have much time to process the situation.

The man with the scar finally spoke. "Mr. Vincent, my employer wants his money back and he wants any copy you made of the picture. And he wants it immediately."

Eddie immediately tried to deny any knowledge of what this man was talking about. "What money? What picture?" Eddie was visibly shaking. "I don't know what you're talking about."

"You know what I am talking about and you do have my employer's money and you do have the copies of the picture. You will turn all of it over to me and you will tell me if anyone else has been given copies of that picture." Wolf reached into his right coat pocket and pulled out a silencer for his gun and began screwing it on the barrel. The slow rotations of the silencer onto the barrel was purposefully done so Eddie could process his fate. Eddie tried one more time to deny any involvement but the situation took an unexpected turn.

"Mr. Vincent, I have no intentions of shooting you. You will die in another manner." Eddie was still shaking but was now confused. Eddie made up his mind that he would not give up the money or the picture. He needed that for his son. Someone would find it and put it to its proper use.

"I don't have your money and know nothing about any picture," Eddie stated in a more assertive voice.

"Mr. Vincent, you can have it your way. If I don't get my employer's money and that picture, you will be dead in a matter of minutes. I will then drive to the hospital and use this gun and this silencer and will shoot your son in his forehead."

Eddie shot out of his seat and yelled at Wolf. "You son of a bitch. You leave my son alone. He has done nothing to you."

Wolf didn't flinch. "Sit back down. It's simple, Mr. Vincent. The money, the picture, and your life in exchange for your son's life."

Eddie slowly sat back down and put his elbows on the table and his face into his hands. He knew it was over. No way would he ever run the risk of bringing even the slightest bit of harm to his son.

"Okay. Okay. I will give you what you want. My son is to not be touched."

"If I get what I want, my job is over and I will have no need to harm your son. If you try to pull any nonsense and I don't get everything, I will not only kill your son but I will make him suffer. You understand?"

Eddie clearly understood. It was over for him and he knew it. His son meant everything to him. With the recent events in Eddie's life, he was somewhat relieved this was all coming to an end. "You will get everything."

Eddie had a few copies of the picture hidden in different places in his home. He retrieved the copies and then went to the safe that was bolted to the floor in his bedroom closet. Wolf was with him every step of the way and the gun was trained on him in case he tried anything stupid. Eddie pulled out a small fire proof box that was contained in the safe and opened it with the key. He handed the pictures and the box to Wolf.

"Mr. Vincent, you will now go back to the kitchen table and hand-write your suicide note."

Eddie had already come to grips with the fact that he was in fact a dead man walking. Eddie sat down as Wolf sat across from him and was counting the money. "There should be a little over eighty thousand left. I spent some on a doctor for my son that offered an unapproved experimental treatment. It didn't seem to have any effect on his condition and that's why he is still in the hospital." Wolf seemed satisfied with that explanation. After all, it was likely the reason he started this blackmailing scheme to begin with.

"Get writing. I don't have all day." Eddie began putting pen to paper. Eddie started thinking about what he wanted to say and how he would say it. Time to start writing.

Friends and Family,

I have been in much pain both physically and mentally for quite some time. I have decided to end my suffering. I apologize for my actions but feel I have no choice. My life has been a good one. My son has been a gift to me and my love for him is eternal. My family has always been there for me and for that I am grateful and I love you all. I may not have accomplished everything I set out to do but I have little to regret.

For my friends- I cherish all of the fun times and memories. I always appreciated all your support for my son and myself. I am just so exhausted. So very exhausted. Please look after WT. I will rest peacefully.

Your son, your father, your friend,

Eddie

Eddie put his pen down and slid the paper across the table to Wolf. Eddie was not shaking anymore. He was at peace with everything. He knew he was going to die but was glad he got to say his good-byes.

Wolf looked at it and seemed to approve. He didn't see anything in there that shouldn't be but he would be sure. "Who is WT?" Wolf asked.

"My son William. He will need to be looked after. I call him WT. Those are his initials. William Thomas."

Wolf was satisfied. He was done counting the money. He placed the money and the copies of the photos in the case and closed it. "Grab your car keys," he told Eddie.

He did as instructed and Wolf walked him out to the garage. The garage door opened and facing outward was a white 1971 Chevy Chevelle. This was no longer the rust bucket from 1983. This was fully restored. No rust. No torn seats. No chipped and faded white paint. The car was now a shiny white color with all polished chrome that could be used as a mirror. It was a beautiful restoration job. This was transformed from a beaten down transportation vehicle to one hundred percent pure American muscle.

Wolf even seemed impressed. "That's a beauty." Eddie wanted to say thanks because of his pride for the car but was that really the appropriate response to the person who is marching you to your death. "Your life will come to an end in the front seat of this car. Get in." Eddie got in the front seat as directed. "Mr. Vincent, you will roll down the windows and start the car. I will be closing the door and will be waiting outside. Once you are dead I will leave. I will check the garage after you are dead. As long as you didn't do anything stupid I will leave you and have no reason to call on your son."

Eddie knew he had no options. He would not take any chances with his son's life. He got in the car and started it up and the engine came to a roar. Wolf handed him the suicide note and told him to place it on the front passenger seat. He gave him a final warning to not do anything stupid or his son would pay the price for it. Eddie slowly rolled down the window. It was a two car garage so Wolf figured it would take less than a half an hour.

Wolf waited patiently. He wanted to call his employer but wanted to make sure everything was officially over. He waited forty minutes figuring that was more than sufficient. He opened the overhead door and saw Eddie slumped over in the driver's seat. The car was still running. He let the garage air out for a minute then went in. He looked around to make sure Eddie did not alter the suicide note or leave any other clues as to the circumstances of his death or about the identification of his employer. Eddie did no such thing. There were no signs of life. Wolf pulled the garage door closed and walked to his car. Eddie Vincent was dead and everything was recovered. Job over.

Chapter 37

As Wolf was paying a visit to Eddie, we were being escorted to the sprawling estate of Carmine Selvaggio. We had driven by this place when we were in school but never entered the grounds. It was a short drive. It only took about ten minutes to get there. There was no talking on the way over despite my efforts to find out what this was about and who we were meeting with. The Selvaggio associates were tight-lipped and didn't respond to anything I asked except to tell me to shut up a few times. The car slowed down as we approached the front entrance. There was an electronic iron gate with a small guardhouse on the inside. I was sure anyone manning that guardhouse would be heavily armed. When the gates were closed there was a large letter S formed in the middle when the two sides of the gate were combined. The large S no doubt represented the Selvaggio name. The driver gave a quick hand signal and the gate began to open. As we approached the house, we saw beautiful gardens and a perfectly manicured lawn. It was obvious that a lot of care and attention was given the grounds at the Selvaggio estate.

We were dropped off at the top of the circular driveway and walked between the pillars that flanked the entryway. The front double doors looked to be solid mahogany and ten feet tall with an oversized decorative brass knocker with a large S in the middle of each door. They sure liked to display that S logo all over the place.

The two men escorted us into the home. We were greeted with a spacious foyer with curved staircases on both sides and an excessively large crystal chandelier hanging from the second floor ceiling. The floor was tastefully done in one foot by two foot Carrara polished white Italian marble tiles. The walls were equally impressive with two-toned gold and brown silk wallpaper.

We were escorted past the foyer and brought into a room that seemed to be part office and part sitting room. There was a large oak desk with a high back leather chair behind it. There were assorted chairs and a couch scattered throughout the office area. There was also a fireplace and various oriental rugs, couches and chairs. We were directed to the fireplace area and told to make ourselves comfortable.

Bo and I grabbed two chairs that were next to each other that faced the fireplace. I looked around the room and the walls were decorated with fine art in the fireplace area and more personal items in the office portion of the room. I also noticed surveillance cameras strategically placed throughout the room. I have no doubt that our every move was being recorded and scrutinized. We sat patiently until our host decided to greet us.

We sat there for about five minutes before two men entered the room. One was the smaller of the two men that picked us up at the elevator and the other was Carmine Selvaggio Jr.

He was no longer the young twenty something year old wise guy with the sweat suit and gold chains dangling from his neck. He had graduated to business suits and a flashy Rolex. He still may have had the gold chains but they would be hidden under his buttoned to the top shirt and two hundred dollar tie. He left the jacket out of the ensemble and his rolled up sleeves showed off his powerful forearms and biceps. The associate walked in side by side with him and said "This is Jack MacMasters and Tim Bollander."

That was the extent of the introductions. Carmine Jr. was a man of actions and not words. It was time to get down to business. No hand shakes. No "thank for coming" was offered. Carmine sat in a high back leather chair while his associate stood by his side.

"I understand that you were at the police station asking about my sister." He didn't wait too long for a response. "I want to know why." Wheeler was right. The Selvaggios have eyes and ears all over the place. It could have been Venters on the night shift desk or Chief Lutz himself. It could have been both or someone else for all we know.

I spoke up first. "Mr. Selvaggio, we knew your sister when we were in college in 1984. She was a friend of ours. We were all very saddened by her death. She was a special person."

"Listen here. That is not an answer to my question. When I ask a question, I want the answer to the question I asked. Now tell me why you went to the police station and asked about Allegra. The next words out of your mouth will be an answer to that question. You understand?"

I did understand. This was his show. He did a nice job of making us feel uneasy. Bo and I could handle ourselves in a nice back alley scrum but this was not that. I came here with the full intention of letting him know what was going on. He had us there to shake us down for information but he didn't know I was there to see if I could find out anything about why my friends were dying. And his sister's death seemed to be at the core of it.

"Two friends of ours died in the last month under unusual circumstances and I think your sister's death may somehow have something to do with it. I came here hoping to find out if there is a possible tie from Allegra's murder to the murders of my friends." I put it all out there for him to digest. "I went to the police station to see if Detective Wheeler could walk me through her case. I have some experience with murder investigations. I am a recently retired Detective."

"What makes you think my sister's death is related?" His tone had changed and now it looked like it might turn into a cordial exchange of information. But people like Carmine Selvaggio Jr. are quite unpredictable so I would be cautious in what information I will gave him.

We had been operating under the premise that Eddie inquired about Allegra's case to Tyler in the conversation that was partially overheard by Jenny Evigan. Then Tyler furthered the inquiry to Donald Keohane. There will be no mention of Eddie Vincent to Carmine Jr. His goons would be out the door the second I mentioned Eddie initiated the questions about Allegra's death.

"One of our friends that died worked for Governor Hainesworth. His wife mentioned to us that he spoke with someone that asked about Allegra but she didn't know who asked him. Our friend then went and talked to the Governor's Chief of Staff about it and a week later he was dead." He was listening and digesting but kept quiet to let me go on. "A few weeks later another friend of ours died in what was made to look like a suicide. We did some digging and know he was murdered. We tied a car to the murderer. It was a rental car out of a suburb of Harrisburg." I could see him putting two and two together being everyone knew the Governor's office was in Harrisburg. "We followed the trail only to find the rental clerk was shot to death. We think that whoever is doing this may not be done. We want to find him before he finds us."

I went on to explain about the surveillance video that we were checking. I also told him that we were followed by two of Governor Hainesworth's associates and that the Governor said he just wanted to keep tabs on us being he had an interest in seeing Allegra's murderer brought to justice. I would not speculate any further on Governor Hainesworth's involvement. I will let Carmine Jr. draw his own conclusions.

"Is that everything?"

"That is all of it," I said.

As I was responding the door was slowly opening. In walked a very old and frail man in a bathrobe and slippers. He had a nurse escorting him through the door who had one hand on his arm and the other one wheeling in his oxygen tank. There was no talking as the man walked toward Carmine Jr. The associate ran to the office and grabbed a chair and placed it next to Carmine Jr's chair.

Carmine Jr. stood up and took a step toward his father. "Pop. Have a seat. Sit here." Carmine Sr. was easily in his late eighties or early nineties and in obvious poor health. He was out of breath but was able to sit down without incident. He seemed relieved to be sitting again. It appeared that walking to this meeting took quite a bit out of him. Carmine Sr. gathered his breath and leaned over to whisper something to his son. Carmine filled him in on what had been talked about already. Carmine Sr. again leaned toward his son and whispered some more words. I don't know if he was intending to whisper or if that was all he could muster up with his current state of health.

"My father is not well these days. He has never been the same man since Allegra was taken from us. As you can see our family has money. We also have power and if we want something we get it. None of those things mean anything to him anymore. What we don't have is Allegra's murderer. My father wants nothing else in life right now except to see his daughter's killer pay for his mistake."

"If we can help in any way, we will. If the person who is killing our friends killed your sister then we want the same thing," Bo said.

"My father said to offer our services to you. Whatever you need, you just call. We have resources that may not be available to you otherwise." I think I knew what he meant but I decided not to inquire.

"We appreciate that, but right now we're chasing a ghost. We don't know where he is or if he is after us or another friend of ours."

Carmine Jr. looked like he was processing things in his mind. He then spoke up again. "Hainesworth" followed by a brief pause," he turned out to be so disappointing. He looked my father in the eyes and vowed that he would get Allegra's case solved. He was in charge of my sister's case. The initial investigation ran through him. He never delivered on his promise."

"I had a hard time getting a read on Governor Hainesworth when we met with him. He seemed genuinely interested in any developments in your sister's case. I was surprised that we found out from his associate that he was in charge of the case. I keep wondering why he just didn't tell us himself," I responded.

"What? You think Hainesworth was somehow involved? If I thought for one second that he had anything to do with it, he would be a dead man already."

"No. Not really. He had no motive. There's nothing we know of that would tie him to your sister before her murder." The old man's eyes cringed every time murder or death was mentioned. He wore his pain on his sleeve.

"He knew her. He definitely knew her before she was killed." Carmine Sr. cringed again at the thought. It also stopped me in my tracks.

"Knew her? Knew her how?" I asked.

"He definitely knew her. I just don't know if he ever met her. He never said. Hainesworth's younger sister and Allegra were roommates in boarding school in their last two years of high school."

I tried not to react but this was stunning to me. It was time for us to end this conversation and get out of here. I think we needed to pay another visit to the beloved governor.

Carmine Jr. gave me his phone number and expects to be the first call if we find out anything. He turned to his associate and nodded towards the door. "Thank you for seeing me. My associate will take you back to wherever you need to go." Carmine Sr. sat there and nodded his agreement but didn't offer any words.

Carmine Jr. has come a long way since he was nothing more than an arm breaking goon for his father a half a lifetime ago. Now he was the boss. He looked the part. He acted the part. Now we were going to have him breathing down our necks looking for answers. I was beginning to know how Wheeler felt.

We decided we would go see Eddie and have Brian and Jessica meet us over there. We would fill them in when we saw them. After seeing Eddie, the plan was to go see Governor Hainesworth again and probe around. Maybe we could make him feel uneasy enough to put him in panic mode. I know from experience that people in panic mode make plenty of mistakes.

Chapter 38

"Brian. It's Mac. I think we need to go back to Harrisburg. I'll fill you in later. Can you two meet us at Eddie's house?"

"We don't have a car. Text me his address and we will Uber over there," Brian said.

"No need. My car is in the hotel lot. We got picked up by Selvaggio's guys. I'll explain later. My spare keys are in my shaving kit. Take my car and meet us at Eddie's. I'll send you his address."

Before I clicked off Brian started up again. "Mac, we got a good look at the guy on video from Flanagan's. It's him. We are sure of it. He's an ugly sucker. Well dressed but an ugly mug. He's got a large gash on the side of his face."

"Nice work, Brian. We'll have to get that video to Rodgers and Wheeler. I'll see you in a few at Eddie's," and then I clicked off.

I gave Selvaggio's assistant the address to Eddie's house and asked him to drop us off there.

*   *   *   *

Wolf was relieved. He was finally able to dial up his employer and report some good news. "It's over. Vincent was the guy. I've got all the copies of the picture and about eighty grand. He said he spent some on some doctor for his kid. I have everything stashed in a storage locker for now." There was a sigh of relief on the other end of the phone.

"Are you sure there are no more copies. I want this over and done with."

"I'm sure. I had some leverage on him. He gave it all up."

"Okay, good. What is going on with McMasters and the rest?"

"They are all at the hotel. I'm in the hotel lot now in case I need to deal with them today, too. I tracked his car to the police station again this morning and now it's back in the lot."

MacMasters was getting too close. Wolf knew McMasters would never let this go. Especially after he found out about Eddie Vincent.

"Good work, Wolf. I want to be sure. Kill them all and I don't care how you do it."

"Even the girl?"

"Kill her, too. No loose ends. There will be something extra for you when we settle up." Wolf wasn't planning to ask for more money. This job hadn't gone as expected and went on far too long. He would have been happy to throw them in for free.

Just as Wolf was getting the go ahead to do MacMasters and company, he saw Kavanaugh and Jessica walking together in the hotel parking lot. No signs of MacMasters and Bollander. Wolf knew just how he would end this job once and for all.

"It must be my lucky day," Wolf told his employer. "Here comes Kavanaugh and the girl walking right to me. I'll call you when it's over." No further conversation as they both hung up.

*   *   *   *

The ride to Eddie's was uneventful. No conversation from the driver but none was expected. He dropped us at the end of Eddie's driveway in the road. We would have to walk up the couple hundred yard long driveway. It would have been nice to get the full ride but I decided not to push it. "Thanks for the ride," I said with tongue planted firmly in cheek. He just grunted and drove off leaving us to walk the rest of the way.

We approached the house and saw Eddie's pickup truck parked near his garage. We felt pretty good that Eddie was likely home. We thought there was a chance he might have already left for the hospital to visit his son. I walked onto the porch with Bo at my side. Bo knocked and yelled Eddie's name. No answer and no one was stirring in the house. Bo turned the door knob and found it to be unlocked. Bo slowly opened the door and poked his head in. He yelled for Eddie a few more times. Same result. No answer and no one stirring about. We were convinced Eddie wasn't in the house. We went back outside and started yelling for Eddie again. Still no answer and nothing stirring.

We leaned up against the back of Eddie's pickup and decided to just wait for Brian and Jessica to come get us. We were talking about the day's events as Bo said, "Do you hear that?"

We stopped talking and just listened. I now heard it, too. It was a feint humming noise coming from the garage. We walked toward the garage door and the sound was more pronounced. It then became clear. It was the sound of an idling car engine. We ran the last several steps toward the garage door and lifted the wooden overhead door. As the door was being raised, it began to reveal a beautifully restored white 1971 Chevy Chevelle, Eddie's lifelong favorite toy. I knew Eddie had restored it but this was the first time I was seeing it in person. He would go to our reunions and flash pictures of that car like a father with new born triplets. The pictures were nice but didn't do it justice. The car was a sight to see. The restoration was perfect and this car sat in immaculate condition. It had come a long way since I first saw that beater in college. My quick reminiscence was short lived. As the door continued to rise we were now staring at the lifeless body of our friend Eddie Vincent. We saw him at the same time and Bo ran to the driver's side door and opened it and turned the ignition off. I opened the passenger side door to get to Eddie from that side. I immediately checked for a pulse or any other signs of life. None could be found. I looked over to Bo and shook my head. He knew exactly what it meant. Another friend of ours was gone.

I told Bo that we needed to leave everything as it sat. This was no doubt a crime scene despite me staring at what looked to be a suicide note. I left the note in place and read it. The hand writing would be checked. I had a feeling this would be a match to Eddie's hand writing. I took out my phone and took a picture of the note and left it exactly as I found it.

Bo was pissed off. I was pissed off. We were both thinking the same thing. Whoever was responsible for this was going to pay for it. We would press on and figure this out. Governor Hainesworth was going to see a very different side of both of us.

I dialed up Brian to see where he was. A male voice answered the phone but it wasn't Brian's voice. The man said, "I have Kavanaugh and the girl. I am going to kill them and then coming for you two."

"Who the hell is this? You're a dead man." It obviously wasn't resonating with him being he began to laugh on the other end of the phone. I had to think fast. I figured this entire mess had started over some type of blackmail. This guy who was killing my friends was definitely working for someone else and was no doubt in search of something. I had to take a chance. "I know who you are and who you are working for and I'm ready to take what I have to the police. I'm at Eddie Vincent's place now and just found him in the garage. I also found something else there. Something you may want." I waited for a reaction but none was forthcoming. "You lay one hand on those two and I'll track both of you down and kill you both myself."

"You say you have the picture?" Now I was sure it was about a picture. I just don't know what picture he is talking about.

"You're damn right I have it. And if one hair on their head is out of place, I'm going to the police with it then I'm coming after you. I know what you look like. You and that big ugly scar on your face." I hadn't actually seen him yet but he didn't know that. At least now I knew he would be taking us seriously.

Wolf paused to think over his options. He didn't want to take a chance that he didn't find all of the pictures. If he missed one then he needed to clean up his own mess. Wolf quickly adjusted his plans and figured a way he would kill all four at once but he needed a little time to put his plan into action.

"Meet me at the old brewery on Stiles Street in two hours. If there is even a sniff of police, your friends will have an unexpected blast. You're a smart man. I'm sure you can figure what that means. Bring Bollander and the picture. We do the exchange and I will let the girl go. You, Bollander and Kavanaugh are still dead men."

I knew where the brewery was. It had been a flourishing business when we were in school but closed several years ago. It was remote but might work for us. Bo had heard everything and was ready to go. Time to get this guy and put him down hard.

"We'll be there. You can count on it."

"If you're a second late, your friends are dead. And just so you know, it would be a mistake to underestimate me." The phone line went dead.

I called Wheeler and told her about Eddie's situation. I told her I couldn't wait for her and I would check in with her later. We didn't have a car. We looked over and saw Eddie's pickup. Bo ran inside and quickly found the keys and said "Found 'em. Lets get going." Bo started up the truck and we drove off. We needed to figure out how we could pull this off.

There was no way I was bringing the police in. This guy was a pro and would sniff it out for sure. The odds of us pulling this off were about the same as a person getting struck by lightning while on the way to the lottery store to cash the winning Power Ball ticket. Regardless of what we figured out, we were going to need a miracle.

I knew this guy with the ugly scar on his face would never let Jessica go. It didn't matter, we had our meeting and we would soon be face to face with this guy. His veiled reference to Brian and Jessica getting an unexpected blast told me he was planning on keeping them hostage with the threat of explosives. This guy was likely a skilled assassin. He might be skilled but I also knew someone who possessed similar skills and someone I trusted with my life.

I dialed up my friend. "It's Mac. I need your help."

"When and where?" Trotter responded.

Chapter 39

We drove back to the hotel in Eddie's truck and regrouped. We really didn't have a plan and didn't think we would be coming up with anything. Our goal was to get ourselves together with this guy in the same building and figure it out from there.

I filled in Trotter with most of the details. He was already in his truck and was heading our way before I got off the phone with him. I told him that we had two hours and it would be a risk to be late even one minute. Trotter had the address in his GPS and told me he was due in at a little after three o'clock. I needed him there by two forty-five and he knew that. He said he would make it there by two forty-five one way or the other. He knew I was going in before that time with or without him. I was not taking any chances with Brian and Jessica's lives. I told Trotter to text me when he was on site so my phone would chime when the text came in. Trotter wasn't much of a text person but he would make an exception for me. He was probably on the phone now with his wife asking her what a text was. He was going to need a clean trip. No red lights. No traffic jams. No cops pulling over his speeding truck.

We switched back to my car in the hotel lot. I checked and made sure our guns were still there. We had put them in a box in the back when we went into the police station earlier. In hindsight it may have been more prudent to have Selvaggio's assistant drive us back to the hotel to get my truck before we went to Eddie's house. That way we would have had our guns with us if we encountered any problems.

The waiting was painful. We figured this guy with the scar needed some time to set up his scene for us. He all but said to me that he was going to be using explosives. I am assumed he was using the time to set up his scene as he wanted it. And I was afraid that included having Brian and Jessica wired up. Trotter was an expert and I was a novice. Bo was below me on the explosives knowledge scale. His only knowledge came from the movies. *Cut the red wire. Cut the blue wire. Cut the yellow wire.* None of which would be any use to us in this situation. Bo grabbed the wire cutters from my tool box and held them up to show me he was ready for anything. I just shook my head.

"What? I'm a boy scout. Be prepared," Bo said.

"Gimme that thing." I grabbed it out of his hand and shoved it in my back pocket while still shaking my head. If Brian and Jessica had to rely on Bo or me to disarm a bomb then we were all in big trouble.

"Hey, you never know." Who was I to argue with that logic?

We arrived at the brewery about fifteen minutes early and parked a block away. I didn't want this guy seeing us and sizing us up before we got together. I called Trotter and he said he was making good time but was still about twenty minutes away. He told us to stall as best as we could.

It was now two forty. We pulled from the curb and drove into the back of the parking lot. I saw a lone vehicle parked near the rear overhead door. The rear of the building had a loading area and some parking but was otherwise flanked by a six-foot-high chain link fence with brush and shrubbery covering most of it. The place was desolate and an obvious good choice for a clandestine meeting such as this one. We did our final prep. Our guns were loaded. Our nerves were flaring but were in check. And, of course we were packing wire cutters. It was show time.

There was a metal door to the right of the loading dock overhead door. We walked up the stairs and saw the door was already cracked open. I pulled the door open and we walked in. At first I didn't see or hear anything. We slowly walked further into the open space and checked out the surroundings. There wasn't much to see. The space was vacant but there were other sections behind walls that had to be checked. There was also a second floor where interior offices were located. This upper office area had steps on two sides.

We walked toward the first set of steps. Still nothing. We decided to not go up the steps and continued on. Around the corner there was another section of the building set behind a large sliding wooden door which was half opened. We stepped into the space. This was the warehouse section of the space. The offices overlooked both the warehouse space and the loading dock space. As we took a look around we saw both Brian and Jessica. They were each tied to a chair which was chained to cement pillar. They were about twenty feet apart from each other. I saw they both had a flashing red light coming from their chest area. As we walked closer it was clear they were both wearing a vest and were fully strapped with explosives.

Bo and I stopped. Brian and Jessica both had gags in their mouths and terror in their eyes. While they may have been glad to see us, they knew their situation has hopeless. These vests looked quite elaborate. I didn't think Bo's little wire cutters would be doing us much good. Still no sign of the guy with the ugly face scar.

It didn't take long. There was a sound of footsteps coming down the metal stairs where the second floor offices were located. As the well- dressed man with the big ugly scar on his face descended the steps, my anger came flooding back. I wanted to pull out my gun and put one right between his eyes. He was walking confidently and was not the least bit worried about gunfire heading his way. He knew we had assessed the situation and wouldn't do anything rash until our friends were out of harm's way.

"We finally meet," the man said. "I have met a lot of your friends as you know." He was baiting me to say something stupid. I decided to stay cool and let this play out. I still had no text from Trotter and needed to stall. "Your friend Vincent did the right thing. He was man enough to trade his life for his son's life. It was almost a shame I had to make him die. If he wasn't so greedy, we probably wouldn't be standing here."

"You son of a bitch. You're a dead man," Bo shouted and made a few strides toward the man. He held up what I assumed was a detonator device. Bo stopped as he thought better of it.

I tried to remain calm and get some dialogue going. "How are we going to do this? I want Jessica and these two guys out of here before we do any business." Bo shook his head to confirm he wasn't going anywhere regardless of what I had just said.

"Business? Is that what you think this is? A business meeting? I am afraid you are sadly mistaken. This is not a business meeting. I am going to get that picture and the four of you will die. If it helps, I promise you it will be quick and painless."

"Let the lady go. She doesn't know anything. She can't cause you any trouble." I tried to make an effort to get her out of here but knew it was a useless plea. I was trying to buy some time. *C'mon Trotter. Where the heck are you?*

"She's not going anywhere. At least not in one piece." The man smirked as he said it. "She is, what we call in my business, a loose end."

"You're making a big mistake. I know you're working for Hainesworth and I have made sure that picture will get to the right people if we don't walk out of here." I took a chance at a bluff. The man looked puzzled.

"Hainesworth? Who? You don't have the slightest clue. Do you?" I can read people and this man was genuinely surprised to hear the name Hainesworth. This was not good. I was hoping the mention of his employer would unnerve him but he didn't flinch. This was something we were counting on. Our little bit of leverage just went out the window. There was no way this guy was working for Andrew Hainesworth and that was going to be a big problem.

The man appeared to suddenly feel better about his position. If I didn't know who he was working for then how could I have the picture that he was looking for? I'm sure the picture was something compromising to his employer.

The man had the detonator in his left hand and reached for his gun with his right hand. He began to wave his gun and told us to take out our guns slowly and throw them to the side. We did as requested.

"If I am reading this right, you have no picture to offer me." The man was right and Bo and I knew where this was headed. Still no sign of Trotter. The time for idle chatter and stalling was over. Whatever was going to happen is going to happen now.

The man started laughing out loud. He knew it was finally over. He would get rid of the four of us now and move on with his life and then on to the next job. Bo was about ten feet away and started a mad dash toward the man. I followed his lead. The man immediately clicked on his detonator and threw it to the ground. That started a clock on the chests of Brian and Jessica. They saw it happen and were squirming about but they could do little to create any movement.

As Bo ran toward the man, he raised his gun and a shot rang out. Bo went down hard. He was hit in the chest, staggered backward and fell back on the cement floor and slammed his head. Bo was not moving.

I was right next to Bo and I kept going and screaming at the man like a crazed man. The man turned to me but I was on him too quick. He got a shot off but I was already swatting at his arm to misdirect any shot. I hit him hard enough to dislodge the gun from his hand.

This man was several inches taller than me and had me outweighed by quite a bit. The man wasn't fat. He was thick. And he was strong. I soon found out he was also agile and skilled at close combat.

I immediately engaged him and got an elbow to his jaw. He was slightly stunned but would press on. He responded with a punch to my face and knee into my stomach. He buckled me over. I immediately launched the back of my head upward and connected with the bottom of his chin. I heard some teeth break. The man was stunned and went to grab for something in his rear pocket. I began punching furiously at his head. He had to take the blows being the hand he should be blocking them with was pulling a knife out and now it was being thrust toward my side. I deflected the arm thrust and was able to grab his wrist. I contorted it to the point of a bone snapping. The man screamed out and the knife was lofted in the air. I grabbed the knife out of the air as it was making its descent and with all my rage built up, I plunged the knife into his chest. He went limp and dropped to the ground. I had no time to check on this guy. I had one friend already down and two more with bombs strapped to their chests. I knew the bombs had been activated but I don't yet know how much time I had. Still no sign of Trotter.

I ran towards Jessica and Brian and saw the clock on the top of the bomb was ticking down and was now under three minutes. I quickly took the gags off but couldn't get them out of the chairs. There was also no way to remove the vests. They were locked on and there was also a likelihood that any attempt to remove the vest would cause it to detonate. I tried to dial up Trotter to see where he was. Even if he wasn't here yet, he might be able to talk me through the disarming procedure when I explained what it looked like. My hand was shaking as I tried to make the call.

I heard Brian scream. "Mac. Look out!" I turned and saw the ugly man with the ugly scar up from where I put him down. The knife was out of his chest and he grabbed the gun from the ground. I thought the man was done so I didn't bother getting my gun. He started to stumble slowly toward me and raised the gun. It was trained right at my chest. The gun went off and I flinched and instinctively closed my eyes. I didn't feel the impact of his bullet. I opened my eyes to find the ugly scar man lying in a pool of his own blood. He didn't have to worry about that scar anymore. Half the man's face was blown off.

Trotter stood there with his forty-four caliber hand cannon extending out from his right hand. "Sorry I'm late, Mac. I got here as quick as I could," Trotter said. Trotter saw Brian and Jessica and ran over to them. He moved quite fast for a man of his advanced years. "Oh, shit," was the first thing he said when he saw what he was dealing with. The clock was under two minutes. Bo was still lying motionless forty feet away.

"Tell me what to do," I yelled to Trotter. Trotter opened a small satchel and handed me a screwdriver. We were running out of time. Trotter didn't have time to disarm both. The two were set too far apart from each other.

Brian sensed the situation and yelled to Trotter. "Get her out of here. Now!" Trotter went to work on Jessica. He unscrewed the top of the timer in a matter of seconds. He exposed the wires and looked it over. He told me to do the same for Brian. The timer was now under a minute and counting down fast. I began unscrewing as best as I could but I just wasn't as fast as Trotter. Under thirty seconds. I got the cover opened. Trotter was done assessing. Twenty seconds. Trotter pulled out his wire cutters and cut two wires. Ten seconds. Jessica's timer had stopped. She didn't have any time to celebrate. She turned her attention to her new friend Brian.

"Cut the blue and orange wires at the same time." Trotter yelled the instructions and slid the wire cutters across the cement floor. With all his adrenaline, he ended up sliding the wire cutters too far. I didn't have time to go after them and get the wires cut. Five seconds. I quickly realized I had my own wire cutters. I reached in my back pocket and pulled it out and did as Trotter instructed. I cut the right wires and the timer shut down with one tick left on it. Somehow Bo knew those wire cutters would come in handy. And they sure did.

I ran over to Bo and he was non-responsive. I called Wheeler and told her we needed an ambulance for Bo right away. I also explained that Brian and Jessica still had vests that would need to be removed by the bomb squad. Soon the one-time flourishing brewery had its most activity since it closed up shop. Sirens were blaring.

Trotter was still assessing Brian and Jessica to make sure they were in no danger. He felt confident that there was no further threat to them at the moment. The bomb squad would take over and make sure they got safely freed from the vests.

I was now kneeling next to my best friend with his head cradled in my chest and using my shirt to apply pressure to help control the bleeding. I was talking to him the entire time. I didn't know if he could hear me or not. The paramedics finally arrived and moved me swiftly out of the way.

I went over and joined Trotter. Jessica and Brian were now being assessed by some police personnel.

Jessica turned to Brian and said, "Thank you, Brian. You're a true friend." She, of course, was talking about Brian yelling to Trotter to save her at the expense of his own life. Brian didn't say anything. He just nodded. She turned to me. "Thank you, Mac. I just knew you would come through for us. How is Bo?"

"He's breathing but has a very faint pulse. He's lost a lot of blood. We can only pray at this point."

Bo was now on a stretcher and presumably in good hands. Trotter walked past the man with half a face and spit on him. He then gathered his things in his satchel and waited with me to be brought down to the police station.

I felt some relief that the man that killed my friends was dead. But it would all be for naught if we didn't ever figure out who hired this thug. I now knew that Governor Hainesworth was not behind this. This was going to be a problem. If not him, then who? I didn't even know where to look at this point.

Chapter 40

The police flooded the scene at the abandoned brewery. There was one dead body on the concrete slab. One other person was unconscious and bleeding from his chest. The EMTs had tended to Bo and transported him to the nearest trauma center. He had lost a lot of blood and his pulse was still faint. His fate was not yet decided. I was not able to go with him as I was detained by the police.

Brian and Jessica were now fully freed from the explosive vests. They were relieved when Trotter and I disarmed the detonators but it took some more time to safely get the vests off. Wolf had the vests locked and added a trip wire in case someone had tried to remove it before his mission was accomplished. The bomb squad went to work and removed the vests. It was a little unnerving watching people work on your friends when they were in their full bomb disarming gear. Once the vests were finally off, they were both able to breathe a sigh of relief. Jessica and Brian exchanged a long hug. I went over and put my arms around both of them.

The police went through the assailant's car and didn't appear to find anything of any evidentiary value. That was no surprise. They would, of course, tow it to their impound yard for further inspection. No clue was left behind to provide any insight as to who his employer was.

The police came over and let us know we all needed to go down to the station to give our statements. They assured us it wouldn't take too long. They knew we wanted to get to the hospital to be with Bo as soon as possible. Then it dawned on me. I needed to call Bo's wife and break the news. I decided to call Katie instead. She was Faith's best friend and she would know how to deliver the news.

I dialed the phone and Katie picked up on the first ring. I hadn't spoken to her since yesterday so she was likely worrying why I hadn't checked in. "Hi, Honey."

"I've been worried sick. Are you okay?" Katie was a little annoyed but this would change in a matter of seconds.

"I'm fine, Honey. A lot happened today. I don't have time to get into everything." She knew something was wrong.

"What happened? Is everyone okay?" she shot back.

"Actually, no. We got the guy but Bo is in the hospital. He was shot." I could hear her heart skip a beat.

"Oh, my God. How is he? Does Faith know yet?" she asked.

"Bo is going right into surgery. He was unconscious and non-responsive when he was taken away to the hospital. He was shot in the chest. He has a pulse and he was breathing." I tried to soften it somewhat but that fact was my best friend was fighting for his life. "Faith doesn't know yet. I told the officer in charge at the scene that I would take care of telling her."

"Text me the address for the hospital. I will call Faith and let her know. I will pack a bag and get right over there to pick her up. We will be up there as soon as possible. Keep me posted if you hear any news."

Katie was amazing. She knew there would be time to get the entire story. Now wasn't that time. Her best friend needed her and she would make sure she was by her side every step of the way.

"Thank you, Honey. I will fill you in on everything when you get up here. I have to go give a statement to the police now."

I clicked off and was taken down to the police station by one of the officers. Trotter was taken there as well by a different officer in a separate car. They were keeping us apart until both statements were taken. Even though it appeared our story was plausible, they were not coming to any conclusions until all statements were taken and the scene was fully processed.

We arrived at the police station and were taken into separate interrogation rooms. Brian and Jessica were brought in as well but were not being interrogated. They were victims and witnesses. Trotter and I were not so we were being treated as suspects until cleared. We were both Mirandized and provided our version of the events. I was done with my interview and they were satisfied with what I had to say. I saw Trotter exiting the interrogation room and was laughing with the detective. The detective appeared to be in his mid-sixties and maybe just a few years younger than Trotter. As it turned out they were both veterans of the Vietnam War and likely walked some of the same dirt. They exchanged a handshake and Trotter came over to me. He knew I wanted to get over to the hospital. He wanted to stay local in case the police needed him again. He told me he would be heading back soon. I gave him my room key and told him he could use my room to clean himself up if he wanted to. He asked me to keep him posted on Bo's health and we went our own ways.

It was nice to have found the person that killed my friends but we were still missing the largest piece to the puzzle. Unfortunately, the identity of the person that had hired that assassin was going to the grave with him. We were out of leads. I highly doubt there would be any trail left behind by him. The police had already processed his phone and other than a few calls to some restaurants and hotels there was only one number he had called more than once. That number turned into a dead end. It was just one burner phone calling another untraceable burner phone. Whoever hired him was obviously smart enough to ensure there would be nothing that could get tracked back to him. The police would search financial records once he got identified. Anyone that was smart enough to communicate through two untraceable burner phones was not dumb enough to leave a trail in the financials.

I arrived at the hospital and saw Katie and Faith sitting in the waiting room outside the operating rooms. They had not received any information yet other than he was in surgery. I went right up to Katie and gave her a hug and a kiss. I moved over to Faith and gave her a long hug. I tried to assure that everything was going to be all right. But the truth of the matter was I had no idea if things were going to be all right or not.

About a half hour later the surgeon came out. He was removing his surgical mask and gloves as he walked toward us. We all stood up simultaneously and started walking toward the surgeon.

"How is he?" Faith asked. She couldn't get the words out quick enough.

"He is going to be fine. The bullet went through and didn't cause any significant internal damage. He was very lucky. A few inches to either side and it would have been much worse." He didn't need to say the last part in front of Faith but at least he opened the conversation with Bo being fine. "We are going to keep him for a few days. He hit his head pretty hard and was concussed. We will monitor that to make sure everything is okay with that."

We all thanked the surgeon and asked when we could see him. He told us it would be at least an hour. A nurse would be out to let us know.

Brian and Jessica had joined us and we gave them the positive update. Brian and I went down to the cafeteria and grabbed some coffee for all of us. We were not leaving until we spoke with our friend. The nurse finally walked in after about a half hour of waiting and said that Bo was awake. She said immediate family only could go see him. Faith grabbed mine and Katie's arms and said we are the immediate family, then looked over to Brian and Jessica and said they were, too.

The nurse knew exactly what was going on but let it slide. She told us he was still heavily sedated and might float in and out. She asked that we keep the visit short. The five of us walked in there and I saw my friend lying there with his chest and shoulder wrapped up and a gauze bandage covering his entire head. He had tubes coming out of everywhere. He had an IV drip pumping morphine into his system to mask the pain. His eyes were open and he managed a small smile when he saw Faith. She went right over to him and gingerly kissed him all over his face. She didn't want to hurt him. She didn't know what parts hurt and what didn't.

He didn't have much strength but managed to extend his right thumb upward to tell us he was going to be fine. He tried to mouth a few words but just didn't have the strength yet. Faith let him know what the doctor said and told him he needed to get some rest. Bo managed another little smile and then closed his eyes. Those few moments with Bo were enough to raise our spirits. We knew he was strong and he was a fighter. We knew he would be walking out of this place in a few days.

As we were about to head out, one of the nurses came in. He said his name was Evan and he was assigned to Bo. He said he would be monitoring him for the next eight hours. He went over to Bo's bed and checked his chart. He checked the monitors and the IV drip. All was good. He told us he would take good care of him and for us not to worry about a thing. Evan stopped in the bathroom before he left the room. He left the door open. He was only using the sink so he didn't seek any privacy. After he was done using the sink he looked into the mirror and pulled his comb out and fixed his hair until every last hair was in its rightful place. He spread his raised arms out to each side to confirm he liked what was he was looking at. *This guy must think he's The Fonz.* He walked out and went on to his next patient.

The thing that had been bothering me since I met with Wheeler and looked at the crime scene photos finally hit me like a ton of bricks. I finally figured out who was responsible for this entire mess. I pulled out the Facebook photo taken of Tyler and Hainesworth at the new hospital opening and took a closer look at it. I had been looking at all the wrong people in this picture. The key to the photo was not Albert Hainesworth or his staff members. I focused in on the elderly couple standing behind gubernatorial candidate Michael Guilford. The old man may have been thirty three years older and forty five pounds lighter but there was no doubt in my mind that I was staring at my old *friend* Bucky G. He was no longer the barrel-chested fire plug of a man of 1984. He was old and frail and looked like he already had one foot in the grave and the other on an oil slick. Everything just fell into place. I finally got it. I knew who killed my friends and why.

I told Katie that I had something to take care of and told her I would meet her back at the hotel later tonight. I didn't give her time to respond. I kissed her on the cheek and took off. Brian and Jessica had been through enough already today. I wasn't going to involve them with this. They had been through quite enough already for one day.

I went outside and did a little checking to find a phone number. I found what I was looking for and dialed the number. I spoke with the man's receptionist and let her know who I was and needed to be put through immediately. She put me on hold and a few seconds later I heard a voice that I hadn't heard in thirty three years. I told him what I had planned and we needed to meet immediately. He said he was about an hour away but would be there. He told me that he would only meet with me and me alone. He said he would be coming alone. *I somehow doubted that.* He seemed as anxious as me to finally put an end to this. I hung up and made two more calls.

The last of the two calls was to Trotter. I filled him in on what I figured out and told him we needed a plan. We met at my hotel room ten minutes later and hashed out our plan.

Chapter 41

Trotter and I didn't have much time to get our plan together. I had to be at Milton's Grove in a half hour. Trotter was already on his way there to get set up. Everything we needed to try to pull this off was in the back of Trotter's truck. Most people don't leave home without their wallets, house keys, and cell phones. Trotter didn't leave home without his Kevlar vests, listening devices, and all sorts of weaponry. We were going to have to very prepared and very lucky to pull this off. I had no doubt that we would be outnumbered when the meeting took place.

I was driving over and going through the plan in my head. I hoped we had anticipated everything but I wouldn't be sure until it played out. I wanted to be the first to arrive and try to dictate where this meeting would take place. I pulled into Milton's Grove and did not see any other cars. The place looked just the same now as it did when we left the Enduro party thirty-three years ago. It was just as I remembered it. It was perfect. No people around and it was completely isolated. At least the first step went my way. I was in fact the first to arrive. I pulled up to the two story storage building that backs up to a wooded lot near the pond. I carefully got out of the car and looked around. I didn't see anyone or feel the presence of anyone. I easily found my way into the building. The first floor was open for the most part. There were some grounds-keeping tractors and equipment around. The lighting was sparse but there was enough. I actually preferred it this way. There were lofts on both the front and back sides of the building. I looked up and saw Trotter peeking his head up to let me know he was in place. No words were exchanged and I didn't fixate on the loft long enough just in case I was being watched. The next few minutes were tense as I paced around waiting for what I figured might be a bloody confrontation.

I'm not a killer. I have never taken a human life in all my years on the planet. I found out earlier that I was capable of it under extreme circumstances. Tonight I was pissed off enough to change all of that. That's what was bothering me the most. I had Trotter if I needed him but I'm not sure if I wanted him to do my dirty work for me. If I gave Trotter the word, he would take out his gun and put one right between the guy's eyes. He had a kill or be killed mentality and lived by his own moral code. One more bad guy getting put down permanently was just fine with him. Trotter liked me, so an enemy of mine is an enemy of his. Hopefully it wouldn't come to that. If everything went as planned, neither one of us would have to do any killing tonight. I needed to do everything in my power to keep my emotions in check.

The one hour mark had come and gone and it was still just me standing in the middle of the storage building. *Was this meeting going to happen? Was I being set up?* I was starting to walk toward the door to see if there was any activity outside when I saw a black sedan with tinted windows pull up. I stayed put in the middle of the room and waited. I had one gun in a shoulder holster and a small snub nosed pistol strapped just above my ankle. I heard the footsteps and it wasn't the footsteps of one person. The door opened and two goons led the man inside the building. The man emerged from behind the two goons and stopped about twenty feet in front of me.

"Hello, Mickey," I said. "I thought this was going to be just the two of us."

"Hello, Mac. What can I say? I'm a politician now. I lied." He gave a half- hearted laugh at his lame attempt at humor. "You can call me Michael now. I always hated when you guys called me Mickey. You assholes were the only people that ever called me that. Truth be told, other than Willie, I really didn't like any of you guys. You and Bollander were right at the top of that list," Mickey said. I never knew his real name was Michael. He was introduced to me as Mickey and that's the only name I ever knew him as. Come to think of it, I never knew Bucky's last name. He was just Bucky G Properties LLC to me.

"Michael Guilford, gubernatorial candidate. You've come a long way from being a punk kid in Wilkes-Barre. Did daddy fund your campaign?" I poked at him.

"I don't need Bucky's money. I did just fine on my own," he said as if it was a source of pride. The truth is I couldn't care less who funded his campaign. "I figured Bollander would be here too. He always did your fighting for you back then. I figured he still does." The mention of him using Bo's name sent rage through every ounce of blood in my body. *Stay calm.*

"Not this time Mickey. That psycho you sent after us shot him right before I put a knife in his chest." I didn't actually kill him but Mickey didn't need to know that.

"That's too bad. He turned out to be such a disappointment." Not an ounce of sympathy for Bo or any questions about his condition. He was just upset that he chose the wrong hitman.

Enough of the small talk. Time to get down to business. "Before this conversation goes any further, I need to make sure you are not wearing a wire." I raised my arms up as if to invite him to check it out. One of his goons stepped forward and pulled out a metal wand from his pocket. "My associate will do a quick check then we can get started." He wasn't checking for guns, he was checking for any radio frequencies. He did his quick pass of the wand on my front, back and both sides and was satisfied.

"So, Mac. You said you had a business proposal for me. Something about a picture." We both knew what we were there for.

The problem here was I didn't have a picture to produce.

"Personally, I want to see you dead. But I also want Eddie Vincent's kid to get the care he needs and he needs money for that. So I am willing to put my needs aside for Eddie's kid. You said you could bring the money but I don't see any."

"I don't see any picture, either," Mickey shot back. The two goons were standing behind and on both sides of Mickey. They both had out their guns and were trained on my head. "Where's the picture, Mac?"

"It's available. It's in a safe place for now. You'll get it when I get the money." I wasn't sure if Mickey thought I was bluffing or not. If he thought I was bluffing, he would have already made his move on me. "Don't you even want to know how I figured this out?"

"Not really. I think you're bluffing and don't have a thing on me." Maybe this was his time to run his bluff. He couldn't be sure what I knew and didn't know.

"The picture is only one piece of the puzzle," I said.

"What are you talking about, MacMasters?" Mickey had a look of concern on his face as he said it.

"I know you killed that poor girl. And I can prove it."

Mickey was taking his time digesting what he had just heard and was figuring his response. "What did Allegra ever do to you?"

"You don't know shit and you can't prove shit," he said.

"Oh, I can prove it. The proof is in the evidence room at Wilkes-Barre Police Department in the case file box. With the advancements in DNA testing since 1984 there will be no doubt your DNA will be traced to Allegra's car."

"Evidence? What evidence?" I had Mickey's full attention now.

"Your comb, Mickey. You dropped your black comb in Allegra's car. I saw it among the evidence in the cold case file. It didn't hit me until just today what that comb represented." I had Mickey's full attention now. "By the way, Mickey, I see you have no need for that comb anymore. Sorry the years weren't kinder to you and your beautiful head of hair." I gave a little smirk along with my dig at his now far from perfect hair.

"Still a smart ass. Laugh while you can, Mac. You won't be laughing much longer." Looks like Mickey was a little sensitive about his hair. He was far more visibly agitated now than he was a minute ago. He regrouped. "If you have so much evidence on me, why don't you just turn me in," he said.

"I told you. I want money for Eddie's kid. That is the most important thing right now. I know how powerful you are and can get things done when needed. I'm sure you already have thought of a way to get that comb out of evidence storage and destroy it." Mickey had a wry smile on his face. He had done just that. Now that he knew what I knew he would figure out how to get rid of me and the photo.

"You're so stupid, Mac. It's very disappointing. I actually thought you were smarter than that. You know you're not leaving here alive. My two associates here have ways of making people do things that they don't want to do. You will tell me where that photo is or you will hand it to me. The amount of pain you endure will be up to you." The two goons started walking toward me, guns still trained on my head.

"Wait. Wait one second. I'll give you the photo. You'll get the photo on one condition."

"Condition? What condition? There are no conditions," Mickey said.

"I need to know why. What happened, Mickey? Did she reject you or something? Does poor little spoiled rich kid Mickey not like rejection? What could that girl ever do to anyone to make someone kill her?"

I could see Mickey getting to his breaking point. This had been bottled up so long in him. He probably wanted to tell someone. I would keep pushing. "What was it, Mickey? I know you killed her. These guys know you killed her. Tell me why and you get the picture." Mission accomplished. He was now pacing and ready to let it all out.

"That bitch. That cock-tease bitch. I drove her car to the swimming hole at the quarry. We were both a little drunk. I know she wanted me. She was sending out all the signals. We kissed a little bit and everything was going great. I didn't drive her car to the quarry so I could get a couple of kisses. I made it clear I wanted more. She made it clear she didn't. I moved in on her and she slapped my face. Who the hell is she to reject me? She started yelling at me and telling me that she was going to tell her father about me. I didn't need that lunatic father and brother of hers coming after me. She started walking back to her car. I ran after her and grabbed her by the throat. I started choking the life out of her. I threw her to the ground and then hit her in the head with a rock. Her body went limp. I knew she was dead." He paused and took a breath. "I knew no one saw me leave the Enduro with her. We went to her car at separate times and left when everyone was watching the keg contest." I didn't sense one shred of remorse come out of his mouth.

"You're such a coward, Mickey" I said. He looked at me and almost nodded his agreement with me.

"So now you know Mac. But it's not going to do you a whole lot of good. I'm going to get that photo and then I am going to kill you myself." He looked over to his goons and gave them a nod. His nod was now setting his plan into motion. Time for me to put our plan into motion.

I looked up into the loft area and yelled out, "Trotter, did you get all that?" Mickey turned around and saw Trotter in the loft with his recording equipment.

"You son of a bitch," he yelled at me. "Kill both of them now!"

Mickey screamed to his goon squad. The larger of the two men turned immediately to the loft and started to fire his gun at Trotter. Trotter already had his pistol at the ready and the goon didn't even get one shot off. Trotter fired and did a quick double tap into the man's head. He was dead before he hit the ground.

The other goon wasn't sure where to give his attention. If he turned to the loft, I would shoot him. If he turned to me Trotter would take care of it. We didn't have to wait to find out. I went to pull my gun when I heard the shots. Trotter wasted no time. He put goon number two down just as fast as the first one. I now stood there with my gun now trained right on Mickey's head.

"You're not going to shoot me," Mickey said. Somehow he was now full of bravado. He was looking around to assess his options. There were two guns lying on the ground near where their former owners were lying dead. He was deciding if he should make a move for one of the guns. I could read his mind just as if he were speaking the words.

"Please do, Mickey. Give me a reason to splatter your brains all over this place." He was convinced. No dive for the gun.

Mickey's bravado was short lived. "Mac, we can work this out. I have money. I have plenty of money for Eddie's kid."

"Mickey, who's the stupid one now? I don't want your money. I've got plenty of money. Eddie's kid will be well taken care of and it won't be with your money."

Trotter made his way down from the loft. He had his weapons and electronic listening devices. Mickey did a double take when he saw this old white-haired man as the one that just took out his two associates with relative ease.

"So what's it going to be, Mac?" Mickey said trying to figure out his fate. "You plan on killing me?"

"Nah. Not my style Mickey. I may have my friend here teach you a few things about pain. But I'm not going to do that either," I told him.

"You going to have me arrested?" Mickey asked.

"No. I have something better in mind." I could see Mickey looking a little puzzled.

"What the hell are you talking about? Something better? What does that mean?"

If I didn't want his money, didn't want to kill him, didn't want him arrested, then what options were left?

In walked a group of men in black business suits and overcoats. The first man through the door was Carmine Selvaggio Jr. The last man through the door was the almost ninety year old Carmine Selvaggio Sr. There was no bathrobe. No oxygen tank at the ready. He was dressed in a sharp creased black suit with a white shirt buttoned to the top and bright red tie. His black wingtips sported a fresh shine. He had two rings on his frail fingers and a Rolex on his all too thin wrist. He did not use a cane but walked close to his associate in case he became unsteady. Carmine Sr. was dressed for his final business meeting. Whatever energy Carmine Sr. had left in his body was kept in reserve for just this occasion. He didn't leave his estate for too many occasions these days. This was just such an occasion. All of the color from Mickey's face had completely disappeared as he dropped to his knees.

"Is this the man?" Carmine Sr. said in a soft voice as he was looked toward Mickey.

The first call I had made after I set this meeting up was to Carmine Jr. I told him that I found out who killed his sister and told him about this meeting. I told him my associate, Trotter, would call him and tell him where he left some receiving equipment so they could hear everything spoken at the meeting. They were about a half mile away listening to Mickey tell all the details of Allegra's death.

"Yes, sir. This is Michael Guilford. He killed your daughter," I told Carmine Sr.

Carmine Sr. walked a few more steps in the direction of Mickey and stopped. "This is the man. The man that called my little girl a bitch and a cock-tease." His voice was now slightly raised in volume. "This is the man that murdered my Allegra."

Mickey was now visibly shaking. He obviously now knew his fate would not be a pleasant one. "I have waited thirty-three years for this moment. To look my daughter's killer in the eyes. To stand face to face with this man. Stand before this man that took everything from me. This man that stole my little girl from me. Mr. Guilford, do you have anything you wish to say to me and my son?" Carmine Sr. had said all he was going to say. Whatever response Mickey decided to come up with would not alter his future.

"I'm sorry, Mr. Selvaggio. I'm so sorry. Please don't kill me. I will make a full confession." Mickey was in tears and pleading for his life. His hollow apology fell on deaf ears.

Mickey started staring at the gun on the floor again. This time it was not for defense of himself. If he could reach the gun, I was sure it would be to put a bullet in his own head. I saw him edging closer. I was closer to the gun than Mickey. I stepped in front of Mickey and kicked the gun far away.

"Sorry, Mickey. That's not an option. You're not getting the easy way out." Those were the last words I spoke to the man that had my three friends killed.

Carmine Jr. came up to me and told me they would clean up and handle things from here. Carmine Jr. had taken over the family business several years ago. His power and reach as a crime boss were unmatched by anyone on the east coast. He thanked me and told me he was in debt to me.

Trotter and I were leaving as Carmine Sr. called out to me. I went over to him to see what he wanted.

"Mr. MacMasters, I am an old man. My body is weak. I will be dead soon but I don't fear dying. I have done many bad things in my life. My chosen profession has called for me to handle things in a certain manner. I have no regrets about my choices in life. My only regret in my life was I was not able to bring my sweet Allegra's killer to justice. Her loss left a hole in my heart that pained me every minute of every day since it happened. Not knowing was tearing me apart inside." He paused to collect his thoughts. "Up until now, I thought I would pass on without ever knowing. Knowing is everything. Mr. MacMasters, you have given me something for which my family will forever be indebted to you. Carmine Jr. will look after you, your family, and your friends. If you need anything, you call Carmine Jr." Carmine Jr. looked over at me and gave his ascension with a short nod.

"I'm so sorry for your loss. Your daughter was a special person and someone I considered a friend. I am glad you have the peace that you've been searching for." After a brief handshake, Trotter and I headed out the door. I could hear Mickey screaming and pleading all the way until we got in my car and rode off.

We got back to the hotel and Trotter looked at his watch and said, "I have to get home. Tonight is chicken pot pie night. No one makes it better than Annie."

"Really? After all we just went through, you're worried about chicken pot pie?" I paused and continued. "Well I certainly won't get in the way of chicken pot pie night at the Trotter household." I was joking with him but could tell be wanted to be with his soulmate on a night like this. "Listen Trotter, I owe you big time. You saved my ass."

"Mac, you don't owe me shit. I like getting out of the house every once in a while." His idea and my idea of getting out of the house were not quite the same. I would prefer bowling or a movie or some cold cocktails or just about anything else instead of what went on tonight.

Trotter packed up his stuff and loaded his truck. "Don't be a stranger, Mac. You ever need anything, don't hesitate to dial me up."

"Thanks, Trotter. Will do." I shook his hand and he sped off. That must have been some pretty darn good chicken pot pie.

Chapter 42

We decided to stay in town in our hotel until Bo got released from the hospital. I'm sure some friendly faces in his room helped his stay go just a little bit better. He was already improving and barking at the nurses to get him released. It should only be another day or two. By then all the nurses would all want to get a hand on that wheelchair and roll him out for good. Bo was stunned when he found out Mickey was behind all of this. He was also filled in on Mickey's likely fate. That put a smile on his face.

The hit man is gone. Mickey has been dealt with. No more of my friends will die at either one of their hands ever again. Mickey's confession confirmed his involvement but I never found out what started this whole mess. I know from Mickey and the hitman that a picture was at the center of this. That piece of the puzzle may never be solved.

I also am having a hard time wrapping my head around Eddie's forced suicide. The hitman said Eddie traded his life for his son's life. That would be the only explanation of why Eddie would so readily agree to lay down his own life. He had to be in an impossible situation. But still I feel I am missing something. His suicide note seemed somewhat cryptic. Was he trying to tell somebody something? I've read it over and over and can't seem to figure out if he was sending a message.

I decided to call Wheeler and asked if it was okay for me to go through Eddie's house. She not only said it would be fine but agreed to meet me over there. The place was locked down by the police as this was likely to be reclassified a homicide. I arrived there and Wheeler was already waiting for me on the front porch.

Wheeler was a good detective and needed a break on this case. I told a little white lie to her to get her pointed in the direction of Michael Guilford as her prime suspect. I told her that I didn't have any proof but thought it might be a good idea to check out Michael Guilford. I told her about my thoughts on seeing the black comb in her evidence photos and that it could belong to him.

"Are you talking about the guy who is running for Governor?" she asked as if not believing what was being presented to her.

"That's the one. He was a student with us back then and knew Allegra. He was also at the Enduro. He used to use that stupid black comb every five minutes. It drove me nuts. I didn't put two and two together when I saw it but I would bet his DNA is on that comb and that could place him at the scene."

"That's a little thin, Jack. No judge is going to sign off on a warrant for me to get a DNA sample." She liked what she had heard but she knew she would be up against some tough obstacles.

"You can go judge shopping. You may find one that doesn't like his politics."

"Even if we get the warrant and get a match, we still have a pretty big hurdle to get over. We need to find evidence that he was in the car on the day of her death. They will argue that comb was left there at some other time."

"We'll see. Let's go in and check this place out."

Eddie had a small ranch-style house that was a bit out of sorts on the inside. The place could have used a good cleaning. Dishes were left in the sink. The kitchen table was loaded with papers and mail.

Wheeler then changed subjects. "By the way, I reached out to Eddie's parents and they will be coming to town. They said they will do whatever needs to be done to make sure their grandson gets taken care of."

"That's great. Glad to hear that. I only met them once. They seemed like very nice people."

I saw Eddie's phone on the kitchen cabinet. I picked it up and was able to see that Eddie must have listened to my messages as there were none pending.

I walked over to the kitchen table and started to look at the piles of envelopes and other items there. I saw a white letter sized envelope with no mailing addresses on it. It was something he filled or something that was handed to him. I opened the envelope and saw it was a report from an oncologist. I perused the letter and test results report. I noted it was dated February 10th of this year.

The report went on to say that Eddie was diagnosed with Stage IV pancreatic cancer. This would mean the cancer had already begun to spread to other organs. That would remove any surgery option. He would likely only have several months to live. I also found some medicine bottles for some opioids and anti-depressants.

Eddie was valiant in trading his life for his son's. I'm sure the only thoughts going through his head were for the protection of his son. He would have done the same thing even if he was completely healthy. It does, however, make me feel better that Eddie did not have to endure what would have been a very painful and uncomfortable last few weeks or months of his life. I will take some comfort in that.

I showed that to Wheeler and she had the same thought I had. I then set my eyes on something I hadn't seen in thirty three years. Sticking out from under some papers was the Enduro bible. Eddie was the last one to hold title to it and he obviously kept it for all these years. The Enduro was canceled the following year due to Allegra's tragic death, so he had no one to pass it on to. He must have been feeling nostalgic after he was delivered the news that his cancer was now in Stage IV.

Eddie kept his health problems to himself. I saw him at Squirrel's services and he was a little thinner and a step slower but nothing that couldn't be attributed to getting older. None of us had any knowledge. Maybe he told Tyler but we will never know that for sure.

I opened up the bible and it immediately brought a smile to my face. Memories from thirty-three years ago flooded back. I saw the first page of our event with all the particulars including the names of the three event organizers. I turned the page and saw pictures of the band, the food pavilion set up, the volleyball game, and people enjoying the pond. When I turned the next page I immediately saw an empty space where a photo used to be. Other pictures on that page were of the drinking contest. I tried to think of what picture might be missing. Then it hit me. The picture of Brian, Bo, and me standing in front of the beer truck with our arms draped around each other. Could this be the picture that had started this whole mess?

I didn't see how a picture of the three of us would have had anything to do with this. None of us obviously had anything to do with Allegra's murder. I looked over the rest of the book and placed it back down. I showed Wheeler the missing picture space. She was intrigued by that. She was aware the hitman was seeking a picture for his employer and he may just have got it. She said, "We gotta find that picture." I couldn't agree more.

I recalled the hitman saying Eddie got too greedy. If Eddie extorted money from Mickey he must have given him the original polaroid photo. If Eddie went back for more that only meant he must have made a photocopy of it. I guess Mickey just decided to try to kill whoever it was that was blackmailing him rather than have that person keep coming back for more money. If Eddie kept a copy then that picture might still be in his house.

I then saw some medical bills pertaining to Billy's illness. Something struck me as I was viewing the patient's name on the invoice head. The patient was William A. Vincent. I immediately pulled out the picture of the suicide note on my phone and read it. *Keep a close eye on W.T.* I first read that and thought he was referring to his son William and middle initial T. I thought for a second and knew exactly what W.T. was and that suicide note was meant for me to find. Eddie had listened to my message telling him I would be coming over late in the morning.

Eddie was telling me where to look. W.T. was no doubt White Thunder. I told Wheeler that I knew where to look. We high-tailed it to the garage.

"The photo is here. It's in the car somewhere." We got to the garage and opened the door. I was again staring in the face of Eddie's fully renovated 1971 Chevy Chevelle. Eddie loved that car. The pride and joy of his life was his son Billy. White Thunder was Eddie's non-flesh and blood pride and joy. It made him happy as a teenager and as an adult. Not many people keep their first car for their whole lives. And not many people love an inanimate object the way Eddie did.

It seemed somewhat poetic that Eddie had left the mortal world in the front seat of White Thunder.

I opened the doors and trunk and turned to Wheeler. "Let's get at this. It's here somewhere. I know it." We started with the usual places. We checked the glove compartment, under the seats, between the seats, under the floor mats, in the sun visors, and a complete search of the trunk. We were striking out all over the place. I would have been surprised if Eddie would have made it easy for anyone to find. We kept looking. We popped open the hood and checked the engine compartment. I got on my back and searched the underneath. Maybe he taped it to the undercarriage or wheel wells. *Strike one. Strike two. Strike Three.*

My confidence level was lowering by the minute. *It had to be here.* The search went on but was quickly turning into an exercise in futility. If it was not in the car then it might be near the car. We did a thorough search of the entire garage. No luck.

"Jack, what do you say? Should we pack it in? I could send a forensics team to comb through this place."

I was listening to her but not really listening. My mind was still on this photo and where the heck Eddie could have hid it. I pulled out my phone and read the suicide note again. *Where's the clue Eddie? I know you put it in here.*

Then I saw it. *"I'm so exhausted. So very exhausted…"* I was wondering why Eddie repeated those two words. *Thank you, Eddie.* I went to the rear of the car and stuck my fingers in the exhaust pipe. Didn't feel anything. I tried to look inside but couldn't see anything. I yelled out to Wheeler, "Is there a flashlight in here?" She went to his work bench and found a small mag-lite and handed it to me.

I shined the light inside the exhaust pipe. "I think it's in here. Wheeler, grab me a screwdriver." She found a long screwdriver on the work bench and handed it to me. I stuck the screwdriver in and immediately felt some resistance. "I think I got it." I pressed the flat head of the screwdriver on what was providing the resistance and slowly dragged the object to the end of the pipe. I got it far enough where I could now grab it with my fingers. I pulled it out and found exactly what we were looking for. It was a copy of the picture that had started it all. It was also the picture that would surely make Michael Guilford the prime suspect in Allegra Selvaggio's murder.

"I got it, Wheeler." She was already standing over my shoulder. I handed her the picture.

"What am I looking at, Jack?"

"You're looking at a slam dunk for getting any judge to sign off on that warrant for Guilford's DNA. Trust me. It will be a match to that comb. It also places him in the car on the day of the murder." I explained what she was looking at in the picture. "This is your evidence but I want a copy of it for myself."

Wheeler was elated. She told me I could have as many copies as I needed. Only one will do. She knew that she would clear the one case off her desk that needed to be cleared. No more pressure from her Chief. No more quarterly status reports to the Selvaggio family. Closing this case would be a huge boost for her career. She was a quality detective and deserved any good fortune that would come her way from this.

"I've got some work to do. I'll get my warrant drawn up and nail this son of a bitch. I will also call Mr. Selvaggio and fill him in that we have a suspect and more info will follow. I don't want to give him any names just yet. You never know what that guy might do. Hopefully I can report to him that an arrest has been made. They have been waiting a long time for this."

"I'm sure they have."

It was highly doubtful any arrest would ever be made. That wouldn't matter though. She would be able to clear the case without actually arresting him. They would be able to secure a search warrant for his home. They would no doubt bag some evidence that contained a DNA sample. The test results from that DNA would surely result in a match to the DNA on the comb in the evidence box in Wheeler's office. An arrest warrant would soon follow.

"This will be a nice one to get off your desk." It didn't need to be said but I'm sure she liked hearing it out loud.

"Thanks, Jack. It was great meeting you. Good luck with everything and give my best to your friend in the hospital."

"Thanks, Wheeler. I wish you the same for your mother. Be well."

Chapter 43

Two weeks had passed and still no sign of Michael Guilford and two of his associates. His gubernatorial campaign had officially come to an end. He at first became a person of interest in the 1984 slaying of Allegra Selvaggio and was presumed to be on the run. I had my suspicions that he likely would not be found. I wouldn't be surprised if Selvaggio Concrete and Construction Company measured his feet and fitted him with a pair of custom cement shoes. Whether he is at the bottom of the mighty Susquehanna River or was passed through some meat grinder is of no concern to me. Whatever his fate was, I will hit my pillow every night and sleep just fine. He earned everything that would come his way. He killed someone who I would consider a friend of mine thirty-three years ago and three friends this year including one of my best friends on the planet. Not to mention almost killing my lifelong best friend. I hope he rots in hell.

The Guilford campaign initially tried to say that the allegations were false and he would look forward to proving his innocence. They reported he was taking a short break from the campaign to tend to his personal needs. They soon got the message that he would not be returning when they couldn't find him or reach him by phone. His wife knew nothing of his disappearance. A few days later, they issued a press release stating that Michael Guilford had ended his bid for Governor and had decided not to run. Being he was presumed to be on the run, the irony was not lost on me.

Wheeler and her chief were the faces of the police department at the press conferences after the DNA match was confirmed and the arrest warrant was issued. The moniker of person of interest was now that of prime suspect. She did a nice job and looked good at the podium. Chief Lutes tried to insert himself for partial credit but ultimately did a good job of giving Wheeler her due.

The Selvaggio family also issued a statement to the press. They wanted to publically thank Chief Lutes and Detective Wheeler for all their efforts in solving the case. They said they looked forward to seeing Michael Guilford arrested and brought to justice.

The Michael Guilford story dominated the headlines for a week or so since his disappearance. Buried in the news was the passing of Carmine Selvaggio Sr. The newspaper article said he died peacefully at his home surrounded by his family. I had no doubt in my mind that he did in fact die peacefully.

Bo was recovering nicely from his wounds. He ended up being in the hospital for four days. The bullet entered the top of his chest on the left side and did not hit any vital organs or arteries. He sustained a concussion after hitting his head on the concrete floor after the gun shot knocked him backward and to the ground. Once he was cleared of any brain injury, he was let go and went back to New Jersey to complete his recovery. His arm is still in a sling and will be so for the next few weeks. He will do a spell of physical therapy and he should be fully recovered in about eight more weeks. He will be joining us for our Men's Club reunion dinner but is not happy about missing the golf.

Our reunion starts today. We are staying at the Tropicana in Atlantic City and are meeting at a nice Italian restaurant for dinner to kick things off. We are expecting a full complement of our Men's Club members this year for obvious reasons. I am driving myself and Bo to the reunion. We were about halfway down the Garden State Parkway when my phone rang. I didn't recognize the number other than it was a New Jersey exchange. I picked up and was half expecting it to be some nonsense phone solicitation. "Hello."

"MacMasters, this is Robert Rizzo." I had left my business card on his desk but never expected to hear his voice again. I hadn't got around to turning in my work phone yet. After hearing Rizzo's voice again, I may have wished I did turn it in.

"What the hell do you want, Rizzo?" I shot back at him. The Bluetooth was on so Bo could hear every word Rizzo was spewing. If he was one tenth the detective he thought he was he should be able to figure out that I had no use for him or whatever came out of his mouth.

"Okay. I deserve that." He paused and I was about to jump all over him then he continued. "Listen MacMasters. I'm calling to apologize. I really fucked this thing up." This was not where I thought this conversation was headed so I stayed silent and let him go on. "I got a call from Chief Rodgers from Palmyra and he filled me in. I got the whole story. He had good things to say about you guys. He seems like a standup guy."

"Where are you going with this, Rizzo? Three of my friends were murdered and another was shot. All I wanted you to do was look into it further," I said.

"Like I said, I fucked this thing up." The arrogance we had heard at the police station was all gone. He was sounding contrite and I even picked up on some shreds of humility. "You see, MacMasters, doing what we do, we can't be wrong. It's not an option. There is too much at stake. When we investigate a death, our conclusions need to be a certainty. It's not fair to the family if we don't get it right." He was accurate and making sense so I let him go on. I don't know if this was part of an apology or the beginning of an excuse. "I stopped by the Colluccis to apologize face to face. I told them that my report had been amended to a finding of homicide. They were gracious about it. They're good people. They didn't deserve the effort I gave them." I was glad to hear he stopped by to see Mr. and Mrs. C. To have any sincerity, an apology like that would have to be in person.

"You owed them that." I wasn't ready to accept any apologies or let him off the hook. This apology would do Rizzo a lot more good than it would do for me.

"I'm not making excuses for my behavior but I haven't been the same detective since my wife left me three years ago. I lost my way. I decided to step back and take some time off. I put in for voluntary leave. I'm going to sort things out and see if I can do this anymore. So anyway, that was the reason for my call. I owed you and your friends an apology."

"I hope you get your shit together," was all I could muster up and we hung up. He managed to get through his entire *apology* without once saying "I'm sorry". There was a part of me that took some satisfaction with his call. I knew if I dropped the ball like he did in an investigation, I would have to find a way to make it right. If I couldn't make it right, I would hang it up.

Bo and I didn't even bother to discuss Rizzo's call. We both heard what he had to say and that would be the end of it.

We talked a little about the events of the past few weeks and aftermath. Bo was happy that he had received a personal visit from Governor Hainesworth while he was in the hospital. Katie, Faith, and I were also there when he visited. He expressed his gratitude for bringing Tyler's killer to justice. He always considered Tyler a great friend to him as well as a long time professional confidant. He was proud of the journey they took together.

He was also appreciative that Allegra Selvaggio's case was finally solved. That case had haunted him throughout most of his professional career. It was the one that got away. It was the one case he declared an utter failure on his part. He took no pleasure in not being able to fulfill his promise to Carmine Selvaggio that he would bring Allegra's murderer to justice. For Andrew Hainesworth that blemish would never be erased from his own mind.

He reminded us several times that we had a *friend* in Harrisburg if we needed one. I had already cashed in one favor with the governor. I told him about Bucky's demand for cash from his tenants dating back thirty or forty-some years. Bucky had many properties and likely had *inaccurate* or *creative* bookkeeping. Governor Hainesworth assured me he would make a few calls and Bucky could expect some IRS grunt to crawl up his ass and plant a flag. The back taxes and penalties would surely bankrupt Bucky G Properties LLC and Bucky himself. His entire slumlord empire would soon come crumbling down.

We arrived at the Tropicana and made our way to the restaurant for a nice dinner to start the reunion. We had fourteen people show up including Tommy Collucci. This was our best turnout ever. Unfortunately, it took losing three friends to get us all there. We said our hellos and gave the perfunctory bro-hug greetings.

Some of the guys still hadn't heard all of the details. The ones that did would listen again. I explained that Eddie had found an old picture from the Enduro bible that he thought could be used as evidence against Mickey in Allegra's death.

When Tyler sent out that picture of Mickey at the fundraiser with the governor, he must have told Eddie who it was or Eddie figured it out on his own. I guess if you look hard enough at the photo you can see a little of the old Mickey standing there as the gubernatorial candidate. He looked so much different with the balding head.

Eddie decided to get something out of this for his son rather than go to the police. Eddie knew he didn't have much longer to provide for Billy. He blackmailed Mickey. It looked like Eddie got a payoff but apparently went back for more. Mickey must not have found out who was blackmailing him so he hired a hit man to find him. Mickey figured out that it was one of us guys being we were the only ones that called him Mickey. Mickey still had access to all his father's old files and pulled out the leases to get all of our full names and former addresses. Ev, Squirrel, and Eddie all lived together and were on the same lease. It was probably just a random selection. He could have started with one the other leases and anyone of us could have been the first targets.

I did not let on about my confrontation with Mickey and his thugs at Milton's Grove. Only Bo, Brian, Jessica, and Trotter knew what happened there and it will stay that way. I told the boys that I found the evidence that Eddie was holding over Mickey. I passed the picture around. Some of the guys saw it immediately and some didn't know what they were looking at.

The picture was of Brian, Bo and me immediately before the keg-drinking contest at the Enduro. Eddie took the polaroid instant photo for the Enduro book. It was supposed to be of the three guys that ran the event for the year. We stood there with our arms draped over each other's shoulders and all had huge smiles as we stood in front of the beer truck. Just off the right in the photo was Mickey. There was no doubt it was him. His perfect hair was still perfect. He was smiling as he was walking by with his beer. And there it was. Plain as day. A four inch in diameter rainbow colored peace sign was hanging out of his front pocket. We had all seen that peace sign before. Allegra was never seen without it. Eddie figured out who left with Allegra from the Enduro. He had no doubt concluded that Mickey was responsible for her death.

Tommy Collucci stood up and asked if he could have the floor for a few minutes. Of course we obliged him. "I have been giving a lot of thought to things since Jimmy's death. My brother was always a generous and charitable person with his money and his time. His death has been devastating for my family and all of you as well. Some good needs to come out of this. First I want to acknowledge Mac, Bo, Brian, and our new friend Jessica." She wasn't there but he wanted to be sure to acknowledge her. "I can not tell you what it means to my parents and myself to know the truth." Tommy was doing great but his eyes were welling up and his voice beginning to crack. "We owe you four a debt of gratitude that we can never adequately repay." A tear trickled from his right eye and ran down his face. "Jimmy loved you guys." He paused and tried to collect himself. The tears were streaming but he would push through it. "And I love you guys. Jimmy was so proud to call you his friends." Tommy wasn't the only one with tears coming down his face. "Not many people can say they have friends that would take a bullet for them," Tommy looked over to Bo. "And my brother's friends literally took one for him."

Tommy took a few seconds to compose himself and then continued. "I have decided to honor Jimmy's memory by starting the James Collucci Foundation which will be a fundraising organization to support children and their families dealing with childhood illnesses. I have started the foundation with a $250,000 donation and hope to have annual fundraisers to keep the foundation going. We have already discussed Eddie's son's needs and rest assured he will be looked after by the Foundation." Tommy paused and took a sip of his martini. "Brian and Jessica Adams have graciously agreed to run the foundation in New Jersey." He looked to Brian as he said it.

Brian had decided to move up from Maryland to New Jersey. Brian is a man with options. After all, due to the sage advice of his grandfather, he is sitting on a fortune in Apple stock. He and Jessica are going to take things slow but will be giving it a go. Hopefully Brian will be able to fill that void in his heart that has been missing in him since 1984.

Tommy had previously told me of his plan to start a foundation in Jimmy's name. I thought it was a great idea and of course I provided my monetary donation. I also told him that we would all be assisting with any and all of the fundraisers. After I learned of this endeavor, I decided to do a little fundraising of my own.

I stood up and walked over to Tommy. I pulled a check out of my pocket and handed it to him. There was a check payable to The James Collucci Foundation in the amount of $250,000 from Selvaggio Concrete and Contracting Company. Carmine Jr. wanted to give more but I didn't want him to outdo Tommy's generous gesture. He assured me there would be an annual donation for as long as the charity existed. He also made it clear that if any of us ever needed anything, he would make it happen. *I'm sure he would. One way or another.* It's not the worst thing having the two most powerful people in Pennsylvania owe me a favor or two.

The reunion wasn't the same. It never will be the same again. We will still have it every year and we will enjoy each other's company for those few days every April. Our same old stories will continue to be told over and over again. We will make sure Squirrel, Ev, and Eddie are never forgotten. We parted ways this year after a few days of golf, drinking, storytelling, laughing, and toasting our fallen brothers. We said our good-byes accompanied with the standard bro-hugs. This year we held the hugs just a second or two longer.

ACKNOWLEDGMENTS

I want to thank several people for taking time to read this book and provide valuable feedback. I did hear and use your thoughts as it served as the basis for several re-writes. I felt much better about the story after implementing the changes that came about due to your comments. First and foremost, I want thank my wife, Trish, as we were in lock-step throughout the entire writing process. She would give feedback after every chapter. She also had to endure my constant bouncing of plot line ideas off her. My other sincere thanks go out to Tom Hendricks, Gerry Nee, Tony Casapulla, Tom MacDonald, Bill Wagner, Frank Mitarotonda, John Peracchio, and Scott Brown.

I also want to thank John Etzil, author of Airliner Down. He was kind enough to provide valuable advice on how to become an author and get a book published. If you haven't done so already, you need to read Airliner Down. It was a fast-paced thriller that was enjoyable throughout. You won't be disappointed.

I would be remiss if I didn't acknowledge my copy-editor, Jim Oliveri, Ye Editor. He did an outstanding job of educating me and putting his keen eye to my novel. Thank you, Jim. Your thoroughness and attention to detail was greatly appreciated. Any remaining errors found in the book are all on me.

While The Men's Club is a work of fiction, I am part of a group of great guys that all met in college. We proudly refer to ourselves as The Men's Club. This book would not have been written without the many stories involving the crew from our college days and beyond. None of the characters in the book are based on any one individual. However, bits and pieces of everyone seemed to make into all the characters. The Men's Club roster includes, in no particular order, John Moore, Scott Brown, John Peracchio, Tony

Casapulla, Frank Mitarotonda, Ken Visconti, Paul Esposito, Willie Perenyi, Frank Healey, Mike Smith, John Mackey, John Chmielowiec, Kevin Knorr, Jim Gordon, Jerry Searfoss, Paul Searfoss and others.

We lost honorary member, Ken Herrmann, early in 2019 after a long and courageous battle with cancer. He will always be fondly remembered for driving his golf cart into the side of my brother, Greg's, company car during our reunion at Foxwoods. He will be toasted at all future Men's Club reunions.

Message for Willie- If you read this- give me a call.

ABOUT THE AUTHOR

Jeff Daley resides in northern central New Jersey with his wife and three children. He has worked in the insurance industry since 1987 for one company. He enjoys any activity with his family as well as golf, travelling and reading. His favorite authors and influences include Steve Martini, Lee Child, Michael Connelly, David Baldacci, James Grippando and Harlan Coben.He credits John Grisham's The Firm as the one book that got him hooked on reading.

This is Jeff Daley's first novel. This book started with an idea formed on one of many trips up and down I-95 through Connecticut while visiting his daughter in culinary school in Providence, Rhode Island. Anyone who has endured that traffic knows there is plenty of time to do some thinking.

He is currently anxiously awaiting the birth of his first grandson, Avery. He can't wait to spoil him and then hand him back to his daughter at the end of the day.

To contact Jeff Daley- email – Jdaleytmc@optonline.net

Made in United States
North Haven, CT
21 March 2024